I0582812

THE RIVER WHISPERS

DEB JORDAN

First published in 2025 by Bloodhound Books.

www.bloodhoundbooks.com

Print ISBN: 978-1-917449-9-39

To my dear Mum, Darrelle Hamlet; who will always be with me,
every step of the way.

PROLOGUE

The sun drove down, its rays piercing the vines, intensifying the colour and sweetness of the fruit. The blueish-purple of the grapes lacked lustre, but they clung in plump bunches, tempting passers-by to reach out and pluck just one. Rain had been a long time coming and the ground was parched, ants using the cracks in the earth as a pathway to who knows where. It was not unusually warm for this time of year, but the balmy weather was still the most popular topic of conversation.

Families, couples, friends – everyone, it seemed – had been drawn on this particular weekend to the Swan Valley vineyards. The prospect of an icy sauvignon blanc, sipped on the shady deck overlooking row upon row of lush, green vines was apparently irresistible. The added bonus of mist from overhead hoses ensured that the veranda of Vins Fantaisistes was filled to absolute capacity. Wisteria dripping in purple bouquets from the aged Marri tree beams added a touch of whimsy and even an element of romance for those so inclined. It was this very feeling that had led to the French name of the vineyard: *Whimsical Wines; Vins Fantaisistes*. Music drifted along the deck, a background medley of instrumental piano. Conversation ebbed and flowed in a relaxed current, diners reclining in satisfied comfort or leaning on elbows in an attempt to remain focused after the intoxicating combination of food, wine and warm weather.

How was it then, that such an anomaly to the surrounds could go unnoticed? A tiny, clenched fist reaching up towards the dangling grapes, sent a ripple through the stillness. Frustrated with not being able to touch the fruit, a gurgle of determination broke the silence. The warmth of the sun that had held this little bundle in cocooned sleep was now dappled and cooling, rousing it to wakefulness. The gurgling gave way to a cry, the baby suddenly aware it was on its own. A light, white sheet had been kicked aside by the reflexive force of little newborn legs. The only audience was the ants, too intent on their own journey to deviate or investigate.

It wasn't until a couple who had been dining on the deck broke away and headed towards the lush rows of vines, that the wailing registered. The woman's shout of shock and bewilderment startled the baby further, their two cries merging in a crescendo of disbelief. Turning in jerky, ineffectual movements, the couple searched for the baby's parents amidst the vines. Apart from the now flailing feet and fists of the baby, there was no other sign of human presence.

In the ensuing chaos of questions and calls made to the relevant services, the calm rhythm of the Swan River continued its gentle pace. Cormorants and cockatoos lined the boughs of the banksia and eucalyptus trees, the honey-like minted scent mingling with the breakdown of branches and rotting vegetation. If anyone from the vineyard had glanced skywards, they may have noticed the perched cockatoos ignoring the activity. Instead, their eyes were trained on the river, their flared, sulphur-coloured crests revealing an alertness that their stillness belied.

Caught in the branches of a tree grazing the surface of the river was the unmistakable form of a female body, her fanning hair a trap for river debris.

CHAPTER ONE

SAM ~ NOW

A screech carried across the rows of vines. Sam flinched. He scanned the area, instinctively assessing the scene that greeted him.

He had been called on his day off and had been tempted to let whoever was officially on call take it, but as soon as he heard the location, he was moving before he even realised what he was doing. He *had* to be there.

Sam stood by his car, unaccountably nervous. It had been a few weeks since he was last at the vineyard. *Two weeks, two days and...* he checked his watch... *four hours.*

He looked across at the outdoor dining area. It was eerily quiet.

Lights flashed from various emergency vehicles, with uniformed men and women moving in every direction. Despite the fact they were professionals, the discovery of an abandoned newborn baby tugged at every maternal and paternal instinct in the vicinity. This was a place where people came to abandon their daily stresses and worries over a micro-brewed pale ale or a chilly chardonnay. It was not a place to leave a baby.

Sam turned towards the main reception area. Not a lot had

changed. He stood in the doorway, observing from a vantage point that did not invite interruption. He knew the room well. The grand piano still sat in the centre, although the top was closed and the keys were covered. How many times had he walked in and heard it being played? Stood in this very spot and watched *her* play, completely absorbed in the pull and flow of the music? The arch of her back; the tilt of her neck as she coaxed an elusive tone from the keys; vulnerability threaded through strength and conviction. He had watched and listened countless times. Certainly, enough that he could pick her mood. Tchaikovsky if she was feeling happy and maybe a little dramatic; Bach if she was trying to work through some knotty and intricate problems; Gershwin when she wanted to push boundaries and Rachmaninov when she was annoyed at someone or something, her frustration evident in every keystroke and chord. Hearing the Russian usually made him want to turn around and escape. Still, he'd take that over the silence, any day.

He walked over to the piano and paused, fingers drifting along the closed keyboard lid. Had Sasha closed it? Permanently?

'Dave,' Sam nodded in the direction of the older man standing by the wine tasting counter, his arm resting on the wooden benchtop, seemingly oblivious to the condensation from the Champagne bowl pooled around his elbow. He was the vineyard's owner.

'Hey, Sam. You're in charge of this bloody mess? Probably a good thing. You know the area better than anyone. And the people.' Dave sighed. The enormity of the situation sat heavily. 'Seriously – can you really think of anyone who'd do this? Leave a bloody baby, for Christ's sake? It's gotta be someone passing through, right?'

Sam drew a long breath as he looked beyond the veranda,

the precision and order of the vines normally soothing but now a maze of mayhem. 'I honestly have no idea. This is a new one, even for me. Anything out of the ordinary stand out to you this morning?'

He knew that making general conversation was the best way to gather facts. He also knew that without fail, Dave was always the first person up and about on the property. He would've been on the grounds long before the doors opened to the public, so if anyone was going to notice anything, it would have been the owner of Vins Fantaisistes.

Sam stared ahead, not wanting to rush him.

'Not a bloody thing, damn it!' exhaled Dave. 'It was the same as every Saturday morning, as far as I can remember,' he said, pausing while he stared at the mix of emergency uniforms in the vineyard. 'Staff were arriving to start the restaurant set-up and there were already a few cars parked at the ends of some of the vines. We have seasonal workers coming in to pick the grapes for the next few weeks, ya know? But they're gone by 8am. Best time for these grapes is to pick them before the sun comes up.' He paused for a few beats, but Sam simply nodded, encouraging him to keep going. 'People like to wander through the vines. They think it's all romantic and quaint and all that shit. Bloody nuisance a lot of the time, touching all the fruit, but if we can keep them to the first row, it's not so bad. If someone was to be there with a bub in a car seat carrier, I don't really know if I would've given them a second glance.' Dave's gaze continued to dart across the rows of vines.

'Don't beat yourself up,' Sam said. 'It's a busy time of year.'

He looked across to the veranda, chairs askew and meals unfinished. He'd sat there often enough with Sasha, snatching a moment of peace. Her touring schedule had really picked up in the past year and time together was precious. Sitting out there was when people focused on the person across from them, cloaked in anonymity, and time momentarily suspended. It wasn't a time where you were on the lookout for suspicious behaviour.

Nodding at Dave, Sam headed down the grassy banks and towards the wooden steps that led to the small jetty at the river's edge. He should've been back with the emergency service workers, but this path pulled at him, just as she had laughingly pulled him along it so many times in the past.

Without the noise and confusion of the diners and sirens and lights, the silence was stark. Where was the birdsong and chorus of crickets that always filled the background harmony?

His skin prickled and instinct drove him forward. Glancing upwards, he could see the white shapes of the cockatoos, sitting straight and erect at the very tops of the trees. Yet they were silent.

And then he saw her, face down and floating, one arm slightly raised as if waving for attention but instead, hooked over a branch. He stumbled over the remaining steps and dove into the murky water.

'Oh, God!' Sam breathed as his head sliced through the surface.

The silence broke with the sudden laughter of a kookaburra; normally a sound to elicit a smile, but this time managing to appear mocking and macabre.

CHAPTER TWO

SASHA ~ RECENTLY

'You got stuck *where?*' The woman behind the motel's reception counter gaped at Sasha.

Sasha blinked, forcing herself to look at the face in front of her, the eyes wide under a wispy fringe of flecked white hair. Which could very well have been streaks of flour rather than the natural hues of ageing, she realised, with another blink.

'By the river.' Sasha set her case on the scarred wooden floorboards in the reception of the motel.

'Oh, you poor love.' A hand raised to her cheek transferred further remnants of the baking Sasha had clearly interrupted. 'That riverbank is a death trap at this time of year. You're lucky you didn't get stuck.'

Sasha sucked in a breath and picked up a pen to fill out the registration form in front of her. 'It was a complication I could have done without,' she said by way of agreement, impatient to finish the check-in process and reach the privacy of her room.

'You're in the building round the back and to the right, love.' The receptionist held out a key tag that looked as if it should have been retired at least two decades ago.

Sasha nodded, trying not to stare at the buttons across the

receptionist's bust opposite her, which strained with the effort to remain anchored in place.

'Don't be put off by the old shower. There's plenty of hot water, which I think is exactly what you need, by the looks of it. My Gerry looks after all the maintenance and he's an absolute whizz with it all. It's all gobbledy-gook to me, but he knows what he's doing, bless him.'

Sasha blinked when the top button lost its battle with modesty, revealing a flash of neon pink lace.

'My name's Dolores Marcus, but everyone calls me Mrs M. The number's on the key tag. Just holler if you need anything, won't you, love?'

Sasha put the pen down and reached across to take the key. Despite the heat, a cardigan was draped over her left arm, making action possible with only one hand.

'Thanks.' Sasha kept her voice steady as she left the reception and headed in the direction of her room. She would not allow herself the luxury of feeling emotion. Not yet.

The Margaret River Region had been a favourite place for Sasha to visit for as long as she could remember. For the two of them, really. Her *and* Abby. Not that Abby would be joining her this time. And not at an out-of-the-way place like the one she had landed in. She looked around, brown paint peeling and flaking like untreated eczema. Succulents drooped from dusty rocks around the base of the buildings.

It matched her mood perfectly. Life, with all its glorious imperfections and inconsistencies, had seen fit to land her in a place reeking of despair and despondency. And by "landed," she meant she had deliberately packed a bag, fuelled her car and headed south from Perth. Instinct had dictated her direction. There had been no plan. No forethought. Just a desperate need to escape.

Sasha's eyes fell to her left hand, her heart rate quickening and her breathing becoming more rapid in what was now an automatic response. A dull ache pulsed from her fingertips, radiating through her wrist. The scars along each side of her hand had faded from the angry red they had been for a long time, to a dark purple. At least it wasn't as obvious as the whopping great cast and metal framework holding pins in place that she had carried around for six weeks after the accident. People were no longer having to drag their eyes up to her face and make the conscious decision to engage in general conversation or inquire about the injury. You could always see the mini war going on behind their eyes as they battled the urge to be direct or circumspect. Whether they were being genuine or just plain nosy would dictate the direction of her answer. It may also have depended just a tiny bit on her mood and how sociable or gracious she was feeling.

She glanced down at the tapered black pants she had paired with a collared purple shirt as she walked to the room. It was plain, practical and button-free. Maybe she needed to change her style and start wearing full motorcycle leathers and knee-high boots with chunky buckles. People would take one look at her and assume the scars were riding-related and not ask any questions. She could be the bad-ass biker chick who didn't invite questions or welcome opinions. Looking again at her ballet-flat enclosed feet, and giving a small snort, she realised she was about as far removed from bad-ass as you could get.

Inside the ageing room, Sasha collapsed onto the bed, chewing the inside of her cheek and barely registering the metallic tang of blood. When would she stop being *angry*? The rage that gripped her chest before plummeting to her stomach in a knotted mass of blame and accusation was exhausting.

There had been a moment earlier by the river where she'd stared down into it. Her eyes sinking beneath the surface. Her mind dragging her to the murky depths. The urge to feel the current wrap around her, cocoon her with ribbons of silken riverweed, to nestle on the silty floor and just... stop.

She rolled over and buried her face in the scratchy pillow. Her whole body ached from the anger; from all she'd lost. No. Not lost. She hadn't *misplaced* something. She hadn't been careless. Her mouth tightened. It had been taken from her. Snatched. Wrenched. With no warning. And now she was meant to get on with life? What a bloody joke. She was supposed to move forward. As if it was as easy as that. That's what everyone wanted. Her mum, her dad, Sam. They wanted her to face the future. It was all so goddam trite. If she could no longer play the piano, the one thing that meant everything to her, how could she move forward?

Was there a way forward?

CHAPTER THREE

ABBY ~ RECENTLY

Something had to change. Things couldn't continue this way. They just couldn't. Abby sat on the grass by the Anzac Memorial in Perth's central Kings Park. She gazed at the city and at Elizabeth Quay laid out before her, sparkling and full of possibility. She pulled her knees up to her chest. Or as far as her belly would permit. Little Dumpling was due in a week, so movement of any kind was cumbersome. Clumsy.

When had she become so clumsy? Stupid question. She knew exactly when. And it was more than clumsy. "Clumsy" sounded cute and quaint; a tiny misstep in the course of a day. Something to be laughed at or noticed with a fond headshake and eyeroll. What she'd done had gone way beyond that.

It wasn't intentional. More of an instinct, really. A conditioned response.

A conditioned response that had cost her best friend everything.

A couple passed her, arms locked around the other's waist, determined to maximise every point of available contact. She shivered. Joe had been like that. Desperate to keep her close, connected to him. *Locked* to him.

She had worked hard to change those responses; to move forward rather than continuing with patterns that had her jumping every time Joe so much as blinked. She had way too much riding on the decisions she made now. Which was why she blamed herself for the accident.

Abby rolled her shoulders and gave up trying to clasp her hands around her knees. She stroked the taut skin of her belly and breathed deeply as a seatbelt-tightening-sensation wrapped itself around her. Her body had been practising for a while now.

Would Sasha ever stop blaming her? Would *she* ever stop blaming herself? One tiny glance down at the backlit phone screen had been all it took. One tiny glance that meant Sasha's career was gone, shattered beyond repair. Just as her hand had been shattered when the car had connected with the tree. Her hand! Sasha's hands were everything to her. Music was everything to her. And Abby had taken it from her. Not literally, of course. Although it may as well have been. She had been behind the wheel. She had been responsible for their safety and wellbeing.

She hadn't meant to look at the screen. They'd been laughing at something ridiculous. Probably about the fact that every time she laughed or sneezed, she pretty much peed her pants. Something Sasha had found hilarious and tried to provoke at every given chance.

But the screen *had* lit up. And she *had* looked down.

CHAPTER FOUR

SASHA ~ RECENTLY

Sasha pushed herself off the unfamiliar motel bed and gazed out at the succulents struggling to find a foothold in the rocks. Untethered, but resilient. Would they mind sharing some of that resilience with her? She had forgotten to pull the blinds last night and the morning sun dared her to ignore it, pushing its way through the gauzy curtains.

Sitting on the edge of the bed, she trailed her fingers over the raised black lines of the new tattoo on the inside of her right forearm. Deliberate lines rather than the puckered and tight scar lines that dominated every single thought and action. Her fingers tapped out the melody to *Beethoven's 9th*, now indelibly etched onto her body for all the world to see. She shrugged. Why shouldn't it be there? The song had been with her for as long as she could remember, so having it visible was not exactly a monumental leap. But it was intentional. Her choice. She had consciously chosen to have it placed exactly where it was, the ink bleeding in a predetermined and deliberate design.

She scowled as she tried to close her left hand, her fingertips itching with the impulse to express her anger with a closed fist, or anything other than the damn state of *nothingness* that was its current favoured pose. She heaved herself off the bed, kicking her suitcase out of the way as she made her way to the bathroom.

Sasha stood at the basin. She slowed her breathing and counted. Except, she always forgot the pattern she was meant to follow. In for three counts and out for four? Or the other way round? Or was it seven and eight? Her mouth pinched into a cat's bum pucker. What the hell did it matter anyway? She bloody well knew how to breathe and didn't need some rehab doctor telling her how to suck in air and count. What she needed was for this whole mess to never have happened.

She wrapped her right hand around her left wrist, willing there to be some sensation. She would welcome pain at this point. Anything, other than the dull ache and neutrality verging on numbness. The doctor said it was normal; residual swelling placing pressure on the nerves that would subside in due course. What the bloody hell was *due course*? It sounded about as technical as *Chopsticks* being belted out on a keyboard by a beginner. If that was the best the professionals could come up with, then why was she bothering with any of the rehab?

Getting the tattoo had been as much about feeling something as anything else. She snorted at her previous stance on never getting a tattoo. Needles meant pain. Why would she inflict that on herself? It had been an impulse, pure and simple, driven by a need to escape the suffocating concern of her parents. They meant well. Of course they did. She knew that; she acknowledged that. But she struggled to accept it. Accepting it meant that life was never going to be the same.

Her fingertips continued to tap the 9th *Symphony* as she thought about the morning she'd got the tattoo. Was it really only last week? She had dragged herself from the self-imposed confines of her room and out to a café. The cast had just come off and her parents' brows were more furrowed than ever. A little space was all she wanted.

'Want some company, Sash?' her mother had asked. A little too enthusiastically. A little too brightly.

She knew her parents were concerned. She'd hate it if they weren't. But perversely, their concern irritated her.

'No, thanks.' She'd grabbed her car keys, thankful she had finally been cleared to drive again. Being dependent sucked. 'Maybe another time.'

Normally, cafés soothed her. She was anonymous. Casual snippets of conversation would ebb and flow around her, allowing her mind to wander; a brief departure from a tricky rehearsal or a new passage she had been trying to master for hours.

That day, there had been no rehearsal to escape from and no tricky new passage to master. The only thing she could hope to master was picking up a coffee cup without dropping it. Something the two-year-old at a nearby table was doing with annoying and unconscious dexterity. She had been about to scowl and look away, but had laughed without thinking when the toddler slammed the mini cup down and plunged his fist into it, twisting it back and forth in a desperate attempt to extract every last bit of milky frothiness. There was no thought for appearance, no pause to ponder consequence. Simply a need to act and produce results.

Sasha looked up at the mother and caught her eye, a look of wry amusement accompanied by eyes raised, before delving into an oversized bag and producing a wet wipe. Clearly, this was not a new method of drink consumption by her toddler.

Sasha looked at her own cup of coffee. A long black with no frothiness. No fun. What was she doing? Sitting around and feeling angry was all well and good, but it grated. It chafed and it was tiring.

She pushed her chair back, sending it crashing over, startling the toddler mid-lick of his fist. Great. She'd descended into scaring kids. She was officially a terrible person.

Smiling unconvincingly at the frowning little boy, Sasha hurried out of the café. She paused a few doors down, her heart rate erratic. A familiar swirl of anxiety started to gather momentum. Who was she, if she couldn't play the piano? She hurried along the sidewalk. Desperate to distract herself, she pushed open the door of the store and stepped inside, without pausing to look at the signage on the window.

She froze as the door closed behind her. *Goddammit!* Could she not have walked into a clothing store? A bookstore? Of all the places, she'd barrelled into a tattoo store. Tattoo *Parlour?* What were they even called?

'Can I help you, hun?' The girl at the counter spoke through a mouthful of green gum, while leaning forward and showcasing tattoos covering barely concealed breasts. Was body ink now considered enough to protect modesty?

She closed her eyes for a second before stepping forward. Getting a tattoo was not something Sasha had ever considered. It was not something she'd thought about or doodled designs for in the margins of her high school diary. But here she was.

Rubbing her palms down the front of her pants, Sasha drew in a shaky breath. Why *shouldn't* she be here? Why shouldn't she do something so completely out of character that it left her breathless? *Step into my parlour, said the spider to the fly,* echoed in her mind. A couple of calming diazepam tablets from her surgeries a few weeks back would really come in handy right about now. Upending her bag by the counter to search for some stray pills wouldn't alarm too many people, surely? Sasha stared, wide-eyed and more than a little tongue-tied. What on earth was she doing? She swallowed. 'I wanted to see about getting a tattoo?' It came out as a question rather than a statement.

'Just take a seat on the couch, hun, and I'll go and see who's free.' The receptionist linked her arm through Sasha's and guided her to the couch, the sound of snapping gum echoing in her ears.

While the couch looked scary and black and had a skull lamp on the table at the end, it was surprisingly comfortable; a balance of sorts, for the ink and artwork in front of her. Knives with blood dripping off them and skulls with flames shooting everywhere, bare-breasted women astride motorcycles; these designs were not going anywhere near her body, thank you very much.

Just as she was about to spring off the couch and straight out the door, a vision in swirling, floor-length fabric swished into the room. "Hiya! You've come for a tattoo?" she asked before flicking a waist-length braid over her shoulder. "I'm Toni." She reached over and clasped Sasha's good hand in both of hers. "Do you know what you'd like?"

To run out of the door and forget this ridiculous idea. "I have absolutely no idea," she instead managed to squeak.

'That's okay,' Toni smiled calmly while sliding herself onto the couch beside Sasha. 'Let's just chat about what you like and see what we can come up with. How does that sound?'

Sasha nodded and took a few more deep breaths. 'I don't want anything big, and I do not want skulls, or anything like that.'

'No, I think not,' Toni agreed, her lips twitching. 'Show me your wrist,' she said, reaching for Sasha's hand. Thankfully, it was her right hand that Toni grasped. She eased up the sleeve and turned Sasha's palm upwards.

'I think something beautiful and delicate between your wrist and your elbow. It's the least painful place to have a tattoo, if you're nervous about that.' She raised an eyebrow at Sasha. 'It'll feel like a teeny angry mosquito.'

Reassured by the knowledge that she wasn't signing up for deliberate pain, Sasha started to see some possibilities. As bittersweet as it seemed, she could not see past a design involving music. Was that asking for more pain, though? A constant reminder of what was no longer in her life? She reminded herself she was meant to be being spontaneous, so now was not the time for deep thinking or over-analysing. She straightened and clapped her right hand against her thigh, gripping her leg tightly.

'Maybe a music staff along here,' she said, nodding at the pale skin of her inner forearm. 'Kind of wavy and then petering out to a small point near my wrist? Would something like that work?'

Toni bounced on the couch. 'That's perfect! You can add notes to a favourite song so that it really means something to you.' She leant forward over the tablet she was drawing on, her hand making sweeping motions as the design came to life. 'And what do you think about a couple of tiny flowers winding around the staff and notes? Maybe a little dot of pink so they look like cherry blossoms?' She added a delicate pinpoint of pink to each of the petals she'd drawn with breathtaking speed and skill.

Sasha was mesmerised. In the space of a few minutes, she had gone from never having considered a tattoo to being utterly in love with the design in front of her and *needing* it. It felt like it should be a part of her, an extension of her.

'Come on,' Toni said, leaping off the couch. 'Let's get this masterpiece underway.' Her excitement was contagious. Sasha found herself following Toni with the tiniest of springs in her step; something she hadn't had in a very long time.

Sasha climbed onto what looked like a cross between a barber's seat and a dentist's chair while Toni lined up the pots of ink she would use. It all looked so incredibly cute – a bit like the tiny paint-by-numbers pots with one of those canvas scenes or replicas of famous artworks.

'Are you ready for me to start?' Toni held the angry-mosquito pen above Sasha's arm.

She had settled on the first two bars of Beethoven's *Ode To Joy,* his 9th Symphony, as the notes that would go on the staff. The irony of the title and her current state of mind were not lost on her, but she was trying to look forward, to find joy in little things while she worked out the big things. A joyous song for a joyous idea, she told herself.

Straightening in the chair and taking a deep breath, Sasha nodded at Toni. 'Let's go!'

As it turned out, it was nowhere near as dramatic as Sasha had anticipated. The pen really did sound and feel like an angry mosquito and the whole experience was more empowering than terrifying. A line from Liszt's *Liebestraum* crescendo'd in her mind. She exhaled and let it build. It was the first time she hadn't squashed the thought of music since the accident.

She'd kept her arm covered with long sleeves for a week and not told anyone about the tattoo. Before the accident, Abby would have been the first person she called, the first person she showed.

What were the chances of Abby ever seeing it now?

CHAPTER FIVE

ABBY ~ BEFORE THE ACCIDENT

'Is death the objective here?' Abby glared at Sasha amidst the pristine green of the New Zealand national park. It should have been illegal to feel the levels of pain she was experiencing when surrounded by so much beauty.

Sasha breezed past her and tossed a smile over her shoulder. 'It was your idea to come to New Zealand, so quit your grumbling and get a move on.' She slowed her pace a little and glanced at the deepening colour of the clouds above. 'If we don't get moving, we're going to get dumped on. Your choice, slow poke.'

Abby looked around her at the steep incline ahead and the towering redwood trees either side of the trail. Yes, it had been her idea to holiday in New Zealand. But her vision had been more along the lines of sipping wine while overlooking the Auckland Harbour, sampling local cuisine or even just a bowl of perfectly crisp potato wedges. She wasn't fussy. Some hot wedges with a healthy dollop of sour cream would hit the spot, right about now. How had she not factored in Sasha's almost obsessive desire to explore the outdoors? The trip had been a spur-of-the-moment decision, an opportunity snatched when Sasha had an unexpected cancellation in her touring schedule.

It had also been a welcome escape.

'Did you have to pick the longest trail around the lake, though?' Abby stopped and crouched under the pretence of retying her shoelace. What she really needed was a chance to catch her breath. 'And since when did you become an elite athlete?'

Sasha slurped water from the tube connected to her backpack while Abby made tying her laces look like a length of macrame with the knots she was absent-mindedly making. Anything to give herself a break. If she'd known Sasha was going to treat the trip as an opportunity to train for *Australian Ninja Warrior*, she would've booked them straight into a retreat; one that specialised in colourful fruity drinks, meditation in hammocks and perhaps a token class of Yin Yoga if activity was at all required. Instead, she'd asked Sasha what she wanted to do. After so many years of friendship, you'd think she'd have known better. But no. The need to get away had clouded her judgement.

Sasha reached out a hand to haul Abby upright. 'Come on. The sooner we get around the lake, the sooner we can head to the hot tubs.' Sasha waggled her eyebrows and gave an exaggerated wink. 'You never know who you'll meet. All that steamy water and the secluded tubs. What do you think?'

'I think you're nuts,' Abby threw back. She didn't *need* to meet anyone. She had Joe. Joe was perfect. Although right now, the thought of sinking into the hot water was more than a little appealing. She leapt to her feet and dashed ahead of Sasha. 'Come on. Who's the slow one now?'

'It's not a race, Abs,' Sasha said, her stride lengthening as she caught up and nudged Abby in the ribs.

Abby ignored her friend and looked around. There was no

denying the beauty of the area. The legendary silver ferns were littered along the edge of the track, the metallic sheen only evident from the underside, something Abby discovered when she was tying her shoes. The sides of the trail plunged steeply towards the lake. Not that a descent to the water would be smooth. Or advisable. Far from it. Blade-like branches protruded with a lethal intent, the profuse vegetation nothing but a thin veil. Wind whistled through the canopy of leaves above, a symphony of sounds absorbed by the verdant lushness. Abby shivered. Hearing the roar of the wind without feeling it was a little eerie. She needed to shake herself out of this mood and enjoy the time with Sasha. Space and solitude weren't things she usually craved, but lately, they had been calling. A seductive whisper worming its way in and taking residence in her mind.

'Where are you off to next when we get back?' Abby shook the tangled threads from her mind and focused on her friend.

'London first and then Frankfurt,' Sasha said.

'Geez, not bad, Sash. Need someone to turn your pages?' Abby knew full well Sasha didn't use music when she was performing. 'Or carry your hair dryer and straightening tongs?' Just as she knew Sasha never fussed with hair styles. 'I'll be a huge help.'

'Like you helped when we tried to go into business playing and recording wedding music?' Sasha raised a not-so-guileless eyebrow at her friend and laughed.

'Yep,' Abby deadpanned back. 'Exactly like that.'

A companionable silence threaded its way between the girls; a soft blanket worn smooth and familiar. Just like the memory. In theory, the idea had been brilliant. Live music options in the small dusty town where they grew up were as sparse as rainbows. Live *wedding* music, even more so. Sasha's piano skills paired with Abby's marketing drive had been deemed an unbeatable combination. They had the confidence and arrogance of youth; that self-belief that once an idea had been conceived, the riches would begin to roll in.

They had pitched themselves outside the local newsagent and busked alongside Saturday shoppers. The fact that the local fund-raising sausage sizzle tent was also outside the newsagent was a mere coincidence. If you wanted to define coincidence as deliberate, that is. There was no escaping the fact that the sausage sizzle tent drew people in and made them stop. And while they stopped and dribbled sauce and charred onions down their chins, their eyes would be drawn to the absolutely *brilliant* piece of advertising Abby had whipped up and stylishly scripted onto a piece of blue poster-sized cardboard. Because everyone knew that blue represented sincerity, loyalty and intelligence, elements all crucial to getting married. Or so it had said in the school library's dictionary when she had checked it earlier in the week.

Newly engaged couples had, indeed, stopped and showed genuine interest. Sasha's piano skills were well known in the small town but so far, had been confined to the Anglican church service on Sunday mornings, as well as the school choir and the odd school theatre production. The idea of having live keyboard music at a bush wedding made the brides feel classy, sophisticated. It made the would-be grooms itch their imaginary collars and stretch their T-shirts as the reality of their impending nuptials became concrete, but it was nothing another sausage fresh from the grill couldn't fix.

Eventually, they saved enough to escape. A trip to London when they graduated from high school was the first of many adventures.

Although if Sasha wanted there to be any *more* adventures, she would have to seriously slow her pace. Abby swore under her breath as her foot shot forward when she stepped on a tree root, its surface slicked to smoothness with moisture and decades of pedestrian traffic.

'We've got four days in Rotorua. Do you think some of it can be spent doing something that doesn't require my heart rate going over a hundred beats per minute?' Abby said, reaching to get her vibrating phone from the side pocket of her leggings.

It was a text from Joe. *Damn.* She had already missed three calls from him. Probably the dodgy service thanks to being in the middle of landscape that was straight out of *The Lord of the Rings.* She hoped nothing was wrong. He was most likely checking in and seeing how she was doing. He could be a bit of a fusspot sometimes. But it was lovely that he wanted to check up on her.

CHAPTER SIX

SAM ~ NOW

Sam hit the water, barely registering the chill, thankful he hadn't connected with any rocks below. The branches of the tree that were hidden beneath the water dug at his arms and ribs as he tried to reach for the body amidst the tangle of leaves and river flotsam. No amount of training or time on the job ever prepared you for the reality of finding a body. He spat out the dirty water as he tried to determine the best way to get to the woman.

Was it an accident? He pulled himself through the water, his chest burning as he held his breath. He broke the branch that snagged her arm in a grotesque wave-like parody. Without the anchor of the branch, the river current shifted her away from the tree. The sound of ripping fabric made Sam spin in the water, alert to anyone else who might be around, but it was her skirt, another branch ripping through it.

Hooking his hand under her armpit, he pulled her towards him, rolling her onto her back as he did so. Through the long, matted hair across her face, he dimly registered that her eyes were closed. She hadn't drowned. Drowning victims sometimes had a wide-eyed look as if they were staring off into space, focusing on a point they knew was inevitable. Or fighting desperately to avoid the inevitable. She had been dead before she hit the water. He was relatively sure of that.

Hauling her towards the riverbank, but mindful of preserving any slim shred of evidence on her lifeless body, Sam was aware that people had gathered at the jetty. He recognised Dave and could see a few uniformed officers.

'What the hell, Sam?' exploded Dave. 'We've got her, mate! Get yourself out now.'

A mixture of moss and mildew caked under his nails as Sam grabbed the jetty's edge. He watched as the officers laid the body on the boards, no heed being paid to the weathered and splintered surface. The woman was clearly dead, her mud-soaked hair covering her face, her body limp.

Dave reached out a hand towards Sam, yanking him out of the water. His clothes were heavy, dragging downwards with the weight of the silted water, the result of a few days of rain last week. A tear in his shirt, courtesy of the hidden branches, revealed an open wound, blood running freely as it mixed with the water streaming down him.

'Christ, Sam,' exclaimed Dave, looking at the bloody water pooling on the deck of the jetty, 'you've got a decent nick there.' He leaned closer and lifted the fabric. 'Seriously, mate, you need to go and get that looked at. All kinds of bloody bacteria in there,' said Dave, motioning towards the river.

Without looking at Dave, Sam grabbed a pair of gloves from one of the nearby officers and checked the pockets of the woman's jacket for ID. Nothing.

'Yeah. Fair enough,' he said over his shoulder.

The sun scorched the back of his neck, his head bowed. How had no one noticed a woman floating face-down in the water? How had she ended up there without anyone seeing a single thing?

Sam headed back up towards the vineyard. He knew the body wouldn't be moved until the police had contacted the coroner, so he figured he may as well get the deep gash seen to.

After a brief conversation with the police who were present, he followed a makeshift track that had been worn away by kids running down the hill, too impatient to use the provided stairs. He made his way towards an ambulance, its lights still flashing and bathing the area in strobes of blue and red light.

Sam lifted his hand and glanced down at the damage. He'd had worse. A scar from when he was three years old stretched almost the entire length of his left inner thigh. Keeping his steps measured, Sam took his time. There was no breeze, but the hairs on his arm prickled. Now, more than ever, he needed to talk to Sasha. Letting her call the shots was doing his head in. But what sort of person gave an injured woman an ultimatum?

Honey, I'm sorry your hand was injured beyond repair, and you can no longer do the one thing you're meant to do, but could you please stop feeling sorry for yourself and let us get back to where we were? That would go down an absolute treat.

Honey, it's not the end of the world. You'll find something else you can do that's even better. Trite *and* condescending. He'd nail it with that one. More like, she'd nail him to the back wall of the cop station if he fronted up with something like that.

Sam prided himself on being a straight shooter, on being professional and efficient. Platitudes and pretty words wasted time. Sasha knew this about him. In fact, she claimed to love this about him. So, why was she pushing him away? She said she needed time. Space. It'd been six weeks since the accident and he'd respected that. But how long did he need to keep accepting it? He wasn't someone who sat by and watched things happen. Not when that person was someone he loved; someone he was meant to have a future with.

Except, now she'd bloody gone and disappeared. She took off a week ago and he hadn't seen her since.

It was beginning to feel like he was being pushed around. A piece of driftwood at the mercy of the ocean's might, jostled around in whatever direction the currents dictated. Not that he could tell her that.

And it was nothing compared to the way she was treating Abby. Every bloody person knew it was an accident. No one in their right mind would ever entertain the idea of Abby deliberately hurting Sasha.

But Sasha was angry and lashing out. Sam got it. He knew what it was like to be hurt and feel powerless. Out of control. Sasha knew this, too. Which is what made her behaviour all the more infuriating.

Sam's thoughts were interrupted by a shout as he approached the van. 'Over here, Detective,' beckoned a woman in blue overalls, leaping out of the back of the van. 'I'll take a look for you.' She pointed at his bloodied shirt.

Sam frowned, momentarily oblivious to the fact he was clutching his side, his fingers sticky and bright red. He needed to pull himself together. 'Thanks.'

'I'll get you to take your shirt off so I can take a better look. You might need to head into the hospital for them to sort you out.' She paused and balled up the blood-and-mud-soaked shirt, tossing it into a plastic waste bag. 'Our driver keeps a stash of shirts up front so I can grab one for you. It's a rare day that one of us isn't spewed on or bloodied. Or worse.' She rolled her eyes. 'Let's not go there. But yeah, I'll toss you a clean shirt when we're done.'

'Thanks,' Sam said again.

The paramedic nodded towards the vineyard. 'Can't say I've had a call-out for an abandoned baby before, poor little thing. What do you make of it all?'

Sam winced as the antiseptic sluiced over the wound. 'Not sure,' he said. He looked at the raised eyebrows opposite him. Clearly, more was expected. 'There's nothing there to say who the baby is. A girl, only a few weeks old, but we can't tell any more than that. She'll be picked up by Child Services and put into emergency foster care.'

'God, the poor thing,' the paramedic said, her head drawn to the group huddled over the baby capsule. 'Who would do something like that? It's so crazy,' she said, biting her lip as she dabbed around the wound with cotton balls pinched between surgical tweezers.

'Yeah. Not what you expect out here. I haven't had a chance to check it out yet.'

Sitting in the back of the van, grimacing as the young paramedic continued to clean his wound, Sam gazed out at the scene around him. How had an ordinary Saturday turned into such a shitshow? An abandoned baby and now a dead woman? From his vantage point sitting on the stretcher, he could see four uniformed men on each corner of a board, carefully lifting it up the stairs as they struggled to keep the incline level. Clearly, the coroner was not going to make it out here and the police had been charged with moving her to the morgue.

Sam's eyes narrowed when he saw something fall from the dead woman. He straightened abruptly. 'Thanks, Liz,' he said to the medic, glancing at her badge. 'Can we wrap this up now?'

'I don't think it needs stitches, but keep it covered and then get it checked out in a day or two. If there's any redness...'

Sam pulled his jacket on and leapt off the stretcher and out of the van. 'Yeah, I know... see someone straight away. Thanks.' There was no time for further words.

'You forgot a clean shirt!' Liz called after him.

Racing past the four men carrying the body, he stopped midway down the stairs they had just walked up. If he hadn't been watching from the top, he would've missed it completely. He pulled on a glove from his pocket and reached down into the gap between the stairs and the grass. Sam picked up the object he'd watched fall from the pocket of the dead woman's skirt, the fabric slipping slightly as the men navigated the steps. A chain pooled in his hand as he cupped it.

It was a familiar silver pendant.

CHAPTER SEVEN

SASHA ~ RECENTLY

Sasha let her injured hand trail along the silver chain around her neck as she steered the car along the dirt road back to the motel. Despite her anger, she hadn't been able to take the necklace off. Just as she knew that Abby would never take hers off.

Something ran across the road in front of her, making her jerk the chain and the steering wheel. A *fox*? Since when were there foxes in the bush here? Possums, rats and kangaroos, maybe. But a fox?

She adjusted the car on the dirt road. Amazing how easy it was to deviate even just the tiniest bit. Her shoulders dropped as the thought looped around her mind. Deviating unintentionally. That was the crux of the issue right there. That was exactly what had happened to Abby. She'd deviated. She hadn't intended to, but she had. And that deviation had cost Sasha her career, her livelihood. As much as she wanted to move on and forgive Abby, that moment of distraction took everything she had ever worked for.

And she really *did* want to forgive Abby. To move forward. But how could she do that when she had no idea what she was meant to move towards? Music was all she had ever known, ever loved. She didn't want to be one of those people who accepted an apology, but then kept bringing it up at the slightest falter or disagreement, a weapon to be wielded as and when she saw fit.

But nothing could ever change the fact that it was Abby who'd been driving and Abby who caused the accident. The knowledge was an incendiary trail, gathering heat and exponential strength as each spark took hold to form an internal crescendo.

She tightened her grip and parked the car by her room, attempting to quash the burning sensation.

'I was hoping I would catch you, love.' The sing-song tone at the car window jolted Sasha. Oh, for the love of God. Did this woman have a camera at the gate? 'This is such good timing,' trilled Mrs Marcus. Had she been waiting and watching for her to come back? There was a pile of towels in her arms, but Sasha suspected the meeting was planned.

Mrs Marcus lifted Sasha's exposed and newly tattooed arm the moment she stepped from the car.

'Oh, love! That is gorgeous! Is it new? It looks new.' She trailed her fingers over the still raised fine lines of the tattoo that was barely a week old. Sasha jolted at the contact. 'So delicate and pretty. It looks like it could be a piece of jewellery.'

Sasha let out a slow breath. She needed to stop being so jumpy. And how did this woman know exactly the right thing to say?

'You really think so?' Sasha held her arm out, suppressing a flinch at the unaccustomed touch. 'It was kind of spur-of-the-moment. I didn't exactly plan it.' She bit the side of her lip. 'It was probably a bit rash.'

Mrs M laughed at her. 'Perhaps.' She adjusted the towels on her hip. 'But if you ask me, love, it's exactly what you needed.' Reading the dubious look on Sasha's face, Mrs M continued.

'More importantly, how do *you* feel about it? Do *you* love it? Are you happy you had it done?'

The tension and anxiety that had tethered itself to Sasha loosened its grip. 'I'm happy with it. I'd never considered getting a tattoo before. I still can't believe I actually went and got one.'

'If you want my opinion, love,' said Mrs M, peering over the top of her glasses and smiling at Sasha, 'you've gone and done something just for you. It's made you happy and I can see, plain as day, that you love it. And what's not to love? Give me another look at those pretty-as-pie pink flowers.' She hooked her arm through Sasha's and pulled her close. 'I'm so glad you added some colour to them. Such a dainty, feminine touch.'

Mrs M was right. It *had* made her happy. It was a decision *she* had made and for the first time in far too long, she felt as if she had exerted some control over the direction of her life. It was something she had not felt in a long time, when so much control had been stolen from her in a heartbeat.

'Anyway, love,' said Mrs M, hoisting the towels to her other hip, 'I need to get these up to reception. How about you walk with me? I know there was something I needed to ask you. Or tell you? Goodness me! It's like Gerry always says...'

'Sure,' Sasha interrupted, falling into step beside her. 'Need a hand carrying anything?' For once, she was not self-conscious about the scar and damage to her hand.

The music hit Sasha the minute Mrs M opened the front door of the main building. It drifted out in waves, the melody light and simple, but with so much feeling and emotion that the skill of the person playing was immediately evident. It wasn't a composer Sasha recognised, so it could have been written by whoever was playing. Her feet refused to move and all she could do was stare at the door where the sound was coming from. Mrs

Marcus was oblivious and kept chatting. 'Well, isn't this a stroke of luck! Looks like young Andrea has popped in for a visit.' Mrs M paused and leant in towards Sasha. 'Her mum's a good friend. Andrea's a bit of a local celebrity with her performances. Travels the world and everything, that girl,' she added in a not-so-subtle whisper, excitement radiating off her in waves. 'I wasn't expecting to see her for another day or two, but isn't this just the best surprise?'

Luck wasn't exactly the word that sprang to mind. The music continued to drift down the hall, and before Sasha realised what was happening, Mrs M had grabbed her arm and was propelling both of them towards a room at the far end of the house. The ability to speak seemed to have completely deserted her. The ability to even think had likewise disappeared.

Standing in the doorway of the room where the music was coming from, Sasha gripped onto the wooden doorframe as if it were in danger of collapsing. Splinters dug at her nailbeds. The girl at the piano moved; she swayed. As if the music was coming from within her, its only escape via her fingers.

Mrs M was practically dancing around the room.

'Sasha, love, come over here and meet Andrea. Oh, this is such a treat.' She dropped the towels and wrapped an arm around the young woman at the piano. 'Well, aren't you just a sight for sore eyes?'

Without missing a beat or note, Andrea smiled over her shoulder at the older woman and continued playing.

Sasha made her way across the room, her legs feeling about as steady as those of a newborn foal. What were the chances of her receiving an urgent call right now? *Anything* that would get her out of the room. Given that she'd pushed everyone away from her lately, not very likely.

'Hiya!' sang Andrea, lingering over a final chord and spinning around on the piano stool before standing in one fluid motion. The long, floral skirt she was wearing continued to swirl around her ankles. Her dark hair fell well past her shoulders in loose waves and, like her skirt, it continued to move, energy and elegance braided in effortless fluidity. She reached out and clasped Sasha's hand, shaking it and smiling with such openness and enthusiasm that Sasha wondered if she had confused her with someone else. 'It's good to see you!' Her eyes sparked. 'What brings you to the area?'

This was a perfectly normal question to ask someone who was staying in tourist accommodation, but Sasha found she had lost the ability to answer. Thankfully, Mrs M jumped in as if it were the most natural thing in the world to answer a question put to someone else. Andrea gave an almost imperceptible frown. It also gave Sasha a moment to remember how to breathe. Andrea turned and listened to Mrs M and Sasha was dimly aware they were continuing on with a conversation.

Sasha glanced around the room, trying to be calm and focus her thoughts. For the past six weeks, she had managed to avoid listening to any piano music. Every fibre of her being screamed at her to sit at the keyboard, and her fingers burned with the urge to play something, to let the music flow and escape from the prison it had been confined to. The baby grand piano was in the far corner of the room and Sasha had to make herself look at anything but *it*.

She concentrated on breathing evenly. Chatter filtered through as a buzz in the background. Her gaze jumped around, drinking in details as a convenient diversion. Two of the walls were lined from floor to ceiling with bookshelves, the books arranged with odd irregularity. There was a handwoven mat on the floor, but Sasha couldn't decide what would have inspired the design, perhaps something Mexican and Japanese with figures and nature merging in vibrant colours. Three chairs in various upholstered colours and designs spanned the third wall,

all at angles that invited people to chat while curled up in comfort, wrapped in the chunky-knit throws draped over the backs.

Sasha continued to absorb every detail as she tried to calm her breathing and thoughts. Eventually, she let her eyes settle on the one object she had been determined to avoid. The piano.

It gradually occurred to Sasha that two sets of eyes were looking at her, clearly waiting for a response. Or maybe just for some indication that she was still capable of speech. She wasn't entirely sure that she was.

'Sorry,' Sasha cleared her throat when it came out as more of a rasp than an actual word. 'What were you saying?'

'You were away with the fairies, weren't you, love?' said Mrs M, with a chuckle. 'I was just telling Andrea about your tattoo and how spontaneous you were. Who knows what'll happen the next time you go into town. Maybe a nose ring? I've actually wondered about getting one of those myself,' she laughed, the idea having caught her fancy.

'Absolutely!' agreed Andrea, clapping her hands. 'You really should, Mrs M.'

'Oh, go on with you,' she chortled. 'You know very well I'm joking. Gerry would think I'd lost my marbles.'

Sasha felt as if she was watching and listening to the conversation from the end of a tunnel. Without warning, she was dragged back into the room, another question being very clearly directed at her and Mrs M no longer saving her with her answers and chatter.

'Do you play?' The words echoed around the room.

Sasha stared at the piano, her heart rate rivalling the fastest setting of the metronome sitting above the music stand.

'I used to.' Her words were nothing more than a whisper.

With her heart still racing at a double-*allegro* pace, she was being wrapped in ribbons of memory. It was a memory of her performing.

She tried not to blink. Her position in the middle of the stage was a target for every eye in the filled concert hall. The lights trained on her were blinding, but only if she looked directly at them, which she'd learnt long ago not to do. Always better to look just below them and acknowledge the audience with a small inclination of her head. The conscious gesture was usually enough to steady her heart rate as she drew a breath and lifted her hands to the keyboard. The moment her fingers connected with the ivory keys, the lights, the energy and the nerves were forgotten. All that existed was the music.

Tonight, it was Chopin, Étude Op. 25, No. 6 in G-sharp minor. An ambitious work, but one that thrilled her, the sense of exhilaration incomparable. Calmness filled her chest and relaxed her shoulders as she flexed her fingers over the keys. *This* was where she belonged.

But instead of the opening bars of Chopin filling her consciousness, shards of light knifed through her eyes. There was a sequence of slow-motion events: Abby yelling, the car wrenched off the road, the trunk of a tree all she could see, her left arm flung up instinctively. Reflexively. White-hot pain piercing her hand.

And then, nothing. She was left with nothing.

Rude or not, she could not stay in this room a moment longer. Without any thought for the women in front of her, Sasha turned and ran down the hall, pushing through the front door and stumbling back to her room.

CHAPTER EIGHT

ABBY ~ BEFORE THE ACCIDENT

Wind wound its way through the outdoor wedding venue, mocking guests' attempts at modesty as they tried to conceal undergarments. It was a zephyr with the heart of a jester. As long as it kept its fingers out of the cheeses and dips, Abby didn't mind. The last thing she needed was for the brie to have a light dusting of dirt. It wouldn't pair at all well with the blueberry coulis she wanted to drizzle over it. The grounds of the Fremantle events' venue were certainly picturesque, but months with little rain had taken their toll.

'Oh my God, Abs, that looks incredible.' Sasha anchored a few stray curls behind an ear and ignored the billowing hem of her dress. 'I've got no idea how you do this. I try to make a cheeseboard and it looks like I've laid out things for a science experiment.' She stole a perfectly scrolled piece of salami. 'This,' she said with a sweeping gesture, 'looks like Monet's *Water Lily* painting.'

Abby beamed and swatted Sasha's hand as she reached out to snag an olive. 'It's going to be short a few water lilies if you keep pinching things.' Not that she minded. And Sasha had nailed the vibe she was going for. She always aimed to have her boards be an oasis in whatever function she was catering for, a refuge from social expectations and conversational efforts.

'That's your fault for making it look so damn tasty,' Sasha linked her arm through Abby's. 'You're really good at this, you know?' She tossed a couple of cashews in her mouth. 'You should do this for a living,' she added with a wink.

Abby resisted the urge to roll her eyes. But she glowed at Sasha's comments. It had been a risk to throw in her office admin job a month ago and take the plunge into self-employment. Gone was the safety net of a regular income, of knowing she could plan ahead and budget, of having co-workers to moan to about deadlines or unreasonable expectations from narky bosses.

She was the boss now, narky or otherwise. And unless you counted her very hairy dog, Vishnu, as a co-worker, she had no one to moan to. Mind you, he was a lot more friendly and empathetic than most of the people she'd worked with in the past. Not to mention slobbery. For all his scary looks and intimidating barks, her German Shepherd was a sheep in wolf's clothing. Abby giggled to herself as she pictured Vishnu as a fluffy lamb, pouncing on shadows in the backyard with his tongue flopping about like a pair of damp Speedos on the clothesline. And she would take his genuine gestures of friendship any day over the faux-sincere overtures that were dished out in the office environment. At least his licks were unconditional and devoid of social currency.

Chucking in her job had been one of her better decisions and she was proud of herself. It was a step in the right direction, at any rate.

'Seriously, Abs.' Sasha turned to look directly at her. 'I'm really proud of what you've done. It hasn't been easy, but you did it.' She whipped her phone out from her back pocket. 'Let me get an action shot of the magic happening for your socials. Gotta keep the fans updated.'

'I post plenty of photos,' Abby said indignantly.

'Of your boards, sure. And they're brilliant,' Sasha got in quickly, seeing Abby's mouth opening to interject. 'But people like to see *you* as well. They want to see the genius behind the creations. They want to know the whole story.'

Abby threw a grape at Sasha who caught it neatly and popped it in her mouth.

'Uh-uh,' Sasha waggled a finger at Abby. 'Now *you're* the one destroying the water lilies.'

'Excuse me,' a deep voice interrupted the girls.

Abby flinched and dropped the gum leaf garland she had been twisting between the boards. Sasha shook her head gently, and Abby steadied herself with a deep breath before turning to face him.

'Hi,' Abby said brightly. Just smile and pretend. You can do it.

'I'm really sorry, but there's only the one table for you to set up the grazing boards.' A young guy with the venue's logo on his shirt did his best to maintain eye contact, but gave up.

Abby's brief had been for four boards and she'd been told she would have two tables; all details that determined the size of the boards, the decorations she used and the quantities of food. One table was going to seriously impact the plan.

'You're sure?' Abby frowned as she ran through the layout in her mind. 'You can't find just one more table?'

'No. I'm really sorry. They're all being used for the reception.' A bead of sweat leaked from his hairline.

Brilliant. Was it too much to ask that she could pull off this event without any complications? This was the one area of her life where she had some degree of control, where she could create order and make decisions that did not invite criticism.

Abby closed her eyes for a second before looking back at him. She knew it wasn't his fault. There was no point in making him feel even more uncomfortable than he obviously was.

'Don't worry about it. I'll make it work.' In the scheme of things, it wasn't that much of a problem. She'd dealt with worse.

The event guy scuffed a shoe along the dusty ground, no doubt wishing he could be back inside setting up chairs. Or even out in the 40-degree heat dragging in portaloos.

It was all very well to make the boards look appealing, but the challenges along the way certainly kept her on her toes. Still, it was a heck of a lot more interesting than sitting in a stuffy office, listening to Darryl in the opposite cubicle hoick back phlegm and snot every three minutes. Abby had itched to leave a Post-It note with details for an Ear, Nose and Throat doctor on his desk. Or a box of tissues, at the very least. She shuddered at the memory and stepped back to look at the table. She was exactly where she wanted to be.

'Anything I can do to help?' Sasha asked as the venue guy inched backwards before retreating inside the building. 'I don't need to be at the concert hall for another few hours. I can stay and help put things out, if you want?' She picked up a container of green olives stuffed with strands of pepperdew and peeled back the plastic seal, rolling her eyes as the smell of garlic and lemon hit her. 'I even promise not to eat anything.' She scooped one out. 'After I do a quick bit of quality control with this one.'

'It's all good,' Abby said, drawing a breath and twisting her silver balloon pendant around her finger. 'Thanks for stopping by, though.'

'Don't forget to take plenty of photos, will you?' Sasha said, swiping a final olive and waving as she left. 'You don't want me having to ask waiter-dude to come and take some, do you? The poor guy would probably expire on the spot.'

'Get out of here, you idiot,' Abby said, giving Sasha a gentle shove. 'Go and spread your hilarious charm at the orchestra.'

It really wasn't that big of a deal. Abby stared at the table for a few moments. Tightening the angled layout of the boards would see them all fit on the one table. It would be a little more squashed, but she'd hover on the fringes and refill supplies as they were eaten. She lifted a vase with white roses from her supply box and placed it on the corner of one of the boards. Small personalised touches were one of her signature elements. She wanted the grazing boards to reflect the event and the people involved. The couple getting married today were mad-keen cyclists and she'd found the cutest little ornamental bike with a tiny white wooden crate on the back that begged to have grapes spilling from the sides. She smiled, satisfied that she could still pull off a decent creation. More than decent. If only all her problems could be solved as seamlessly, with just a slight amount of adaptation.

Is that what she was doing with Joe? Adapting? Abby winced when the wire from the leaf garland she was twisting around the boards pierced her palm and the thin latex food-prep glove. Blood beaded, a drop the size of the ruby on her finger, a gift from Joe a few weeks ago. She peeled the glove off and turned her hand over. The ruby on her finger mirrored the blood, the colours deep and mesmerising. She knew why he'd given it to her. It wasn't exactly the apology she'd been expecting after his... outburst.

When he'd explained it to her, it had made sense. Couples had to adapt, grow, change. No one could stay the same. It was a sign of the connection they shared if they could absorb the challenges and obstacles thrown in their path. Those were the words he had used. *Challenges. Obstacles.* Is that what she was? A challenge that Joe needed to conquer?

She shook her head and blinked, grabbing a serviette and

balling it into her hand. The last thing she needed was to add further challenges to her day by getting blood on the food. Besides, Joe was sweet and thoughtful. She needed to shake off her mood.

Immersing herself in the new condensed layout of the table, and drawing all the food and decorations together, Abby didn't notice her phone vibrating in her pocket.

CHAPTER NINE

SAM ~ NOW

Sam stared at the pendant pooled in his hand. It told him all he needed to know.

He raced up to the men carrying the stretcher.

'Wait!' Sam's vision clouded. He ripped back the sheet covering the body.

'Detective, you know you can't–'

'Sir, just a minute–'

Sam ignored the voices around him and the hand grabbing his shoulder. He tried to swallow, but there was no moisture in his mouth. A light breeze caught the corner of the sheet still covering the feet, causing a whisper of movement. Nothing more. He stared at the face he'd uncovered, now devoid of its usual animation, its muscles slack. Lifeless.

How had he missed it? How could he not have known? If he'd known, would it still have been too late? Of course it would have been too late. Still... He'd been so preoccupied with getting the body out of the water that he hadn't stopped to consider whether he recognised the victim.

But he *did* recognise her. And all too well. The matted and mud-soaked hair had obscured her face as he'd hauled her to the dock. His focus had been on getting to the body and then getting it out of the water.

Even in his haste, Sam was aware of the dangers beneath the surface; toppled trees and broken branches with jagged ends; rocks at varying depths thanks to the tidal flows; even snakes had been known to make a river crossing. Adrenaline had urged him forward, the dangers nothing more than peripheral.

The glimpse he got of the closed eyes in the water had been cursory at best, barely enough to register that she may not have drowned. He hadn't paused to push the hair aside and see if he recognised the person. Why the hell would he do that? Or, more to the point, why the hell *hadn't* he done that?

'Detective?' The voice snagged Sam's attention. The sergeant at the head of the stretcher had an impatient air about him. Sam recognised him from the city station, his bald head pitted like the skin of a rockmelon. Greg? The name rang a bell.

He shoved his hand in his pocket to cover the shaking. 'Sorry,' Sam said finally. 'Just needed to check something.'

Neither man moved for a moment, both looking at the body. In the glaring sunlight, Sam could see her skin had turned blueish-grey and started to wrinkle. How long had she been in the water?

'Any idea what happened?' The sergeant wiped a dribble of sweat from his jaw. The air was stifling. The light breeze from lunchtime had all but disappeared.

Sam stared at the face – the familiar face – a leaf stuck to her cheek. His fingers ached to pull it off. 'No idea. The coroner will have to confirm, but I think she was dead before she hit the water.'

Abby. *Fuck.* It was Abby.

'Shit.' The sergeant looked over towards the ambulance where paramedics were still checking out the baby. The one that had patched Sam up was cradling the baby. 'Any idea if the

47

two were related?' He jutted his chin. 'People don't just up and leave a baby in the middle of a bloody vineyard for no good reason.'

Sam let the sheet fall over the face, covering her features, as if the act of hiding the identity would make it less real. 'No,' he said. 'They don't.'

Fucking hell. Was the baby Abby's? The thought – no – realisation punched him in the gut.

'Maybe whoever did this,' the sergeant gestured at the stretcher and Sam flinched, the reality tightening his throat, 'is still in the area. Could be, they stuck around for the kid.'

He had a valid point. Although Sam doubted that was the case. He shook his head in an attempt to clear it.

'Could be,' the sergeant continued, straightening his back as the idea gathered momentum, 'he's hiding and waiting. Or walking around in bloody plain sight. How long's it been since they found the kid? If the mother was around, she'd be making herself known, don't you think?'

'She would,' Sam said, his eyes still glued to the covered body. She damn well would.

The sergeant nodded at Sam and looked down at the stretcher. 'You done here, Detective? Best we get a move on.'

Sam dragged his eyes away from the covered contours of the body. 'Yeah.' He paused, his voice hollow. 'Thanks.'

A few minutes passed while Sam stood, unmoving, staring out at the river. The sun seared the back of his neck, but it didn't register. How the hell had she ended up in the river? Surely, someone had seen something? Heard something? Even bloody *recorded* something? People were so damn obsessive about recording every little staged detail around them that something had to have ended up on someone's phone, surely?

A team from the forensics unit had arrived and was moving methodically along the water's edge, processing the area in minute detail. He watched them take photo after photo of seemingly innocuous patches of grass, clumps of weeds and sections of riverbank. Would any of it help? Give them answers? Would it tell him how she'd ended up in the water?

And where was Dave? He wasn't just the owner of the vineyard. Sasha and Abby meant the world to him. He was Sasha's father, but he was also a father figure to Abby. Had he seen the body? Did he know, too?

Sam spun around, scanning the people still milling in the area. Tables had been abandoned, with food still piled high on the plates, now congealing in the heat, the misting hoses above creating a sludgy soup. Chairs were shoved on their sides thanks to the scrambled chaos and commotion. A lot of the diners had left. A few remained, details still being taken from officers. Some were standing in small groups. There was also a lot of head shaking, shoulders being shrugged, brows being furrowed. The atmosphere was one of confusion. Shock.

There was no sign of Dave.

He opened his hand and stared at the pendant, a silver balloon with a short loop of chains threaded through the base that dangled like the tail of the real thing. Both women had one. Sasha's had a red enamel bow on the balloon; Abby's was green. They had been a gift from Sasha's mum two years ago at Christmas. Abby had been part of the celebrations. It's just the way it was. Abby was a part of the family; she always had been. He'd been part of it too. His first Christmas as Sasha's boyfriend.

He'd been welcomed from the moment he'd set foot in the vineyard. He'd been a little nervous. A *lot* nervous. Meeting the parents of someone he'd met while issuing them with a speeding ticket was a first for him. Issuing speeding tickets wasn't something he'd done in a long time, either. He'd briefly debated ignoring the car flying past him in the reduced speed zone and continuing home. Duty got the better of him, though. And he was glad that it had. The driver wore a sleeveless red dress and hadn't tried to make excuses or explain in excruciating detail her reasons for speeding. She hadn't tried to flirt her way out of the ticket. She had accepted it, smiled in resignation, and promised to pay more attention.

And that would have been that, if it hadn't been for the fact that a mere ten minutes later, Sam pulled into the parking lot of the Perth Civic Centre at the same time as his ticket recipient.

'Was there something else?' The amused voice greeted him as he got out of his car.

'Just a coincidence,' Sam had said. 'I'm here for the concert.'

'A coincidence, indeed,' she had responded. 'So am I.'

They had parted ways, Sasha heading in the opposite direction and Sam assuming she was meeting friends. It was an assumption he had very quickly revised when the pianist walked onto the concert stage. A pianist wearing a sleeveless red dress that swept the boards, trailing in her wake.

Tickets to the West Australian Symphony Orchestra had been his secret Santa gift from the station. He'd been tempted to pass them on to someone who might appreciate the culture a little more than him, but had changed his mind at the last minute. It was about time he started doing something other than returning home at the end of each shift.

If someone had asked him what was performed that night, he would've had no idea. So much for being a detective and exercising keen observational skills. His observational skills had been otherwise employed, taking in details about the pianist on stage. Her composure, her elegance and her confidence drew him in. But it was more than that. He found himself thinking of her smile in the parking lot, the attraction that had tugged at him.

Since he was already acting out-of-character by being at the concert in the first place, Sam figured he may as well continue the theme and attempt to see her afterwards. Thankfully, she had laughed at the coincidence of the meetings and had agreed to go out for a coffee the next day.

Spending Christmas together despite only having dated for a month felt natural. He'd been content to sit back and soak it all in. The laughter, love, and affection was evident in the banter. Both girls were only-children, but had chosen the other as their "family." They were probably closer than many actual siblings, devoid of the contempt and bickering often born from familial proximity. They were inseparable.

Or they *had* been inseparable. The accident had changed everything. Sasha had been so wrapped up in anger and desolation that she'd lashed out at the person closest to her. At the *people* closest to her. Sam got that she was angry and mourning the loss of the one thing she knew; her livelihood; her passion. But surely, she had to know that Abby would never deliberately do anything to hurt her? And that *he* only wanted to help her, to be there for her? Wasn't that what partners were supposed to do? Support one another in times of need or crisis?

Bloody hell. Where was Dave? He needed to find him before someone else did. Sam strode through the dining room and into the small office tucked beside the shelves of wine for sale. Dave was standing behind a desk, staring out of the window that afforded him a view of the entire vineyard; row upon row of carefully tended plants, a rose bush at the end of each one before the lawn sloped towards the river. He looked up, eyes blank. Dull.

'If I'd been standing here, I'd probably have seen what happened, ya know?' Dave said. 'I could've *done* something. Stopped it.'

He knew. He knew who it was. He'd seen the body. Of course he had. Sam stood still.

'Shit, Sam. What the hell am I going to do?' Dave raked his hand over his head. 'How am I going to tell June? Abby's like a second daughter to her.'

'She's here?' Sam looked around for Sasha's mother. This was going to kill her. Poor choice of words. But it would.

Dave's shoulders slumped. 'Any chance it's not her?' Hope threaded his voice.

Sam opened his hand and looked again at the necklace. 'No.' There was no chance at all.

CHAPTER TEN

ABBY ~ BEFORE THE ACCIDENT

Abby's phone vibrated in her back pocket as she hoisted dripping grocery bags onto the kitchen counter. The dark clouds that had loomed all morning erupted just moments before Joe had swung the car into the driveway. Not that it had prompted him to pull the car further under the cover of the open garage. She jerked her ladened arms higher and winced when her shoulder protested. God, she really needed to add some upper body exercises into her workout. Which she'd do, just as soon as her shoulder felt better.

'Can you get that, babe?' Abby jutted her hip towards Joe, keeping her tone light to mask the discomfit.

Joe looked up from his own phone, his hands otherwise free. And dry. There had been no offer of help lugging bags from the car. Instead, he'd dived into the garage and through to the kitchen, busying himself with the myriad of notifications he'd missed while driving. If the groceries were going to make it inside, it was going to be up to Abby. A practised grin chased a flash of annoyance from his face. It was a flash most people would have missed. He put the phone face down on the entrance table.

'Sure.' He reached across and fished the phone from Abby's soggy pocket. He held it in front of him, angling it so the only thing Abby could see was the back of her lilac case. His nostrils flared and his lips tightened.

Abby gave a final heft, and let the bags drop with a thump. She hoped the eggs weren't in either of them.

'Who is it?' Abby held her hand out, keeping her tone light. He was doing nothing to mask his irritation. The hairs on her arms stood to attention as the phone kept buzzing in Joe's hand. Drops of moisture dribbled down the phone towards his fingers.

He tossed the phone over to the couch where it skittered across the cushions before slipping onto the floor. Rain smacked against the panes of the lounge room windows; sharp angry raps doing their best to find a way in, trying to find a point of weakness where they could worm their way through. Abby's stomach clenched. She rolled her shoulder unconsciously, the pain in it twisting in sympathy with her stomach.

'It was nothing.' Joe crossed to the fridge and yanked it open. 'Just Sasha. Probably wanting to whinge about fuck knows what. I guess you've missed her.' He jutted his chin, daring Abby to contradict him.

Abby cringed, more at Joe's tone than the language. She considered moving to retrieve the phone, but hesitated. Instead, it lay on the carpet, a tiny coloured brick of unexploded surprises. She had no idea what Sasha wanted. Probably checking in to see if they could do something over the weekend. Nothing important. Nothing that should make Joe angry. Except it did.

Joe suddenly spun from the open fridge and cupped a hand around Abby's cheek. 'I really don't know why you keep hanging out with her.' He rubbed his thumb along her jaw. Tenderly. Gently. And then with increased pressure. 'You're so much better than her, hon. Can't you see she's using you?' He kept his tone soothing. Syrupy. 'You don't need someone like her, hon. You've got me.'

Abby turned away from him and reached blindly into one of the grocery bags. *Using* her? What was Joe talking about? Sasha didn't *use* her. 'No worries.' She swallowed, an attempt to quell the moisture building in her eyes. Trying to work out what Joe meant was confusing. Trying to guess his moods was exhausting.

Joe slammed the fridge door so hard that it bounced ajar again before finally settling back to being closed.

'Christ, Abby. There's nothing to eat.' Joe moved to the pantry and peered in, the gentle tone of mere seconds before, gone. 'I thought we just went bloody shopping?'

Abby swallowed and bit down on the inside of her cheek. She could point out the obvious – that the groceries were still in the bags, if he cared to help. Or she could settle for the path of least resistance.

CHAPTER ELEVEN

SAM ~ NOW

Sam sat on a wooden bench by the winery's restaurant the next morning. It gave him a perfect view of the river and of the branches he'd dragged her from.

The pre-dawn light cast a hazy filter along the river's surface. Sleep had eluded him after 2am and following a couple of hours of tossing and turning, he'd found himself driving out to the vineyard. He'd also emailed his supervisor about his connection, removing himself as the lead investigator. Since it wasn't a direct family link though, he planned to stay involved. *Very* involved.

How was it no one had seen anything? The place had been packed at the weekend; the restaurant buzzing; people out for a stroll, soaking up the atmosphere. Sam got up and made his way towards the water. It wouldn't hurt to go and take another look. Police tape ringed the area and it wouldn't be long until officers were back to continue the investigation. The path was shadowed, but he knew it well. He ducked a fraction when he felt the breeze of a cormorant gliding in to land on a branch by the riverbank. The wings extended slowly and precisely, the feathers separating so they could soak up the sunlight. It was an unconsciously theatrical performance.

Sam's foot slipped on the slope covered in dew-slicked grass. The cormorant turned its head further in the opposite direction, shunning even a hint of interaction. Sam could relate. He didn't feel like interacting with anyone either. Questions drummed through his head. What the bloody hell had happened? Loose stones slipped under his shoes as the grass gave way to gravel. Was it really only a few months ago that he'd walked along here with Sasha?

He grabbed a branch and swung himself down a small drop on the bank, landing on a smooth rock ledge hidden from general view. He instinctively reached for a dangling rope without looking up, his hand sliding along layers of moss and mildew.

Sitting on the rock that had enough space for two people, Sam breathed deeply. Damp earth and decaying vegetation filled his lungs, the summer scent of the Swan River. Patches of exposed bank invited the local birdlife to delve deep into the rich soil. A twisted red drink can was obscured by a tangle of twigs and leaves. Sam reached down to pull it out. Secluded areas along the river's edge were a magnet for couples to share a drink and a few private moments.

Had the place been chosen deliberately for its seclusion? Was that how she'd ended up here? Sure, there had been dozens of people in the area. But if you knew what you were doing, where you were going, then you could do anything. Get away with anything.

Was that what had happened? Had she been deliberately targeted?

Sam felt a pang of longing twist in his gut. Sasha should be here with him. This was *their* spot. He could see her, sitting beside him: her laugh, staccato bursts of joy, sunlight hitting the stray streak of grey at her temple that had only just emerged. He rested his hand on the vacant rock surface beside him, his fingertips ignoring the damp leaves, instead remembering the wayward curls he liked to delve his hands into.

Her voice was clear. She was always daring him to do something. *I dare you to jump in.* He'd looked at the murky river water and laughed. Of course, he wasn't going to jump in. *I'll make it worth your while.* She'd teased him, her fingers dancing a melody along his arm, over his shoulder and finishing with an intricate trill below his ear. It was as easy as that. It always was. He'd ended up in the water. But he hadn't ended up alone. He wasn't a complete pushover. At least, that's what he told himself.

Truth of the matter was, he would've done anything for Sasha. He knew they'd been happy. He hadn't imagined that.

Sam looked over his shoulder at the sound of footsteps crunching along the gravel path.

'You down here, mate?' An indistinct curse followed the question.

Sam didn't recognise the voice.

'You bloody lazing on the job again, ya slacker?'

Sam cleared his throat and stood up on the rock ledge.

'Oh, shit. Sorry, mate.' A blaze of hi-viz pink came into view, stopping at the police tape. 'Thought you were me useless partner.'

'Nope,' Sam said. 'I'm not him. Or her,' he added.

The woman in front of him pulled a two-way radio from the pocket of her vest, the Velcro straining at its anchor points. She hooked a thumb through a belt loop and hoisted it over a copious amount of stomach flesh. The cormorant turned its head to gaze at the other side of the river, a light breeze twitching the feathers on its still immobile wings.

The woman snapped a piece of gum against the roof of her mouth.

'Me mate has bloody done a disappearing act, the useless tart. She's about as helpful as tits on a bloody bull some days.'

Did she just *wink* at him? 'What brings you down here?' Sam said.

'Down here? Well, it sure as hell ain't to go swimming. No siree.'

'Makes sense,' Sam said, not feeling the need to add anything further.

The vision in hi-viz slapped the radio against her thigh and then rubbed it against her chest. As if polishing it with her boobs was going to help. 'Anyway, I'll leave you to...' She waved in the general direction of the water before holding the still silent radio up to her ear. 'I'll be on me way now and let you get back to...' She flicked her hand again. '...whatever it is you were doin'. Gotta get things packed up from the race on the weekend and back to the warehouse.' She turned and kept muttering. 'Bloody idiots runnin' all over the place and swimmin' and shit. Got better things to do with me time than that, I'll tell ya that for nothin'.'

'Nice to meet you,' Sam said, by way of farewell as she puffed her way up the inclined path towards the carpark.

The race. Of course. There'd been a local run yesterday, earlier in the day, before everything had happened. A lot of the people eating lunch on the vineyard's veranda had probably taken part in the event first. He'd need to get in touch with the event organisers and get a list of who took part.

Even if they hadn't witnessed someone entering the water, there surely had to be some details, however minor, that might help. He wasn't sure if his conviction was more to do with hope or fact.

Sam headed back up towards the vineyard and his car. He needed to get into the station and talk to the coroner.

―――――――――

Sam looped through the station's small kitchen and poured a coffee, wincing at the bitterness as he took a gulp. It would have to do. He didn't have the time – or the inclination – to stop and get something decent from a café. He needed to see if the autopsy results had come through. Despite the detour to the vineyard, he'd still arrived early and the office was operating at a low buzz rather than submerged in the usual morning mayhem.

A few droopy plants balanced on edges of desks, but if ever there was to be an exercise in futility, that was it. The poor things had no idea what direction sunlight was meant to come from. Instead, they turned in on themselves, inviting the piles of folders and paperwork to swallow them up.

Sam headed in the direction of the coroner's office and knocked on the door. The blind on the door's glass pane was raised and Sam could see Paul Green at his desk. This wasn't Paul's only office; his main one was at the Central Law Courts, but he liked to have somewhere to work in private when he was at the station.

'Morning, Sam,' Paul nodded in greeting when Sam entered.

'You're here early.' Sam reached across the desk to shake Paul's hand.

'Could say the same about you. Best time of day to get things done though, right? Try and clear the decks a bit before the daily chaos starts. I'm due in court at nine and I wanted to go over the notes you sent through from the vineyard.' Paul shuffled a few things around on his desk, pulling out the papers he'd printed with the initial findings, along with the reports that had been filed. 'I'll be able to go and examine the body as soon as I'm done here.'

'Any thoughts on cause of death?' Sam cut straight to his reason for being there. No point wasting time that neither man had to spare.

'Not yet,' said Paul, drawing a breath. 'She was moved sooner than I would've liked, but it was the only way. Couldn't exactly leave her at the scene. I'm still going through the photos and notes that were taken. Looks like there was some head trauma.'

'Any sign of sexual assault?' Sam asked. The question burned his throat.

'Too early to tell.' Paul peered at some of the photos and frowned. 'I can see a lot of superficial cuts, but they could've been from the branches that caught her in the river.' Pointing to a spot on her shoulder, he continued, 'This one here looks deeper. Can't tell yet if it's a stab wound or not. I'll let you know as soon as I've had a look.'

'Thanks.' Sam ground his teeth, forcing his mind to focus on facts. There'd be time later for emotion.

Sam looked at the photos that Paul had spread out across his desk. They were the usual ones that were taken at a crime scene; shots taken from all angles of the body, where she'd been found, imprints in the ground, the surrounding area, close-ups of wounds and abrasions and then a few taken when she'd been laid out in the morgue. Lifeless. Alone.

Oh, God. The thought of her pain and terror churned through him. Had the injuries occurred when she was conscious? Had she been aware of what was happening to her?

CHAPTER TWELVE

ABBY ~ BEFORE THE ACCIDENT

The teacup crashed in perfect freefall. Scalding liquid splattered in every direction, droplets of chaos covering every surface in the day spa's massage room. Joe's name flashed across Abby's phone screen.

'Jesus, Abby,' Sasha leapt up from the depths of her massage chair recliner.

Good grief. This wasn't the start to the day she'd envisioned. A foot rub at the day spa in the shopping mall was supposed to be calming. Grounding, even.

Sasha grabbed the towel that had been under her legs. 'Are you okay?' She dried the peppermint scented liquid off her legs and blotted damp patches from her rolled up pants. 'Geez, if you didn't want the tea, you just had to say so.'

The phone in Abby's hand continued to vibrate. Could she just ignore it?

'Put your phone in your bag,' Sasha said, leaning over and patting the towel against Abby's damp ankles. 'If you can't see it, you can't be bothered by it.' She hadn't asked who it was. She hadn't needed to.

If only it was that easy. This was meant to be a fun day out.

An escape. A chance to catch up with her friend between her tour dates. Sasha's time back in Perth was limited and she wanted to make the most of seeing her. Any time with her was fleeting and a tiny bit frenetic. Sasha had always been like that. You got swept up in her energy and were left feeling revived, as if a dose of her energy was exactly what the doctor had prescribed.

Abby badly needed a dose of Sasha's energy and optimism right now. She'd been open and upfront with Joe about her plans. Well, kind of. If "up front" meant she'd said she was ducking out to do a few chores, then that's what she was doing. Sometimes, it was easier to be just the tiniest bit evasive. Mentioning Sasha just irritated him and she hadn't been up to dealing with that this morning. Joe wasn't the biggest fan where Sasha was concerned. He thought she had too many opinions; that she was *independent*. As if that was a bad thing. It wasn't that Joe didn't like opinions. He only had a problem if they didn't match his own.

As Abby opened her mouth to reply to Sasha, the door to the shop swung open.

'Well, well, well.' The squat figure in the doorway was shadowed, but there was no mistaking the mocking tone.

Abby froze. Prickles shot along her spine. Shit! Shit, shit, bloody shit. Joe. How did he know she was here?

'Joe,' Sasha said, not bothering to hide her distaste. 'What brings you here? Did you have a sudden urge for a foot massage?'

'I got worried when Abby didn't answer her phone.' He frowned and shook his head at Abby, an outwardly indulgent reprimand. 'Wasn't it lucky I installed a new tracking app?'

He what? Abby's heart started racing.

'Do you want to join us?' she offered, weakly. *Oh, God. Why did he have to show up?* She tried to keep her tone neutral.

Accommodating. Sweat prickled at her armpits. He knew she had lied.

'Now, why would I want to do that?' Joe asked, lifting his hands. 'You girls need some time together.' He smiled. Abby knew it wasn't sincere. 'You've had a busy morning... chores, was it? It's the least you deserve. I'll see you at home later, baby.'

He bent over Abby and cupped his hand behind her neck, brushing his lips from her cheek to her ear. 'I can't wait,' he whispered.

Abby shivered.

CHAPTER THIRTEEN

SASHA ~ RECENTLY

Sasha stood in the doorway of the café. Should she go in, or continue walking? She flung the door open with a little more energy than needed. Papers taped to the glass panels fluttered in protest.

'Morning, young lady,' grinned the man behind the counter. At least, it *sounded* like he was grinning. It was hard to see much of anything behind the greying beard that was a masterclass in hirsute waywardness. 'What can I get you started with?'

Sasha blinked and looked at the list of coffees behind the counter so that she wasn't staring at the beard and what might possibly be hiding in it. 'A long black with three shots, please.' Something extra was definitely needed this morning.

'Excellent choice.' He flipped and twirled a pale blue cup with the panache of a bartender working for tips. 'You'll really enjoy the flavour of the new roast we're trying.'

'Mm-hmm.' Sasha feigned interest in the menu. She didn't want to be rude, but she also didn't want to get into a conversation about the merits of coffee roasting.

She should never have gone back to the vineyard after the accident. Going home had been a mistake. But she had been in such a daze of drugs, pain and loss that she had let her parents make the decisions. And they weren't necessarily *wrong* decisions. They just weren't the right decisions *right now,* for her. Getting away had been the only thing she could think to do.

Who was she kidding? She had full-on run away. The sudden decision to leave had been an impulse driven by necessity and panic. The urge to scrub her skin bare and erase all that had happened clawed at her. Eyes staring. Voices choking her with their concern. People smothering her with attention and sympathy.

And the expression in her mother's eyes? It was too much. It was *all* too much. She wanted to swipe her hand across people's faces and clear them like the Magna Doodle she used to draw on as a kid. The increasingly familiar look from her mum added so many knots to her already twisted insides, they could have resembled a macrame belt. A belt that was being yanked tighter and tighter with each glance, each word, each sympathetic sigh cast in her direction.

'How are you feeling, love?' her mum had asked on the morning Sasha had fled.

'How do you think I'm feeling?' Sasha had snapped.

'What about a drive to the coast?' her mum had suggested, her voice controlled. 'We could stop and get a coffee or go for a stroll.' It moved to brightly contrived. 'Whatever you feel like.'

'Does it *look* like I want to go to the bloody coast?' Sasha had let the words fall without censor. 'God. Could you just *think* about how it would make me feel?' Unfair words. 'You just want me to hurry up and get back to normal so you can get on with your life.' Hurtful words. 'Admit it. You're sick and tired of looking after me.' Hateful words.

Words had spewed from her mouth, leaving her with a bitterness that no amount of determination or feigned positivity could remedy. She needed time to work through things and she couldn't damn well do that with everyone closing in on her.

Now, Sasha stood at the café counter, lost in thought, oblivious to the queue forming behind her. Was it too much to ask that everyone leave her the hell alone and stop with the stupid questions? Being at the vineyard with all their hovering had been claustrophobic. She was being strangled by their overt solicitousness. By their love.

Sasha sighed. Her stomach rolled in what was becoming a familiar wave of anxiety and something that was now feeling suspiciously like guilt. Why on earth had *guilt* appeared?

Sasha drew a deep breath to refocus her thoughts and hoisted a canvas tote bag onto her shoulder as she looked again at the bearded face standing behind the counter. She took the table number from his outstretched hand, inhaling as she reached over a pile of still-warm blueberry muffins. Their scent loosened a thread from the knot in her chest.

'Go and find a table and I'll bring this right on out to you,' the guy said, adjusting a well-worn cap with a hand the size of a dinner plate. 'Can I tempt you with one of these little gems, fresh from the oven?' He nodded at the muffins, the scent still dancing around her. 'I baked them myself,' he said, eyebrows raised before throwing a wink in her direction.

'Thanks,' Sasha said, wondering how fingers that size could possibly navigate kitchen utensils or even the coffee machine.

Fingers were the first thing Sasha always noticed about a person, the same way a basketball player might assess someone's height. At least he could *use* his hands. Bitterness blended with self-pity seeped through her. Was there an appropriate coffee roast to match her feelings? Crushed Dreams Dark Roast?

'They smell great, but I'm fine.'

Who was she kidding? Her stomach growled in protest at her refusal of the baked goods. Why had she felt the need to be churlish and say no? Was she becoming one of those people who were contrary, simply for the sake of it?

The beard in front of her twitched as if holding back a smile. Was the guy a mind-reader as well as a baker of divine-smelling creations? She swung around and wove her way to the back of the café before she could make a further spectacle of herself.

Bookshelves anchored the corner and a leather couch with worn patches in all the right places invited her over. Fairy lights trailed a fanciful path through vases, volumes of worn books and a variety of knick-knacks on the shelves, adding an air of escapism. A coffee table scarred from decades of hot mugs placed atop it rested in front of the couch. A dark green rug was laid on the floor and light filtered through a cream lampshade tucked into the corner of the bookshelf. Sasha dumped her bag on the arm of the couch. The space whispered serenity.

Her mind screamed unfairness.

When she left the hospital, she should have picked somewhere completely out of the way, where people couldn't talk to her. There were too many expectations at home, too many questions. Questions she couldn't deal with right now. Questions like; *How are you feeling today? What do you think you'll do now? Have you thought about what you're going to do instead of performing?* Well-meaning, well-intentioned questions, but ones she had no idea how to answer. She had a feeling that *I have no fucking idea what I want to do. Why can't you leave me the hell alone?* was not an answer that would go down well. At least, not with her mum and dad. Or Sam.

Sasha sank onto the couch and buried her head in her hands. God, she'd treated him appallingly. The poor guy didn't deserve the attitude she'd dished out. It had been like a leaky tap, though: self-pitying, accusatory, toxic words that gathered momentum until the droplets turned into a deluge. It was why she'd turned away from him. No. More than that. She'd pushed and shoved herself away from him, hurling words that she knew would hurt.

Haven't you got anything better to do than hover over me? She could still see him standing by the piano last week. He'd driven out after work to see her, just as he'd been doing every day since she had been discharged from the hospital. *Standing there like a bloody puppy isn't helping me in the slightest.* Her words had been scathing. Being mean was becoming her default setting. Anything to stop the pain. Not that it worked. She had momentarily traded the pain of her lost career for the pain of discarding Sam. The constant concern, questions and attention had been more than she could cope with.

But how was she meant to move forward when every turn her mind made took her to music? Music was what she knew. What she lived for. What did she have to live for now? It was so damn unjust.

Sasha slouched back into the armchair, wrapping her beige cardigan around her even though it was comfortably warm. Why couldn't she have broken an ankle? Or even a leg, for God's sake? She could handle an injured leg. If it meant she couldn't run again, so be it. Or skip. Or twirl a bloody hula hoop. What did any of that matter?

Sasha laid her hand on the table, pushing up the cuff of the cardigan that was fast becoming a wardrobe staple. She tried to flatten her palm against the table, barely resisting the urge to thump her right fist on top of her useless left hand. Anything to see her fingers splayed out in front of her. Instead, they were curled, turning in on themselves, unable to flex or close. Useless.

She took a breath and counted while she listened to the hiss of the coffee machine in the distance. The scent slipped around her, briefly silencing her mind. The moment of focus stopped the impulse to hit her hand, but that was about it.

So, where did it leave her? Everyone wanted her to face what had happened. Accept it. Move on. But how could she move on when she had no idea where she was going?

She couldn't even bear the thought of facing Abby. She knew Abby hadn't deliberately hurt her. Of course she hadn't. But every time she thought she could maybe see her friend, rage rose inside her – a crescendo of irrational, illogical emotion that no amount of dampening could subdue. She knew she was going to have to face the messages Abby had been sending. There were only so many ways and times a person could apologise. Abby had found them all. But the searingly hurt part of Sasha wanted Abby to keep finding more ways.

There was also the matter of Abby's baby. Her goddaughter. Her mum had told her when Sophia was born. But still, she'd held back.

A tiny part of Sasha's brain registered that her friend had gone above and beyond with her persistence. Her contriteness. Especially given everything she herself was going through. Sasha would find her thumb hovering above the phone's screen, trembling with indecision whenever yet another message from Abby pinged. But then she'd look at her left hand and her scalp would prickle. Rage and anger wove a web so intricate that she was unable to see a way through. Even now, just the thought of seeing her friend, facing her and listening to her was prompting the contents of her stomach to travel up her throat. She grabbed a glass of water, her hand shaking as she raised it to her mouth.

No. She wasn't ready to see Abby. But was it fair to relegate Sam to the same emotional Siberia?

Sasha jolted when a cup and plate was placed in front of her.

'Here you go,' said beard guy, his thumb and forefinger pinched between the cup's handle. 'Thought you looked like you could do with one of these as well,' he added, sliding a muffin towards her.

Sasha raised her eyebrows. She leant forward and breathed in the fruity, buttery aroma, touched by the thoughtful gesture. 'Thanks.'

'Enjoy the treat.' He straightened, the fairy lights glinting against the silver strands of his beard, making him look like Santa masquerading as a barista.

Sasha offered a tentative smile, the action unfamiliar. The load on her chest lightened a fraction.

She knew now what she needed to do.

CHAPTER FOURTEEN

ABBY ~ BEFORE THE ACCIDENT

Abby arrived early at King's Park and swung her Mazda into a parking space, only to see Joe's car in a far corner. She wasn't surprised. Although, she'd hoped to have a few moments to ease into it all. Yes, she was nervous. But it was a good kind of nervous energy. Not like the nervous fear she'd become accustomed to feeling each time she saw him. This time, she was reclaiming something. She was doing something she needed to do. Had to do. Should have done before now, if she was being honest with herself.

She was reclaiming herself.

She kicked herself for not realising this sooner. For not realising she was being manipulated and used. Abused. That was all about to change.

It wasn't like she was oblivious to domestic violence. But she wasn't a downtrodden victim, utterly dependent on her partner for financial security. For anything, really. Sure, her catering business might still be in the toddler stages. But like a toddler, the wobbly steps were developing with an instinctive confidence. She believed in herself. And that belief in herself was addictive. Her eyes had opened. It never occurred to her she was a victim. Until she was.

It was so subtle. Gentle, almost. Until it wasn't. Discreet degrees of manipulation. Coercion. Until she was trapped. Not literally trapped. There were no actual locks and chains. She could've left at any point. Got up and marched out. No. She'd been trapped in a mental slide of normalisation.

Why hadn't she been smarter than that? It made her sick to her stomach when she stood back and could see it for what it was. It was like surfacing from the bottom of the pool without swimming goggles, everything distorted and fragmented at the bottom, but stunningly clear when she broke through the surface. She had her head above water now.

In the past, her first thought had always been about how Joe would react, what he would think, what he would say. *You're wearing that?* Or, *God, can't you make something edible for me to eat?* Or, *Why the hell would you say something like that?* It was always delivered where no one else would hear if they were in public, hissed into her ear, usually with a painful pinching and twisting of the flesh on her inner arm. He had perfected the art of leaning into her curtain of hair, an illusion of a caring, loving partner. A solicitous boyfriend, always by her side. Making sure she was never alone.

This time, he was going to listen to *her*.

A dragonfly settled on the blade of her windscreen wiper, perched with balletic elegance and a supreme confidence in its ability to not falter on the narrow strip it had chosen. Its translucent and delicate wings belied its strength and poise. That's what she needed to do. Be confident. Be strong. Not falter. *Be* the dragonfly.

Oh, God. *Could* she? She twisted the hem of her shirt between her fingers. Or would Joe squash her, swat her away, as he had become fond of doing? Abby shook her head, cleared the doubts. Regained her balance.

Joe had his back to the carpark, hands resting on the lookout railing by the giant boab tree. It was early but the sun had risen, lasers of morning light shooting through the city buildings and bouncing off the water.

The park was one of her favourite places in Perth, especially the paths that overlooked the city. The Swan River, more of a sea from this vantage point, seemed to offer freedom and possibilities. Escape.

She used to find Joe's habit of arriving early endearing. Respectful, even. A sign of valuing her and her time. She knew better now. Arriving early meant he could control the situation. Have the upper hand, while looking like an all-round great guy who didn't take people's time for granted. Abby gave a snort. What a joke that was. The only time Joe valued or respected was his own. Certainly not hers.

And just like that, another tether to Joe loosened.

Abby sat in the car and scrubbed her palms along her jeans, as if the act would be enough to remove the unease. Had he seen her yet? He hadn't turned or given any clue he was aware. But again, that was all part of the game to him. That air of being unaware, of letting people think he had no idea they were looking at him. When really all the while, he craved their admiration, their acknowledgement of the outstandingly handsome and good guy that he saw himself to be.

She blinked and glanced around the carpark. There were a few vacant spaces, but for the most part, there was a steady stream of people arriving; locals getting their day off to a virtuous start along one of the many trails in the park; tourists wanting to beat the crowds and walk along the treetop glass bridge, only to discover there were gates that prevented entry until later in the morning. Enough people to generate a sense of safety.

Joe hadn't moved. Abby kept her eyes on him as she pulled the keys from the ignition. His shoulders were relaxed as he faced the river, his chin raised just high enough to afford passers-by a view of his profile. She had watched him adjust it often enough. Out of necessity, she had become intimately aware of its shifts and twitches; its flickers and clenches.

For now, though, he was relaxed. And why *wouldn't* he be relaxed? As far as he was concerned, Abby was coming to apologise. To grovel. To prostrate herself, if not physically then certainly figuratively, at his feet. It was the pattern she had perpetuated, the behaviour she had repeated and perfected. Why would he expect anything different this time?

Joe turned and stared directly at Abby, his eyes landing immediately on her car, no searching required at all. Yes. He knew all along she had arrived.

Abby pulled her phone from the bag beside her on the passenger seat. The battery bar was reassuringly solid. She pulled up Sasha's text thread and loaded the bomb emoji, ready to be tapped at a moment's notice. Her friend had been thrilled when Abby told her she was ending things with Joe. *About bloody time! I'm so proud of you, Abs.* Abby let the words circle around her mind a few times, adding another layer of resolve. Leaving Joe was something she had to do for herself. But it helped to have the support of her best friend. She reached up and rubbed the pendant between her thumb and forefinger.

She slid the phone into the pocket of her jeans and wrapped her fingers around it, a small metallic security blanket. Sasha was at a nearby carpark by the park café. Out of sight, but close by if needed.

The morning was cooler than Abby expected when she

opened the car door. That was fine. It would keep her focused. Attuned to Joe's tactics. He had an entire playbook of tactics and liked to rotate them, shuffle them with apparent indifference. Except there was no indifference. There was only ever calculation, manipulation and control. Fine. Let him think he had control of the situation. Hopefully the shock would make her words all the more clear. She was no longer going to be the one caught unawares, at the whim of his moods.

'Babe!' he called across the carpark. A smile was pasted in place, his eyes narrowed ever so slightly. But only if you knew what to look for. Abby knew what to look for. 'You're looking good.' His gaze swiftly assessed the top she had chosen. 'That blue is a much better colour for you.' Another smile.

And there it was. The judgement, ever so subtle, wrapped up as a compliment. It was a comment that used to bring about a sweet rush, relief flooding through her with the knowledge she'd got something right and that Joe was happy with her. Today, she bit back a smile of her own. Yep. She knew what he was all about. Seeing it clearly was such a thrill.

'Did you get stuck in traffic?' His brow creased. An approximation of concern, the mask was in place for ears close by. A passing elderly couple smiled obligingly when Joe nodded in their direction.

She wasn't late. This was a standard Joe move to establish control. Make her pause and question what she'd done. Too bad, Joe. She was done questioning herself.

Abby picked her way between the parked cars and onto the pavement, stepping aside when Joe leant in to kiss her.

She watched his step falter and his left eye twitch and narrow.

'Hi, Joe.' She kept her face neutral. No smile. She knew he would notice. Her hand snuck into her pocket and gripped the phone.

'I thought we could head over to the café and have some breakfast,' Joe continued, again moving towards her and reaching out to take her arm.

Again, Abby side-stepped him. 'I don't think so.' Be definite. Own the situation. 'No,' she added. Don't over-explain. Don't over-elaborate. She bit the inside of her cheek. The impulse to add more almost overwhelmed her, so ingrained it had become.

Joe shrugged, aiming for indifference. 'That's fine, babe.' He straightened and tightened his lips. 'Whatever you feel like.'

Except it was never what she felt like. It was always what Joe felt like.

Abby took a breath. 'This isn't working, Joe.' Oh my God, oh my God, oh my God. She kept her face impassive. There was every chance she would vomit on his feet. Although even that would be an improvement from grovelling there.

Joe chose the route of confusion. *Feigned* confusion. She watched his chin jut in and out a couple of times. 'And what might *this* be? Abby?' He said her name quietly, drawing it out, before casting a smile at a couple of joggers weaving between the two of them.

Abby walked over to the railing and grasped hold of it, looking at the boab tree, at its naked strength and solidity. 'Don't play dumb, Joe. It's not a good look on you.' *Shit! Did she really just tell him he was dumb?* 'This—,' Abby gestured back and forth between the two of them. 'You and me. We're not working.'

'Abby,' Joe hissed, covering the distance between them in three rapid-fire steps.

Abby turned her back to the view and felt the railing digging against her spine. Wind blew her hair back from her face, exposing her with no shield, no curtain, no mask.

Joe's mask melted and the blisters bubbled, putrid words spewing out. 'You fucked up, stupid little cow.' He stepped closer and Abby held her ground. 'What the fuck do you think you're trying to do?' He barked a laugh and the mask melted some more. 'Is this you trying to *leave* me? Seriously?' His voice was incredulous. 'You're *nothing* without me.' Balls of spittle formed at the corners of his lips, corrosive beads of anger and impotence. 'Do you hear me? Nothing!' More spit.

She squared her shoulders and looked directly into his eyes. There was to be no ambiguity. No confusion. He *would* hear her.

'I'm not *trying*, Joe.' Abby let go of the railing and leaned towards him, no longer backing away. 'I'm telling you. This. Is. Not. Working.' Oh my God. That felt so good to say! 'And yes.' She lifted her chin. The air left her lungs and her shoulders relaxed. 'This is me, leaving you.'

Joe slipped his spare key into the lock and sidled through the door. Not answering her phone yesterday was such a lame move. It had annoyed him initially, but it was actually kind of cute, when he thought about it. She wanted his attention, pure and simple. She knew that ignoring his call would get under his skin. Which it had. For all of two seconds. But she couldn't fool him that easily. He was ready for her games.

It was simple. If she'd answered her phone, he wouldn't have had to be here now.

He ran his index finger along the entrance table, frowning when he noticed the blue bowl that he liked to put his keys in, was missing. He must remember to find it and put it back before he left. He picked up a new frame that was angled on the corner. Abby and Sasha laughing under the Eiffel Tower and holding balloons. One red, one green. He leant closer. What was she playing at? She knew what he thought of her so-called friend: arrogant, entitled, condescending bitch. It was how anyone with a grain of perception would see her, her with her stupid look of judgement when she talked to him. Abby was ignoring him by flaunting the picture. She'd soon learn. This little visit was proving to be very enlightening.

Her little stunt with saying they were over was nothing but a game. He was certain of it. Oh, sure. She might whinge and whine and make token gestures of not liking it or some such bullshit. But when it came down to it, she loved that she had a man who knew his mind, who knew what she liked. For God's sake. If she didn't like it, she sure as hell didn't have to stay with him. He wasn't a monster, for crying out loud. The bitch had free will. She could leave anytime she wanted to leave. He wasn't going to beg her to stay. Sure. He got a kick out of it when she begged, but again, that was her choice. She *chose* to do it. To plead, to prostrate herself before him. That was on *her*. He was simply giving her what she wanted.

He paused in front of the fridge. The contents of a fridge could tell you so much about a person. His dumbass girlfriend, for example. Or *ex*-girlfriend, if he was to listen to her. But why would he do that? He knew she didn't mean it. It was just her way of messing with him. She thought she was keeping him on his toes, keeping him guessing. Didn't the stupid bitch know he was one step ahead of her? He always was. And that was being conservative. Truth be told, he was more like five or six steps ahead of her. But he wasn't a monster. He didn't want to hurt her feelings.

Her fridge was such a bloody joke. How could she not see that? God. All the time and energy he'd put into educating her and she still refused to pay attention. Didn't she realise how lucky she was to have someone like him paying attention to her? He picked up a round of brie cheese. Who was she kidding? Brie? Was she trying to pretend she was bloody Italian? Or

French? It was pretentious. People needed to be genuine. To act with the truest intent. That's what he was doing. His intentions were true. Pure.

He shut the fridge door carefully and sighed. Checking out Abby's place was all well and good.

But he wouldn't find what he was looking for in the fridge.

CHAPTER FIFTEEN

SAM ~ NOW

Sam made the drive back to the vineyard for the second time that day. Was it really still only morning? He needed to talk to Dave. Sam pulled into the lower carpark by the river, the bonnet of his car nudging the checked police tape cordoning off the area.

He rolled his shoulders as he got out of the car, barely noticing the stiffness. The dressing on his ribs pulled with the movement and he winced. He hadn't thought to check it last night. There had been other things on his mind.

A year and a half ago, Sam had met Abby's boyfriend Joe for the first time at this same spot. Sasha had been home briefly from wherever she'd been touring and he hadn't been thrilled about sharing the rare time they got together as a couple. It was one of those crisp winter days where the sun was out but the chill in the air encouraged action. Or so Sasha had said. All Sam had felt encouraged to do was slouch in front of a crackling fire with his girlfriend, a beer and the rugby on TV. Time off was scarce. Time *together* was precious.

But Sasha had wanted them to hang out with Abby and her new boyfriend. Sam had yet to meet the guy. He'd suggested drinks and watching rugby on the big screen in the vineyard's lounge. Instead, they'd gone kayaking.

The afternoon had rolled around and Sam had stayed on the couch until the last minute. The Western Force were playing the Canterbury Crusaders and it was not the result he'd been hoping for. It never was with the Force. Which kind of made kayaking feel somewhat more appealing. But only marginally. He would've taken the couch and fire combo over the kayaking date any day.

He knew Sasha was not overly fond of Joe. *The guy's a bit off. I can't really put my finger on it. I want to get your take on him.* They had been her words when she'd thrown out the idea of them all getting together. He liked Abby. She was family, as far as Sasha was concerned. Which was all Sam cared about. Taking the kayaks out had been an inevitability.

Watching rugby and gauging a guy's reactions was as good a way as any to determine character, if you wanted to get right down to it. If Joe complimented a prop for great body position in a ruck, then he was astute. But if he berated that same prop being out-manoeuvred by an agile winger, then he really had no idea what he was talking about and should learn when to keep his mouth shut. Did he really need to make small talk with a stranger – while kayaking – to form an opinion?

Abby and Joe were waiting at the vineyard's jetty. A light band of rain had washed through an hour before.

'How's it going?' Joe had lunged forward, thrusting his hand at Sam, his head and shoulders moving as one in the absence of a discernible neck. 'Bloody brilliant day to be out here, isn't it?' His smile was wide. A bit forced, but it was the guy's first time out here.

Abby leapt forward and wedged herself against Joe. 'I can't believe we finally get to spend some time together.' Her eyes darted from one person to the next in the group. 'Thanks so much for suggesting this, Sam.'

Sam raised an eyebrow at Sasha and leant forward to kiss Abby's cheek. 'Good to see you, Abs.'

'Isn't this the most beautiful place?' Abby said, sweeping her arm for Joe's benefit. 'Don't you just want to, I don't know, kind of let go of everything in a place like this?' She drew a deep breath, smiling as she looked up at Joe.

'Hon,' Joe said, shouldering her to the side as he stepped forward, 'a river's a river, am I right?' He grinned at Sam and Sasha, expecting collaboration.

Sam watched Sasha bristle. Joe planted his hands on barrel-like hips. He had the torso of a prop, but the skinny legs poking out from long cargo shorts did nothing to suggest he liked physical activity.

Sasha looked directly at Joe. 'I think Abby's right. This one is pretty special.'

'Yeah, yeah,' Joe said, his smile not faltering, but not quite reaching his eyes. 'Trees, water, fresh air. It's brilliant.'

Abby giggled uneasily. She grabbed Sasha's arm and jumped down to where the kayaks were tied to the jetty. 'Just ignore him,' she said. 'He's nervous about meeting us all here.'

Sasha snorted. 'If he's nervous, then I'm shy and demure.'

'Please, Sash,' Abby pleaded. She grabbed hold of the first kayak and unlooped the rope. 'Be nice,' she said over her shoulder.

Sam headed towards the second kayak. 'You follow rugby?' he asked Joe. There was still a slim chance they could turn around and head back inside.

'Nah,' Joe said. 'I'm more of a lacrosse man, myself. Now *there's* a sport that needs skill. Finesse.' He kissed his fingers.

Lacrosse? What the hell kind of answer was that? Wasn't that a college sport in the US?

'Mm-hmm,' Sam said, not trusting himself to say anything more.

'Babe,' Joe called across to Abby, 'are you ready yet? Getting into a kayak isn't rocket science.'

Abby laughed hesitantly and darted her eyes at Joe. Sam saw Sasha's lips tighten. So far, the outing was not off to a great start.

Sam jumped in before Sasha could say – or do – anything. The guy was going to end up in the water before they even left if he kept going the way he was.

'What keeps you busy during the week, mate?'

'Bit of this, bit of that,' Joe said, turning abruptly and yanking a rope out of Abby's hands, 'you know how it is.'

'Wanker', Sasha muttered as she passed Sam. 'Not sure I do, Joe,' she said more audibly. 'Maybe I'm not very good at understanding. Can you help me out?'

Uh oh. Sam knew that tone and it did not bode well. He watched Sasha's shoulders square up, ready to engage.

'Can you help me out over here, Sash?' Sam interrupted. Sometimes, intervention was the wisest course of action.

She stood her ground for a moment before glancing at Abby and then stalked over to Sam. 'See?' she muttered under her breath. 'The guy's a dickhead.'

'You invited them, so let's just make the most of it,' Sam said. Not that he disagreed with Sasha. The guy wasn't doing himself any favours.

'What does Abby see in him?' Sasha struggled to keep the distaste out of her voice. She slipped into the kayak and held the paddle while Sam manoeuvred himself into the front.

'You're not making this easy for me, babe,' Joe's voice rang across the water. 'Can't you stay still while I get in?'

'Sorry,' Abby said, reaching out to hold the edge of the jetty in an attempt to steady the rocking kayak. Rocking that was being caused by Joe's ineffectual efforts to get in.

Joe entered the kayak with the same level of finesse as a two-year-old climbing onto an inflatable castle.

'Let's just get going,' Sasha said, with a vicious dig of her paddle in the water.

Sam gripped the checked tape while he stared at the water, the memory washing over him. His opinion of Joe hadn't changed since that first meeting. Not that they'd socialised much. He didn't see the point in spending valuable time with someone who needed to build themselves up at the expense of putting others down. What had Abby seen in the guy in the first place? He'd been pleased to hear Abby had ended things with him about a year ago.

Sam pulled his phone out of his pocket and tapped the screen. Joe might have been out of Abby's life for some time, but it would still be worth chatting to him.

His eyes followed the track down to the river. How had she ended up in the water? If she had been dead beforehand, how had it happened? Had there been a struggle on the path? And if there had been, why had no one seen it? She could have slipped, but that didn't account for the wounds. And she sure as hell couldn't have put herself in the water. His gut twisted again at the thought of her, facedown and lifeless.

Sam squashed the image. There would be time later to deal with his thoughts. He locked his car and headed up to the cellar door store where he knew he'd be likely to find Dave. He rolled his sleeves down, anticipating the air-conditioned chill that Dave maintained as a year-round constant for the storage of the wines inside.

Sure enough, Dave was inside. Greetings and small talk were minimal. He stood beside a couple of old barrels that acted as display platforms for the vineyard's wine with cheese knives, platters and glasses styled around them.

'Have you spoken to June?' Sam watched Dave's face as he wiped the wine bar's counter. 'How did she take it?'

'How do you bloody think she took it?' Dave snapped. 'Sorry,' he said quickly, leaning against the counter. 'Sorry, mate.' He pulled a bottle of last year's cabernet sauvignon from behind the counter and raised his eyebrows at Sam before pouring two glasses. 'To hell with the hour. It's a lot to process, ya know?' He put the bottle back under the counter. 'Probably should get inside and check on her.' Dave looked towards the main house but made no real effort to move.

Sam listened as Dave's thoughts and words jumped all over the place before he interjected. 'The race that was held here over the weekend,' Sam said, switching topics. 'Did you have anything to do with that?'

Dave frowned. 'Not really.' He passed a glass to Sam. 'The racecourse only passed through the property. It didn't start or finish here.'

'So, no one concerned with the event would've been hanging around by the jetty?'

'A couple of race marshals were wandering about, pointing people in the right direction, but that was about it,' Dave said, tipping his glass back and draining half of it. 'I dunno. Can't say I was paying too much attention to them.' He finished the rest of the wine and looked up suddenly, the time of the race aligning in his brain. 'Do you think one of them would've seen something?' Desperation filled his voice.

Sam set his glass down on the barrel. 'That's what I'm hoping.'

'Just give me a moment,' Dave said, his voice suddenly

urgent. 'I'm sure I've got the organiser's details in my office.' He rounded the bar and headed for the door. 'Shit. I completely forgot that all took place earlier in the day. They'd all cleared off before lunch and the bub being found.' He disappeared into the next building.

Sam's thoughts circled back to Abby's ex, Joe. It was not unreasonable to think the guy had kept tabs on her since they'd split. There was something about him that snagged at Sam. Had he done more than that?

CHAPTER SIXTEEN

SASHA ~ RECENTLY

Sasha sat on the small porch outside her room. This time in Margaret River was exactly what she needed. She plucked a sprig of lavender from the pot beside her, squashed it between the fingers of her good hand, and inhaled. She might know what she needed to do, but it was easier said than done. Making things right with Abby wasn't simply a matter of saying, *"I'm all fine now. Let's put it behind us and move on."* She wasn't fine and she didn't know how to move on. It was still all too new, too raw.

Her thoughts were interrupted by excited shouts from a family arriving at the lodge. A couple of teenage girls, one blonde and one brunette, tumbled from the back seat of an SUV as if they were emerging from a month-long period of solitary confinement. They stretched, squealed, stretched some more and then nudged each other along the gravel path while the adults headed towards reception. Slim, tanned limbs indicated a summer spent outdoors and the scuffed Converse suggested they had spent many hours and covered many kilometres together.

Sasha looked down at her own pasty legs. Good grief.

Would it hurt them to look less like a bowl of scone dough? It was the result of too many days under artificial hospital lights and even more days hiding herself at home. The blonde-haired girl suddenly performed an impromptu pirouette, spinning in front of her sister – or maybe her friend – releasing energy and emotion for the pure sake of it. How long had it been since she had felt that carefree?

Sasha gave herself a mental shake. Self-pitying thoughts were not getting her anywhere. They were indulgent. She drew another breath of the lavender and focused on feeling calm while she watched the two girls make their way along the path. She stretched her legs out and rolled up the cuff of the shorts, inviting another inch of sunshine. She felt like the disc at the end of a yo-yo, being controlled, released and then rewound according to an external force. What were the chances of finding a pair of scissors to sever the piece of string?

Those girls could easily have been her and Abby. Her breath caught at the realisation, as if she had mis-judged the location of a seat. How often had they walked along after school, lost in their own world, a shared connection that came from being so in tune with one another?

Pulling her phone from her pocket, Sasha opened the text thread from Abby. The same text thread she had silenced a few days ago. The constant pinging was an intrusion she hadn't been able to face. She knew they were there and had glanced at them, but had not felt compelled to answer or respond.

Each time she came close to replying, the image of Abby glancing down at her phone in the car and pausing to read what was on the screen, took over. Abby knew better than that.

When Abby found out she was pregnant, there was surely no better motivating factor than the thought of protecting that precious baby. Sasha's goddaughter. And there was never any doubt she'd be godmother, either. To be honest, Sasha didn't even remember Abby asking her. It was just assumed. An unspoken knowledge that they would be godparent to the other's child. They had reached that decision at a long-ago sleepover.

The fact remained. Abby should have known better than to look at her phone.

Sasha gingerly lifted her legs, which had begun to stick to the chair, and looked down at the next text.

> I'm bringing Sophia to the vineyard on the weekend. I really need to see you, Sashi. Please? Xx

Hmm. It seemed a little more insistent than the previous ones.

Sasha's thumb hovered to start typing a reply. But it was the point she could never get past. Just *one* thumb on the screen. She felt a familiar prickle working its way along her scalp, a ripple of tingles that made her want to yank her hair out by the roots. Anxiety burned in her chest. She slammed the phone face-down onto the arm of the chair.

She exhaled a puff of air, blowing hair from her face. She flipped the phone over, indecision making her fingers tremble. The last text on her screen was a mix of chirpiness and something more... desperation?

> Hi Sashi 😊 I still miss you. I really need to talk to you. Please let me see you. I can't do this without your help. xx

That was the final text. What was it Abby couldn't do without her help? There hadn't been anything since. As much as Sasha tried not to think about Abby, it was difficult to turn her thoughts off. How did you stop thinking about someone who knew you better than your parents?

Sasha's injured hand began to throb. She reached automatically into her bag for some painkillers, but stopped. Was the timing of the pain a coincidence? Or a consequence of the thoughts? She wrapped her right hand around the scar and squeezed. The ache receded and she relaxed back against the chair and looked out into the unkempt bushland surrounding the property.

Was it time to let go of some of those feelings? She was still angry at Abby. And Sam, for that matter. She squirmed in the chair. Why did everyone have to push her? Rush her?

Sasha knew she had cast such a targeted bolt of blame at Abby that there was no escaping the fallout of her vicious words and accusations. But she missed her. She missed the one person who knew her.

'Hello, pet!' Mrs M's cheery voice cut across the porch.

Sasha yelped and jumped from her chair, flicking aside a wayward tear.

'Hi, Mrs M. A new family all checked in?' she said hurriedly, before Mrs M could ask how she was.

'That they are.' Mrs M brushed some flour from the sleeve of the yellow dress she was wearing. 'I was wondering if you'd be around. I was going to ask–' Mrs M paused and tilted her head to the side, no doubt noticing the tear drying on Sasha's cheek. 'Never mind,' she said, pulling a hankie from her bra.

Sasha wasn't sure what was more startling. The fact that Mrs M tucked it in her bra, or the fact that it was an honest-to-goodness handkerchief.

'How about we go for a walk?' Mrs M suggested, again interrupting the jumble of thoughts that had landed with no warning in Sasha's mind. She handed the hankie to Sasha. 'It's such a pretty day and Roey has been pestering me all morning to get out,' she said, looking down at the white ball of fluff dancing between the two of them. 'We can have a nice little chat. Or you don't have to talk at all. The Lord and Gerry know, I talk enough for a whole room full of people.'

Roey pranced about on her hind legs, a dance of uncomplicated excitement about nothing more than the prospect of a simple walk. Sasha reached out and took the blue piece of fabric. It was embroidered with flowers and pieces of felt secured with the tiniest blanket stitches Sasha had ever seen. It should have been behind glass in a display cabinet.

'I can't use this, Mrs M,' Sasha said, weaving the soft fabric between her fingers.

'Go on with you,' Mrs M clucked. 'What good are pretty things if you can't feel them and use them? I made this one when we were living in Peru. It kept me busy and out of mischief.' Before she could voice any questions, Mrs M continued. 'What do you say, love? Fancy a walk with the two of us?' she said, reaching down to scratch the dog behind her ears. Roey obligingly spun on the spot before planting herself at Sasha's feet.

Mrs M laughed and nodded at the two girls turning cartwheels on the lawn. 'I don't think you'll get much peace and quiet here.'

They headed along the driveway before Mrs M detoured left through a gap in a row of shrubs, chatting about nothing in particular. Gravel crunched rhythmically. There was a comfort to it that Sasha hadn't felt in a long time. How long had it been since there were no expectations placed on her?

Just as they rounded a bend in the path, a miniature dollhouse came into view. Not an actual dollhouse. Although it did look like it could have been one in a former life. Sasha stumbled as she turned to look.

'Steady on, love,' Mrs M said, reaching out to hook her arm through the crook of Sasha's elbow. 'You'll come a cropper if you keep going like that. You've got enough to deal with at the moment.' Mrs M picked up Sasha's left hand gently and turned it over. 'This looks all very recent, love.'

Sasha's heart raced, the prospect of talking about anything personal twisting her stomach in knots. But wasn't she here to make some changes? It was why she had decided to take the trip to Margaret River in the first place. *Be honest. You totally ran away.* She gripped the phone in her pocket, thinking about the texts from Abby. Maybe it was time to stop running.

Sasha gulped. No time like the present. 'They're from a car accident a few weeks ago.'

'Oh, love.' Mrs M patted Sasha's hand, still tucked through her elbow. For once, she didn't flinch. 'I'm so sorry.'

A light breeze whipped curls across Sasha's cheek. She hooked them behind her ear before continuing. She outlined the accident. What had caused the accident. *Who* had caused the accident. And what she could no longer do. When she finished talking, she snuck a glance at a silent Mrs M. A tear trailed down the older woman's cheek.

'You think I'm a terrible person for the way I'm treating Abby, don't you? And my parents. And Sam.' The words tumbled out of Sasha. 'And you're right. Of course, you are. Abby didn't mean to hurt me. I know that.' She hiccupped on the last word.

'It's not what I think that matters, love.' Mrs M pulled Sasha close, squeezing her against her side.

'But Abby shouldn't have looked down at her phone. If she had just kept her eyes on the road, she wouldn't have swerved.' Sasha couldn't help some residual anger sparking through.

'Or maybe she would have.' Mrs M sighed. 'You don't know what would have happened. And,' she paused raising her eyebrows at Sasha when she tried to interject, 'it's not going to get you anywhere playing the *If Only* game, is it?' Her normally dancing eyes were serious.

It was the same message her mum had been trying to get through to her in the past weeks. And her dad. And Sam. But she hadn't been willing to listen.

'Mmm hmm,' she said, with deliberate vagueness. Mrs M had a point. Although none of it changed the fact that she could no longer play the piano. Abby might not have meant to hurt her. But she had still taken Sasha's livelihood. Her passion. How could she move past that?

Sasha pointed to the first thing to catch her eye in an effort to distract herself. And Mrs M. The woman's gaze was intense. It was the dollhouse sitting on a post, the clear front windows affording a view of dozens of books inside. 'How amazing is this?' *Yep. Excellent choice. Totally seamless.*

Mrs M flicked a quick glance at her, but went with the segue. 'Those little libraries are a brilliant idea, all right.'

For a moment, Sasha forgot about her hand and about Abby. It was honestly one of Sasha's favourite things to see when she was out walking. She sat down on the bench seat next to the little library while Mrs M ran her fingers along the spines, pulling out the occasional book for closer inspection. The dollhouse rested on an old wine barrel, which intrigued her. Holes were cut into the side of the barrel, allowing a profusion of pansies to spill from the gaps. It was a brilliant idea and would be perfect at home. She whipped her phone out and snapped a photo.

'Dad's going to love this,' she said to Mrs M. She'd think about sending it later. And maybe letting her parents know she was okay. She grimaced and shoved the phone back in her pocket along with the feelings of guilt. She hadn't been fair to them. To any of them. She knew that. But did every tiny bit of self-awareness have to swamp her right this very minute? A little time to get used to the idea of what an absolute cow she'd been would be brilliant.

Sasha jumped up from the bench seat and went over to where Mrs M was still pulling books from the little library. The older lady gasped and leant in for a closer look. 'Ooh, would you look at that? It's the latest by Holly Craig!' She reached in and plucked it from the shelf.

Sasha let Mrs M's chatter wash over her. It was a lazy river of words, unthreatening and undemanding, allowing her to float along with minimal effort. She felt her shoulders increase their distance from her ears, the tension unfurling.

An indefinable calmness drifted in the air, gentle tendrils weaving between the women. Beyond the little library there were charred stumps of eucalyptus and gums, flattened by an earlier bushfire, but now covered in patches of green. New life sprang unapologetically forward. Sasha reached out to brush her fingers over the springy leaves. Bush fluff, Sam called it. Could she bring herself to call him? Talk to him? If she could consider calling Abby, was she ready to face Sam?

CHAPTER SEVENTEEN

SAM ~ NOW

The following day, Sam sat in his car, stuck in traffic. He thumped the steering wheel. 'It's a bloody mess.' His anger ricocheted around the car.

He swiped the back of his hand across eyes that felt like sandpaper. It wasn't even midday yet. Sleep had been minimal the night before and he was running on adrenalin. He was on his way out to talk to Abby's ex, Joe Porter.

'Yeah,' Paul Green, the coroner, agreed through the car speaker system. 'It was a blow to the side of her head that killed her. The other wounds weren't exactly defensive and can be explained by her falling into the river. Any residue left in the wounds is from the river water. She was dead before entry.'

'Do you know what was used for the blow to the head?' Sam hated saying those words. Who would have deliberately hit her? Who had the most to gain by wanting Abby dead?

'Something rounded and even. She would have been dead before she hit the ground. I'll let you know more as soon as I have the details.'

'Yeah. Thanks.' Sam disconnected the call. He needed food and coffee. But something was scratching his mind about Abby's ex-boyfriend, Joe Porter. Sam knew they'd separated about a year ago, but there was something about him. Couldn't hurt to go and have a chat with him. His details had been easy enough to find with a quick search at the station.

Sasha hadn't said a lot about him since Abby had made the decision to end things. Only that she thought it was about time. With everything going on in both their lives, he hadn't felt the need to delve deep into the details of a broken relationship. If Sasha was happy, that was all he needed to know.

He wondered if Sasha's parents had told her about Abby yet? They couldn't put it off much longer. She might not be in the best frame of mind right now, but she had to know.

This side of Sasha was not something he'd anticipated. To be fair, no one anticipated a catastrophic accident. Just as no one anticipated the death of their best friend. *Fuck*. What would this news do to Sasha?

Was it wrong that he wished things could go back to the way they were before the accident? Before everything got so fucked up? He wasn't normally one to wish things could have been different. Things happened and you dealt with it. That was life. Sticking your head in the sand didn't fix anything. But Abby dead, on top of Sasha losing the ability to play the piano – how were you meant to deal with that many disastrous events?

Sam gripped the wheel and slowed his breathing. Vineyards flashed by on both sides of the road. They weren't as picturesque as *Vins Fantaisiste*. A memory hit him from three months ago. It had been just before the accident. Before everything changed.

He'd met Sasha out at the vineyard. It wasn't for anything special, no anniversary or special day. Just a chance to hang out together and spend some time with each other. He remembered looking at her and thinking how lucky he was.

They had headed down the path to the river. She was like something out of *The Hobbit,* all earthy and natural, candid and cute. Sam swallowed and scuffed the riverside path, a shower of gravel arcing in front of him. It was probably best he didn't share that little insight with Sasha. It would be right up there with telling her that her hair was as soft as cows' ears. Which, for the record, it was. But it wasn't a comparison that had gone over especially well. He rubbed his shoulder, remembering the whack she'd delivered when he'd shared that observation.

'I'm just saying,' Sasha said as they continued to wander, 'that you have a very logical way of looking at things.'

They continued along a well-worn path, heading upstream from the vineyard. Spring was already making an appearance, not so much tapping at the door, but announcing its arrival with a proud unrepentance. Despite the fact it was still technically winter, green shoots wove a tapestry along branches that had grown impatient with resting during the cooler months. Sam counted eight ducklings scurrying after their mother. At least, he assumed it was the mother. He spied a second adult duck making lazy circles in the water.

He reached out and laced his fingers through Sasha's. She pursed her lips, frowning.

'Just because it makes *sense,*' she put air quotes around the word and Sam rolled his eyes, 'it doesn't mean that we should.'

'Should what?' Sam asked, knowing full well he'd get a whack on the arm for it.

Sasha nudged his shoulder. 'I know you're winding me up, you idiot,' she said, sliding her arm around his waist. 'It doesn't mean we *should* stay home at Christmas. Don't you want to go away somewhere? Just the two of us?' She reached up and kissed the side of his neck.

'I'll give it some thought,' he said.

As it turned out, there hadn't been much thought involved. Or any, really. Of course, they'd gone away. Not far. Just to an Airbnb in Fremantle. It was just for a change of location.

Sam blinked rapidly. The traffic was light and he was almost at the Malaga Warehouse. Watching Joe's reaction in front of colleagues would tell him a lot more about the guy, regardless of what he said. Joe may have thought he had power in playing with people's perceptions and emotions, but Sam had power in being able to recognise when someone was hiding something.

Pulling into the warehouse carpark, Sam sat and watched the activity surrounding the building for a few moments. It was an industrial area and was one of many similar looking, uninspired concrete boxes. There was a small office at the front – a demountable that had been dumped on the spot. It had the ubiquitous window-mounted air conditioner that would no doubt be blasting freezing air into the confined space while rattling the window with enough white noise to drown out any other surrounding sounds.

Sunlight reflected off the white cladding on the warehouse walls with blinding intensity. Sam pulled on his dark glasses. The entire industrial area probably reflected enough heat and energy to power a small electricity sub-station. There were four loading bays along the side of the building, with ramps so customers could wheel or carry their purchases to their cars. Sam could see the daunted look on a customer's face as he struggled with a crated coffee table.

Standing about three metres inside the warehouse and back from the roller door of the first loading bay, Sam could see someone leaning against the shelves, a clipboard tucked under one arm and the other hand hooked lazily into his pants belt loop. It had been a while since he'd seen Joe, but from the car, it looked a lot like him. Another staff member jogged over and gave the customer with the coffee table a hand to manoeuvre the crate towards his car, while the one with the clipboard merely watched. Yeah. Definitely Joe Porter. Sam remembered the lazy arrogance.

Sam tucked his phone in his pocket and got out of the car. The rush of heat was as brutal as he expected.

'G'day,' called the staff member who'd been helping with the coffee table. 'Got a receipt to pick up something?'

'No, mate.' Sam reached into his pocket for his badge. He looked at the young guy in front of him but watched Porter in his periphery. The slouched pose straightened a fraction of a degree and he pulled down the blue cap he was wearing. Porter kept his head angled towards the clipboard, but Sam could tell he was alert and listening. 'I'm here to see Joe Porter.'

'Oh, yeah.' The young guy looked about. 'That's him over there.'

'Thanks.'

Sam crossed the distance from the ramp to the shelves in a couple of strides. It was like watching a light switch being flicked. In the space of time it took for Sam to be standing in front of him, the man had gone from looking impassively at his board with just the slightest narrowing of his eyes, to lifting his chin and directing a smile towards Sam.

'Sam!' Porter exclaimed. 'Long time, no see, mate. What brings you down here?'

Sam kept his sunglasses on and watched him closely. 'Just wanted to stop by for a chat.'

'Yeah?' Joe said. 'It's a busy day, but okay.' He darted a glance left and right before he drew a slow breath.

Sam looked around the warehouse and loading bay. Three workers sat at a table, one with his feet propped up on a chair. Activity was minimal. The summer heat demanded conservation of energy.

'I won't waste your time,' Sam said. 'Have you seen Abby recently?'

'Abby Sinclair?' Joe frowned.

'Your ex-girlfriend.'

There was a silence. Joe's fingers clenched around the clipboard.

'Yeah, yeah,' Joe said quickly. Sweat tracked a trail from his temple to his jaw. 'I know who you mean.' He leant back against the shelves and made a show of thinking. 'You know, I can't remember when I last saw her. Ages ago, mate. Why are you asking about Abby?'

Sam waited a moment. Nervous people rushed to fill silences.

Joe swallowed. 'You know we broke up, right? I haven't thought about her in, hell, months.'

Sam doubted that. There was a crash from across the warehouse. Joe jumped. Laughter ricocheted around the high-stacked shelves. One of the workers was on the ground, his chair on its side. Plastic chairs and smooth concrete floors were never a great combination if you were going to swing back on them.

'Give me your best guess,' Sam said.

'If I had to give you a date, then it'd probably be about a year ago.'

'Why did you see her?' Sam asked. May as well see where he went with it. There was a fine sheen of sweat on Joe's upper lip.

'God, this is gonna sound ridiculous,' Joe said. 'I don't want to be disrespectful, you know?' His left eye twitched as if he was about to wink and then thought better of it.

Sam didn't answer. The guy was a bigger dickhead than he remembered.

'I had to call things off about a year ago. She'd gotten a bit too clingy and needy, you know?'

Sam stared at Joe. Joe puffed out his cheeks and ran a hand across the back of his neck. Or where his neck would have been. His ears were doing their best to rest on his shoulders. The fizz of a can being opened by one of the three workers in the vicinity punctured the silence. They had ceased their conversation.

'I mean,' Joe continued, 'if things aren't working, you gotta do what you gotta do, right?' He bobbed his head at Sam.

Did the guy want affirmation?

'Can you be specific?' Sam asked.

Joe frowned. 'Not sure what you want here, mate.' He tried to prop the clipboard against his hip, sensing he needed to get the upper hand.

'What did you *gotta do*?' Sam said. 'Explain that for me.'

Joe's lips tightened. 'I'm not sure what you're getting at.' He straightened. 'What are you doing out here asking me all these questions for anyway?'

'Are you aware Abby was killed over the weekend?'

'No way!' Joe said, his eyes wide. 'Wait. Why are you telling me? Do I need a lawyer, or something?'

'You're not under arrest,' Sam said. 'But that's entirely up to you.'

'Right. Okay.' Joe looked around.

The three workers were still at the table, but they all had their heads bent over their phones, clearly listening. Sam stayed silent.

'So,' Joe said. He lifted his chin towards Sam. 'Abby's dead? Shit. How did that happen?'

Sam glanced around the warehouse. He ignored Joe's question. 'Worked here for long?'

Apart from the one meeting he'd had with the guy back when Sasha insisted on the kayak outing, he'd only seen him a handful of times. He recalled Joe carrying on about the logistics involved in his line of work. And then something about what a pain in the arse it was to coordinate deliveries when shipping container schedules were at the mercy of dock workers. To be honest, he'd tuned out and focused on the river. The local birdlife had way more to offer.

Joe shook his head, feigned confusion darkening his eyes. He looked at the group of three men still glued to their phones, and opened his mouth. He closed it again, rejecting the impulse to shout at them. Finally, he looked at Sam.

'A few years.' Joe took a slow breath and straightened his shirt. 'Any reason you need to know that?'

'Just curious,' Sam said. He waited.

Joe rushed on. 'I mean, it's not the most exciting gig, but it pays the bills.'

Sam glanced at the watch on Joe's wrist. It clearly paid a lot more than the basic bills. It was a TAG Heuer that retailed for well over five grand. Which he only knew because he'd eyed it a few months ago when he'd been at the mall with Sasha. It felt like a lifetime ago. And if he wasn't mistaken, the guy was also wearing a brand-new pair of RM Williams boots. They definitely weren't standard warehouse-issue work wear.

Sam watched Joe fidget and become more and more agitated. He was being deliberately vague with his responses. This was a guy who liked to be in control. Remove the control and he floundered. Sam knew from Sasha that Joe hadn't been the one to end things with Abby. It had been Abby's decision. Abby had been the one to take control. How had Joe responded to that control being taken? Joe was the kind of person who wouldn't think twice about redirecting the narrative to suit himself.

'So, the last time you saw Abby?'

'I told you. It was about a year ago.'

Sam stayed silent.

Joe filled the gap. 'Like I was saying, we needed to go our

separate ways. Hated having to break her heart like that, but it was for the best, you know?' Joe swatted an imaginary fly. Clearly, the need to hit something, *someone*, was strong.

'Did you, you know, bump into Abby during the past year?' Sam asked. It was almost too easy to push Joe's buttons.

'Didn't I just answer that?' Joe snapped. He closed his eyes for a fraction longer than necessary. 'Look, man, I'm sorry Abby died and all that, but I really don't see what the shi...' He stopped and pressed his lips together. 'I still don't see what it's got to do with me.'

Sam pushed his sunglasses onto his head and looked straight at Joe.

'I know you're with Sasha, mate,' Joe barrelled on. 'And I know the two girls are –*were* – tighter than tight, so I get why you're invested in this.' Joe reached across to clap Sam's shoulder, but stopped at the last second, his hand dangling in mid-air. 'Abby's been busy with her kid and all. Why would I want to get in the middle of all that shit, you know?' Sam nodded. Joe kept talking. 'I mean, it's a bloody nightmare. Who's gonna want to take on someone with a kid that isn't theirs? Not everyone's gonna do the right thing.'

Sam fought the urge to react. He knew a blank face yielded more results. It was a battle, though.

Across the warehouse, a chair scraped along the floor. Joe swivelled, his torso and head turning as one. Conversation amidst the three men at the table had failed to resume and one was levering himself slowly out of his chair. His face was a study in someone who was doing their best to not attract attention.

'Where were you Sunday morning?' Sam asked, drawing Joe's attention away from the workers trying to extricate themselves from the area.

Joe frowned, pretending to think. 'Sunday morning? Probably still in bed, you know?' Again, he began to wink before thinking better of it. 'Yeah. I was at home. Just having a lazy day.'

'Can anyone confirm that?' Sam asked.

Joe lifted his hand to the back of his head and hesitated. Sam watched him. 'Of course not,' he snapped. 'I just told you; I was by myself.'

He hadn't said that. But he was clearly rattled. Sam had a feeling Joe Porter knew a lot more than he was letting on.

And if he hadn't been in touch with Abby, or seen her in the past twelve months, how did he know she had a baby?

CHAPTER EIGHTEEN

ABBY ~ BEFORE THE ACCIDENT

Abby positioned the grazing board on the table overlooking the ocean. The soft dawn light had faded and sunlight was bouncing off the still surface of the Indian Ocean, no white peaks being wind-whipped. It boded well for setting up.

She'd arrived early to ensure she snagged the public picnic table she wanted. Availability was never usually an issue at 9am, but when she was counting on this particular one for an event, it paid to be cautious. And early. Besides, most people who stopped at this spot only did so to take a selfie as proof of their morning fitness regimen.

She smiled briefly at the twenty-something-year-old who had trotted up and was doing her best to angle her takeaway coffee cup with just the right amount of newly-lacquered nail showing. Abby bit back the impulse to roll her eyes.

'Hold this for a sec, would ya?' the selfie-shooter demanded, suddenly shoving a bumbag in Abby's direction. As if Abby was simply waiting there to leap at the chance to do someone's bidding. 'And would ya move that chunk of wood?' She pointed a perfectly filed nail at the grazing board. 'I'm gonna sit on the table so I can get better lighting on my good side.' She glared at the board in question, not-so-subtly implying Abby had put it there purely to vex her. Without waiting for Abby to move it, the selfie-shooter pushed the board aside and sat her bum on the table.

That was just excellent. Now she'd have to sanitise the surface. Again. Abby hoped the solo photoshoot was nearly done so she could get back to work. She stood to the side with the bumbag dangling from her wrist. The action shots seemed to have stopped, but the girl was now hunched over, both thumbs flying over her phone screen with the practised perfection of a Gen Z influencer.

'Do you mind if I keep setting things out on the table?' Abby ventured, when the girl looked as if she was settling in, despite screwing her face up after taking a sip of her coffee.

Abby received a vague flick of a wrist in her direction. And very possibly a *humph*. Clearly, actual words were being saved for whatever important message was being crafted on the screen.

Abby pulled her phone out of her back pocket to check the time. There was still an hour before guests for the baby shower were due to arrive, which was more than enough time to get things laid out and arranged, so there was no need to panic. She had a feeling that engaging further with the entitled selfie-shooter would only result in unwanted confrontation.

But a healthy dose of passive assertion never went astray. Abby bit back a smile as she sat down on the bench seat attached to the table, right next to pristine white sneakers at the end of crossed Lycra-clad legs. She stretched back and placed her elbows on the table behind her. The onscreen nail tapping stopped. Nothing like invading the personal space of someone who thought genuine contact and interaction only existed via a screen.

'Do ya mind?' Lycra legs were uncrossed and the phone was

slipped into the side pocket of the woman's leggings. The selfie-shooter slithered off the table when Abby angled a smile over her shoulder but made no attempt to move. Her smile grew as the girl stomped away, snatching her bumbag from Abby's outstretched hand and tossing her coffee cup in the bin. Abby mentally fist-pumped.

This was an important job, and she needed to nail it. Positive feedback and reviews were the lifeblood of her business. Especially one as fledgling as hers.

Abby spritzed disinfectant spray over the table and swiped a cleaning cloth over it again, rubbing vigorously where the Lycra-clad derriere had deposited itself. There had been one not-so-positive review so far. She'd been taken aback by it initially. Grumpy reviews weren't unheard of in the hospitality industry. They were to be expected. But it didn't mean she had to like getting them. She gave the table a final sanitizing spritz.

She moved the board back to where she had originally positioned it, taking the time to run her fingertips along the grain of the wood. The board had been a gift from Sasha when Abby had, well, made the changes she needed to in her life. She tried to reframe the thought in her mind. She didn't want to associate the beautiful board with Joe. The gift had been a celebration of change, of new beginnings.

But there had been something about this one review. It had scratched at the edges of her mind, unable to be dismissed as easily as the mediocre ones that were written by people who made a career out of finding faults. *Career dissenters*, Sasha called them.

For a company specialising in bespoke boards and creating the perfect atmosphere, I was seriously underwhelmed. The only atmosphere created was one of amateur pretension. My five-year-old's effort at making an afternoon snack plate

looked better than the board of over-priced cheeses and
stale crackers that I ended up with.

She knew it was Joe. The bit about the five-year-old was the
slip-up. One of his favourite putdowns had been to say, *A bloody
five-year-old could do this better than you.* Or some variation on
that. But it had always centred around that exact age. It was his
go-to phrase. Her skin prickled again.

She hadn't spoken to him since the meeting at King's Park.
Voice messages and texts had filled her phone for the first week
after she ended things, until she blocked his number. She
shivered. The thought of his rage at being ignored filled her with
nervous unease.

It wouldn't have been difficult for Joe to leave a snarky
review, either. Her catering business wasn't a secret. And with
her ignoring his calls and texts, undermining her business was
not something he would've thought twice about. But the review
hadn't helped. There had been two cancellations since it went
up. Not that people said it was the reason they cancelled. What
else could it have been, though? His words were toxic. *He* was
toxic.

But she had to move on. It was time for a new beginning.

Abby stepped back and looked at the table and the space
she'd be able to use. The area would be filled with ten women in
just over half an hour. She needed to get it absolutely spot on.
And hopefully she'd get at least one decent review out of it that
would make the bad one fade into oblivion. The actual setting
up didn't take long. She had refined the routine and loved seeing
it quickly take shape. She snapped a photo of the shimmering
ocean view and added a few hashtags: #beachlife #magical
#bespokeboards. And she tagged the location, so potential
clients would realise how accessible she was.

She paused for a moment as an idea struck her. Did she

have time to set her phone up and film a time-lapse of the setup process? That would work well as a post. If she could condense it to a ten second clip, people would get a tiny glimpse of the process coming together. Abby liked thinking of it as a kind of magic. Ooh – a song idea to go with the clip! Queen's *A Kind Of Magic*.

Abby spun towards the railing to set her phone up. If the timelapse clip turned out as she hoped it would, maybe she could use it on her website as well. Distract and deflect potential clients away from the negative review. She angled the phone so that the ocean formed the background. Clouds wafted at the side of the screen, knowing they were bit-players to the star attraction of the water. There was no filter that could compete with the sparkles that shimmered along the corrugated surface of the vast ocean. And was that a dolphin? *Yes!* She whipped the phone up to zoom in.

'Would you look at that?!' A deep voice interrupted only centimetres from Abby's ear.

Abby jumped and flung her phone in the air, only just managing to lunge and catch it before it plummeted over the railing and into the ocean. 'Shit!' She breathed heavily. 'God, you scared me.'

An arm reached out to steady her. 'Sorry,' the culprit said, eyes wide. 'I just couldn't resist stopping. No matter how many times I see them out there, I never get tired of it.'

'Yeah,' Abby said, her breath still coming in rapid little puffs. 'I know what you mean.' She forced herself to inhale calmly and focus on the dolphins still breaking through the surface in graceful arcs. It wasn't Joe. Between the online comments and the knowledge that Joe didn't let go of things – her – easily, she was perpetually on guard.

'Geez, I didn't mean to scare you,' the guy said, turning to look at Abby and frowning as he registered the lack of colour in her face. He shoved dark hair from his eyes, crouching and peering up at her.

Abby stepped back. She still wasn't a fan of people being too close. Personal space issues had become something of a *thing*. 'You're all good,' she said, turning to line her phone up again, hoping the guy would take the hint and keep moving.

'Setting up for a picnic?' he asked.

'Kind of,' Abby said, moving to the other side of the table and digging into one of her chiller bags. She reached in blindly, not caring what her hand landed on. It could be a whole fish, for all she cared. Just as long as it prompted the guy to get on his way. She pulled up a toy baby's bottle.

'Well, now you've gone and intrigued me,' he said, smirking at the bottle. He waggled his eyebrows. 'A teddy bear's picnic?'

For the love of God. Why did she have to be landed with people who could not take a hint? First the selfie-shooter, and now dolphin-dude. Although he was just the tiniest bit cute in a tousled and unkempt kind of way. She slammed the miniature bottle down on the table and pressed her lips together. No! There was no way she should be noticing things like that. If Joe had taught her anything, it was that she couldn't trust first impressions.

If she ignored him, would he take *that* hint and be on his way? And there was no way she could now pull out the cute plush bear she had packed as a prop for the baby shower theme without encouraging him.

'Do you want some help?' he asked when Abby kept digging around in her various bags. 'Have you lost something?'

For crying out loud. What *was* it with this guy?

'Come on,' he said, shooting her what she presumed was meant to be a disarming smile. 'The least I can do for scaring you is to help.'

Abby clenched her jaw before taking a deep breath. 'Do you know what would help?' she said sweetly.

The guy straightened. If he had a tail, it would have been wagging madly. It was almost enough to make Abby switch gears and agree to let him assist her. Almost, but not quite.

'See the table down there?' Abby said, pointing to another picnic table about fifty metres along the path.

He turned eagerly. 'Yeah. Do you need me to take something to it?'

God, this was like kicking a puppy. She gritted her teeth, about to tell him to jog down that way and then keep going. But she couldn't. She wasn't that person. 'No,' she said, closing her eyes briefly. Would it hurt to let him help for a few minutes? Maybe it was time to start letting people in again. Abby chewed her lip. 'Actually, you know what?'

He bobbed his head and raised his eyebrows, expectation and anticipation creasing his forehead.

'I could do with some help setting up this frame,' Abby said, pulling out a collapsed garden arch she always set up as a backdrop for her tables, winding pieces of greenery and special elements that reflected the event. For the baby shower, she had secured a selection of blue booties, tiny blue teddy bears, some dummies and oversized powder blue safety pins with florist wire. It was her first time catering for a baby shower and she'd had a ridiculous amount of fun making this particular garland. Ideas were already buzzing around her head for a baby girl-themed garland and a gender neutral one. Photo opportunities resulted from the unique arch, meaning clients would – hopefully – tag her in their Insta-worthy posts, generating further interest and new clients. 'Only if you're sure? You really don't have to do this,' said Abby.

'I'm Cody, by the way,' dolphin-dude said, leaping forward and thrusting his hand out.

Abby gave a small jump. Sudden movements still startled her. She reached out hesitantly and took his hand. 'Abby,' she said. 'Thanks for this,' she passed him the bag containing the pieces of the arch-shaped frame.

God, would she ever stop feeling so jittery? Abby watched Cody pull out the poles and snap them together as if he'd done it a dozen times before. He had an ease about him that encouraged her to relax, which wasn't something she had felt for a long time.

'You been doing this for a while?' Cody asked, inclining his head towards the table.

Abby snaked a trail of pumpkin seed crackers around a wheel of brie cheese. 'A couple of months,' she said, popping a couple of blueberries on top the cheese. 'What about you? What do you do when you're not scaring people?' She screwed up her nose and tried to smother her discomfit with a flurry of scooping hummus into small bowls.

'I'm a landscape gardener,' Cody said, with no hint of irritation.

Abby was so used to second guessing everything she said. It was proving to be a difficult habit to break. Something about Cody's easy manner began to tug at and loosen one of the knots. Her inclination had always been to avoid engaging in conversations with men. It wasn't worth the grief from Joe. But Joe wasn't a factor anymore, so what did she have to fear? Wasn't this about new beginnings? New opportunities? It was the premise of her whole business, after all. There was no reason why she couldn't ask further questions. Who was going to stop her?

'What made you get into landscaping?' She kept her back to him and arranged a pyramid of dried mango spears on the board.

Cody reached down to snap two more poles together. 'A Tonka truck,' he said.

'Riiiight,' Abby replied, wondering if she'd heard him correctly. *A Tonka truck? She hadn't asked him what his favourite toy was.*

He laughed – a deep, uninhibited sound enveloping the small area. 'I'm not kidding,' he said. 'Or so my mum likes to tell everyone. She said I was landscaping the sandpit with my trucks before I could even walk. Bridges, waterways, rock gardens – the lot.'

Abby didn't know whether to laugh or melt. She'd never met a guy who was so unabashedly open. She looked at him for a moment, used to reading Joe's features with split-second precision, gauging and assessing fleeting looks, muscle twitches and even blinks. There was no sign of him being anything other than genuine. She fanned out some pre-sliced apple on the board. It was all very confusing. Why was she even thinking about what his expression really meant?

'So, you've made a career out of playing with Tonka trucks?' Abby said, tipping too many olives into a small bowl and then madly trying to contain them. She sneaked a sidelong look at him, attempting to gauge his reaction.

'Damn straight, I have,' Cody said, laughter colouring his words. 'And, do you know what the icing on the cake is?'

'Uh, no?' Abby still kept a safe distance between them, but the easy banter encouraged her to keep talking as they worked.

'I get to wear a toolbelt all day.' He stepped back to look at the arch. 'It's like I never had to grow up. If I didn't think I'd look like a complete dickhead, I'd wear my Batman cape as well, which used to complete my look when I was a kid.' He struck a mock superhero pose.

Abby snort-laughed and immediately swiped her hand

across her mouth at the unexpected sound. How long had it been since she'd been this relaxed with a stranger? With someone new?

'You could always make a cape with your company's name on the back,' Abby ventured, openly smiling. She tucked her hair behind her ear and raised her eyebrows, daring him to engage.

'You know what?' Cody said, suddenly still. 'That's a bloody brilliant idea. I'll have them made for the rest of the crew as well. Do you think it would be over-the-top to make up a shield-type logo well?' he asked hopefully, as if Abby's opinion really mattered.

Abby bit her lip to stop another snort escaping. Here was someone who had made her feel more at ease in three minutes than she'd ever felt in all her time with Joe.

'You definitely need a shield,' she said, dropping a blue-topped baby bottle into the centre of a pile of macadamias with a flourish.

Cody secured the garland around the arch and turned to Abby. 'I think you'll have to help me come up with the design now,' he said. 'Should we make a date to work on it?'

Abby froze and almost crushed the crostini she'd scooped up. Could she really go out with someone she didn't know? A complete stranger?

She loosened her grip on the brittle crackers and looked at him. He had a hole in the shoulder of his T-shirt. His shorts were spattered with paint and his cap looked like a freebie from a liquor store. There wasn't an ounce of artifice about him. Even for a casual run along the waterfront, Joe would have worn the latest lululemon line of men's clothing, each item perfectly coordinated. As if expensive activewear made up for his less-than-athletic stature.

If she was serious about making changes and embracing new beginnings, now was the perfect time to put it all into practice.

'Yes,' Abby said, simply. 'We should make a date.'

At that exact moment, a man in perfectly coordinated activewear slowed his pace as he ran by the picnic table. Abby didn't notice. She was smiling at Cody.

CHAPTER NINETEEN

SASHA ~ RECENTLY

Sasha kicked her leg out and flung the quilt off. Her room was stifling. She pushed a hand through her hair, now damp with sweat. It took her a moment to orient herself. She groped for her phone in the dark. It showed 5.15am. How had it got so hot? She'd set the air conditioner to run at a constant nineteen degrees before she went to bed, knowing she liked that sweet spot of cool-yet-cosy. She threw the covers further back and flapped the sheets, trying to create some breeze. So much for Gerry maintaining...

Sasha bolted upright when she heard scraping outside her door. Her heart vaulted into her throat, and she held her breath, every fibre of her frozen. What the hell was that? She flicked the switch of her bedside lamp, but it was dead. That was odd. It had been working last night. Her heart hammered against her chest, pounding as if desperate to escape its confines. Was someone trying to get into her room? Sweat trailed down her neck, her T-shirt sticking to her back and armpits.

She grasped at the bedside table for something she could use as a weapon. All she could feel was her phone or the TV remote. Where was a bloody baseball bat when she needed it?

Or a cricket bat? She'd whacked enough balls in the backyard and at the beach to know how useful one could be.

Tiptoeing across the room to the door, Sasha brandished the TV remote in front of her. She glared at it. What was she going to do? *Click* the intruder into changing his mind? With any luck, it was just a possum. She paused and listened, her ear angled to the door. And where the hell was the peephole that hotel doors the world over had? The scraping sound disappeared. Was it safe to open the door and peek out?

She froze. There was no way she could hold the remote *and* open the door at the same time. Her left hand was completely useless. She couldn't clasp the remote. Neither could she turn the lock on the door. For fuck's sake! She shoved the remote under her left arm, and used her right hand to unlock the door, yanking it open wider than she intended. That was just brilliant. Why not invite the intruder or thief or serial killer in for a cup of tea while she was at it? She looked around, the dawn light barely casting a dim glow over the area. Long shadows spilled from every angle. She flicked the patio light switch. Nothing.

There was no sign of any movement and everything was quiet. She inched her way across the patio and looked across the property towards the main house and reception. There were no lights on inside the house. Maybe there had been a power outage. Although there was a light shining from above the garage. Either it was a security light with battery back-up, or they still had power.

Sasha chewed her lip. Was it too early to go and knock on Mrs M's door? The sun might be on the verge of making an appearance, but it was barely after five o'clock. The only place a sane person would be, was in bed.

Still gripping the TV remote as if it were a weapon, Sasha scanned the area for any sign of movement. Nothing. Her breathing slowed. She went back inside, locked the door, hopped into bed and pulled the sheet up to her chin. There was no need for the quilt while the power was out. The TV remote stayed in her hand as a precaution.

A few hours of sleep later, and with sunlight flooding the room, Sasha stretched and took her time waking up. Birdsong added a cheerful backing track. She lay still and let it wash over her, breathing slowly and evenly. She glanced at the remote control still in her hand and unwound her cramped fingers. If it weren't for the imprints on her hand, the early morning scare might have been a dream. In fact, the whole episode now felt faintly ridiculous. She blamed it on the semi-lucid state that magnified middle-of-the-night thoughts.

And using a TV remote as a weapon? What the hell had she been thinking? Abby would find it hilarious. Except she wasn't talking to Abby. Or Sam. And barely even to her parents. She had no one to share her ridiculous thoughts or moments with, no one to laugh with, or to tell her when something was nonsense.

But she could stop the loop. It was a new day. There were choices to be made. Her heart began to race again. Maybe later. The difficult choices could wait a little longer.

She decided to spend the morning away from the motel. The power was back on and her air conditioner was once again breathing chilled air into the room. She was still feeling a bit jittery after the early-morning wake-up call, or whatever the heck it had been. In the clear light of day, it had no doubt been a possum scratching at crumbs. Crumbs that she – just possibly – may have dropped yesterday when she stuffed the last of an exquisitely flaky almond croissant in her mouth before going inside. She had planned to tell Mrs M about the possible intruder, but it suddenly seemed silly. The power was on, the crumbs explained the scratching, and it was time to start the day.

Wandering down the main street in Margaret River, Sasha found herself pausing outside a café called Green Goodness. Green vegetables weren't her food of choice, but the sign on the sidewalk was so colourful and exciting that it had stopped her in her tracks. There was also the chance it might cancel out the almond croissant from yesterday. She might not quite be ready to contact Abby, but if she was serious about pushing outside her comfort zone, it made sense to head on in and try something green.

The door to the shop tinkled as a customer came out, frothy green drink in hand. Sasha ducked in before she could overthink things.

'Hiya,' sang the girl from behind the counter, her corkscrew curls scraped back with a fluorescent green headband that did nothing to stop them dancing about her head. 'What can I make for you? Did you see the new matcha-frappuccino on the board outside? It's *soooo* good!' She practically vibrated as she spoke. If she wasn't a walking billboard for green energy and vitality, then Sasha didn't know who would be.

'It does look good,' Sasha admitted nervously.

'How about you try one of our samples,' suggested the green-drink poster child, passing across a tray of shot-sized eco-friendly cups brimming with green goodness.

'Thanks,' Sasha said, raising a small cup to her lips. The smell of freshly cut grass registered at almost the same moment as the taste of mulched and decayed grass clippings hit her tongue.

'So,' the green-goodness energiser bunny said. 'What did you think?'

'Um, I really don't think it's for me,' Sasha said, her eyes still watering. She wanted to add that the only place for it was in the hutch of a guinea pig. Or a rabbit. And only if the rabbit was extremely desperate. She tried to think of some redeeming features she could add to soften the blow of practically spitting her drink at the little energiser bunny but she drew a complete blank. 'Do you make hot chocolate?' she asked instead.

The corkscrew curls stopped mid bounce and a frown appeared beneath them. "With, like, actual *real* chocolate?"

Sasha turned and headed outside. She needed a drink that was *not* green. One that contained a decent amount of caffeine.

'Sasha!'

The sound of her name carried along the street. Shit. Who knew her in Margaret River? Sasha spun around and saw Andrea from Mrs M's sitting room closing the distance between them. And reaching out.

'What a coincidence, running into you,' Andrea delivered a hug.

Sasha tried to rally. She knew she'd been rude, running out on her and Mrs M the other night. The fact that Andrea was still being openly friendly to her now spoke volumes about her character.

'Good to see you,' Sasha swallowed and pasted a smile on her face. She knew she should probably apologise for the other night. 'Hey, I'm really–'

'Oh, don't give it a second thought,' Andrea interrupted, correctly interpreting the direction Sasha was heading in. 'Everyone has something they're dealing with. I don't think I'm being full of myself to assume it had nothing to do with me.' She raised an eyebrow at Sasha. 'I seriously doubt I could've made that much of an impact on someone in such a short space of time, right?' She nudged Sasha with an elbow. 'Hey, why don't we grab a drink and you can make it up to me? I'm trying to distract myself. Mrs M has talked me into giving a small concert tomorrow night and I'm nervous as anything! I've felt sick all morning.'

'I know all about that feeling,' Sasha said without thinking. Shit.

Andrea shot her a small questioning look, but continued when Sasha didn't say anything more. 'I haven't played at home or in front of people who know me in years and years and I'm so bloody nervous.' She grimaced and gave a small shudder.

Sasha knew the feeling well. Or, she *used* to know. She would get nervous before every performance, whether she knew audience members or not. No matter how many times she played a piece, every single time she set foot on a stage, her skin and scalp began to prickle. It always disappeared as soon as she lifted her hands onto the keyboard, but she'd never been able to stop the sick feeling in the hours before every single concert.

'Come on,' Andrea said and grabbed Sasha's arm. 'Let's go in here.' She led her into a café. It was only once they were inside that Sasha saw the seats were not of the squishy, armchair variety. They were of the trendy, cool-crowd, bar stool variety. *High* bar stool variety. High enough that a running leap would be required to mount the stupid things.

Sasha glanced across at Andrea who had managed to navigate the stool with ease after ordering two coffees.

Still, sharing a coffee with someone had to be a step in the right direction. Knowing that Andrea played the piano and did so for a living made Sasha want to run for the hills. But facing it was something she had to do. Maybe a croissant with the coffee would help settle her stomach.

'How long are you back in Margaret River?' Sasha said, venturing into the territory of adding something to the conversation. *Excellent start. Totally original.*

'I've got another ten days before I head off again. WASO – West Australian Symphony Orchestra–' Andrea raised an eyebrow at Sasha to check she knew what she was talking about. Sasha nodded faintly. 'They're doing some joint performances with the Salzburg Symphony Orchestra. And then I think it's London after that–'

'That's amazing,' Sasha exclaimed, cutting her off before Andrea could finish with a question of her own. It was much easier to be the one asking them. 'Have you been to Salzburg before?'

Most people loved talking about where they'd travelled to. Sasha hoped Andrea was no different. She would be willing to look at a few photos, if necessary.

'A few times,' Andrea said. 'I love the place. I mean, what's not to love? The buildings, the bridges, the chocolate,' she said, taking a slurp of the cappuccino in front of her. 'What about you? Have you been?'

Andrea wasn't as easy to redirect as Sasha had hoped. She was clearly one of those people who genuinely wanted to listen to a person and find out more about them. Either that, or she was incredibly nosy. Somehow, Sasha couldn't see it being the latter.

The thing was though, Andrea only knew her as *Sasha*. Which was short for *Alexandra*. And Alexandra Andrews was the name she used when she was performing. *Used* to perform. Her stomach twisted. God, would it ever stop hurting? The classical concert community was relatively small as well. Especially those pianists who were lucky enough to tour with orchestras. Which Sasha had been doing – very successfully – for many years. Andrea would have definitely heard of *Alexandra Andrews*. Recognising her face was a little more of a stretch since her face wasn't exactly plastered all over posters. She wasn't about to give Taylor Swift a run for her money in the recognition stakes.

'Yes,' Sasha said, finally answering Andrea's question, 'a few times.' She meant it to sound casual and light-hearted, but from the lines creasing Andrea's forehead, she figured she may have missed the mark. 'Sorry. Yeah, I've been a few times, but it's not something I want to talk about right now.'

'Fair enough,' laughed Andrea, not at all put out by Sasha's unwillingness to share. 'Everyone has stuff they don't want to talk about. I get it. But you know I can listen at any time, right? I know we've only just met, but sometimes, talking to someone who doesn't know about all your baggage and dramas can be a good thing.'

Sasha wriggled on her stool. 'Thanks. Everything's still a bit, um, recent.' Which it was. But interestingly, the idea of telling Andrea didn't fill her with dread. She tore a strip off the just-delivered croissant and dunked it in some strawberry jam, leaving a trail of crumbs across the table and down her shirt. It had been a long time since she had felt this relaxed.

She looked down at her phone sitting lifeless on the table. Was she ready to start moving forward? Perhaps it was time to start acting, rather than thinking.

CHAPTER TWENTY

SAM ~ NOW

'I tell you, Joe Porter bloody knows something,' Sam said into the phone, well clear of the warehouse. He adjusted his sunglasses against the glare. He'd made another call to Paul Green, the coroner, as soon as he was out of earshot. 'He was twitchy as hell just now.'

'You think he was involved?'

'His reactions didn't add up.' Sam turned and looked back at the warehouse. There was no sign of Porter. He knew he didn't have a lot to go on. A few twitches didn't exactly make the man guilty. But Sam couldn't let it go.

'Can't help you much on my end, I'm afraid,' Paul said. 'The morning has been crazy. But I'm on my way to the morgue now. I'll call you as soon as I know anything.'

Sam ended the call and crossed the warehouse parking lot to where his car sat baking in the midday sun. Sheets of corrugated iron provided some semblance of division from the crumbling wasteland beyond the property. Chunks of concrete with pokers of steel reinforcement protruded like a junkyard octopus. If Porter had the disposable income for flashy watches and shoes, he sure as hell wasn't getting it from his salary at the warehouse.

Furnace-like heat blasted Sam as soon as he opened the car door. He hopped in, wincing as his legs made contact with the blistering seat. Long pants helped, but not a lot.

Sam switched the air con to maximum fan speed and wound down the windows to let the trapped heat escape. He pulled out his phone and stared at it. Could he call Sasha? His fingers itched to tap her name and make contact. *Keep being you,* Sasha had said. They were the last words she'd said before she left the room. Before she left him. Well, that meant following his gut. And his gut was telling him to call Sasha. He needed to hear that she was okay. His thumb hovered over the screen.

Who was he kidding? Once she heard about Abby, of course she wasn't going to be okay. Indecision gripped him. He hated it. On the one hand, he knew Sasha needed to know. But on the other, she would want answers. Answers he couldn't provide yet. Would it hurt to wait a little longer?

Sam made a decision. He would go to Abby's place. He needed to see if there was anything there that could shed some light. He had no idea what he was looking for, or what he even hoped to find, but it had to be worth a short detour.

Once he'd done that, he would call Sasha.

He stabbed at the switch to close the car windows and grimaced.

Okay. He'd *think* about calling Sasha.

Abby's house was bare and bereft. Shadowed. Tall tuart gums in the neighbouring nature strip had accepted an unspoken challenge to reach their maximum height, taking all available sunlight. The trade-off was ground that lacked the energy to produce anything more than a token offering of sparse weeds.

Sam gripped the wheel while the car idled outside the non-descript suburban brick rental property. It felt wrong to be here without either of the girls. He looked at the front door, half expecting to see Abby burst through it. The shaded veranda was small, but it had been a favourite place for the girls to sit and chat, the constant shade providing a welcome cool. Two blue Adirondack chairs sat to the left of the front door. They had been Sasha's house-warming present to Abby. He knew, because he had assembled the bloody things after a trip to Bunnings. Sasha had insisted on the wooden chairs, having fallen in love with them on one of her tours in the US. She'd tried to convince Dave and June to put them in the outdoor dining area at the vineyard as well. But the campaign to acquire them had screeched to a halt after the accident. Like everything else.

'Can I help you there, mate?' Sam jumped as a pair of hands slapped against the car window. Some cop he was, letting someone sneak up on him.

Sam wound down his window. A thin arm with papery skin leant on the edge of the glass. 'Hiya, Rob.' Sam recognised the elderly man as Abby's next-door neighbour. He'd cleared the old man's gutters about six months ago. He didn't want to share the news about Abby yet. 'How's things going? Anything going on around here that I need to know about?' Sam squinted into the light. He knew Rob liked to fill him in on Neighbourhood Watch-type things. Was it too much to hope he'd have something useful this time?

'Sam!' A grin erupted. 'Time for a cuppa? I've been makin' notes, all careful, like. None of that electronic bullshit for me.' He gave a phlegmy cackle and pulled a mandarin from the pocket of a threadbare dressing gown. 'Gotta keep an eye on the neighbourhood, right?'

Sam shook his head. 'Sorry, Rob. It'll have to be another

time. Why don't you get the notes and I'll take a look at them at the station.' He paused and then added, 'Maybe I'll get them typed up.' He guessed – correctly – that the official nature of having his notes typed and documented would appeal to Rob.

The older man's stoop straightened a fraction. 'Good idea. I'll go and find them.'

'Thanks.' Sam switched the engine off. 'I'm just going to pop into Abby's place, then I'll come and get your notes.'

Rob shuffled off, his dressing gown flapping. He stopped and looked back at Sam. 'Tell that young lass in there to come across for a piece of shortbread soon. I've been keepin' an eye out for her, but haven't seen a peep of her. Or the bub.'

Sam sighed and got out of the car. Tomorrow. He'd come and tell Rob what had happened tomorrow.

The garage was closed and the driveway was vacant. Abby's car had been found at the vineyard, obscured as one of many parked on the grass verge during the day, but a solitary beacon once everyone had left. It had been towed to the impound yard.

Sam climbed the few steps up to the veranda. The blue chairs were coated in rain-splotched dust. It had clearly been a while since anyone had used them. If he had to guess, he'd say the day before the accident had been the last time they had seen any human contact. Just over six weeks ago. A light breeze swept through, dislodging leaves from beneath the chairs.

Abby's door had one of those keyless entry pads. Her house was a rental, and it had been a new addition she had put in at her own cost about a year or so ago. It was linked to a couple of security cameras and had let her see when someone came to her door, or attempted to get in. He hadn't thought too much of it at the time. Only that it was sensible, given she was the only occupant in the house. Had someone tried to get in recently? Someone that had scared Abby? He'd get IT at the station to pull footage.

He keyed in Sasha's entry code, briefly hoping it still worked. It had been a few weeks since he had been to the house. The electronic click and release of the lock sounded instantly.

The room was dark and the curtains pulled. Sam reached for the light switch. Stale cooking smells lingered in the lounge. A baby crib was next to a grey couch. A handful of small cloths and bibs were scattered on the couch, along with a blanket draped over the back. Sam recognised it. The gumnut green and beige colours crocheted into patchwork squares had been one of many Sasha had made before the baby was born. Sasha loved to crochet in her downtime. "Active rest", she called it. Her fingers were never still. It only now occurred to him this would be something else Sasha could no longer do; something she would be missing.

Sam stepped over a plate with half a piece of toast on it that had been left on the floor by the couch. The place was a mess. Hardly surprising, when it had been just Abby with a newborn baby.

He crossed to the bookcase on the opposite side of the room. There were three framed photos between piles of books. He picked up one of a middle-aged couple, both laughing at the camera. Abby's parents. Her mother had her hand raised, as if beckoning someone – Abby? – to join them. They had died about five years ago, from memory. A car crash where the driver of the other car had fallen asleep at the wheel and veered straight into them. He replaced the frame gently. It was a small consolation that he wouldn't have to tell her parents their only daughter was dead.

The frame to the left showed Abby and Sasha. There was no posing in this shot, both collapsed on the ground in a tangle of limbs and laughter, the Eiffel Tower in the background. The photographer had missed the girls turning cartwheels, instead capturing the aftermath. Sam hadn't been on this particular trip, but he had heard all the stories. And sat through evenings of photos shared on the TV. Those two had shared so much. He breathed heavily. Not anymore.

His eyes moved to the frame on the right. Abby and her baby daughter Sophia. He picked it up. Abby was looking at her hours-old daughter, love and tiredness tugging at her features. She had her index finger resting against the baby's tiny pursed lips, as if smoothing away Sophia's annoyance with being plunged into a world of blinding lights and bewildering noises. Seconds later, tears had been streaming down Abby's face. Sam knew this because he'd been the one to take the photo. June had come later, laden with flowers, fruit and hugs. Lots of hugs. And Dave had hovered in the doorway, unsure whether to ask about the birth or talk about the weather.

Sasha had stayed away. But she had snatched Sam's phone when he'd visited her that evening. She'd swiped through the photos, her mouth set in a tight line. Until it wasn't and her cheeks were lined with salty streams. Was that really only three weeks ago?

Sam set the photo back in its place on the shelf. A heaviness settled in his stomach. Sasha. They might not technically be together at this point in time. But he needed to talk to her. *Shit.*

His throat clogged as he looked around the small living space. Why hadn't he gone back to visit Abby again? Checked to see if she needed anything, or any help? He recognised June's flowers from the hospital visit, now withered and drooping, barely a centimetre of dank yellow water in the bottom of the vase.

He moved across to the tiny kitchen and paced around it. It took three seconds. Three seconds where he saw dishes piled in the sink, stuck together with congealed and crusted remnants of whatever food Abby had seen fit to throw together. Three seconds that revealed the overwhelming tiredness and exhaustion of early solo parenthood.

It was so fucking unfair. A life interrupted. Taken away.

Sasha's life had been interrupted. But she was still here.

He paused by the four-seater dining table. A blue notebook covered in butterflies sat in the middle with a pen on top. He knew Abby always had a journal with her. He opened it. *My dear, darling child*, it said on the first page. And there was a tiny ultrasound image taped below the words. It was her pregnancy journal.

His throat constricted even more. He needed to leave. Sam picked up the journal and left the house. He closed the front door and drew a ragged breath.

'There you are, Detective,' Rob called from next door. 'I've got the notes I made for you.' He beckoned Sam over, flapping a yellow-checked Spirax notebook at Sam. 'May as well take the lot. It's all dated and got the times written in. I know how much details matter.' Rob had the quivering excitement of someone who knew his years of neighbourhood vigilance might finally pay off.

Sam crossed over to the old man's veranda. Rob leant against a weathered plastic picnic table that held an ancient Wilbur Smith book and a tube of haemorrhoid cream. His dressing gown sagged open and did nothing to disguise the loose pyjama shorts.

'Thanks, Rob,' Sam said. He took the notebook and tucked it under his arm with Abby's pregnancy journal. 'I'll get onto it back at the station.' He waved a farewell to the old man as he headed towards his car.

'Not much happening in the last couple of days,' Rob said, keen to prolong the conversation. 'Not since the lad in the blue car banged on her door and tried to rattle his way in.'

Sam's step faltered.

Didn't Joe drive a blue car?

CHAPTER TWENTY-ONE

ABBY ~ 9 MONTHS AGO

Abby slid her shaking finger along the end of the small cardboard box, almost dropping it in the process. She juggled it briefly and turned wide eyes towards Sasha. The last thing she needed was to contaminate the test with God-knows-what from the floor of the waterfront toilets. She needed the answer. Positive or negative, she needed to know.

'Have you locked the door?' Sasha asked, turning to check it.

Could you even lock an entire public restroom? Abby sat on the wooden seat that ran along one side of the beachfront facility. Her legs were not going to keep her upright for much longer. The smell of saltwater blended with urine wafted around her. Her breaths came in shallow, rapid bursts. How had this happened?

Idiot! You know how *it happened.*

She let her head fall forward and tried to slow her breathing. The urge to vomit pooled in her stomach. Despite the cool interior, sweat dripped down her inner arms. There was no way she was going to be able to hold the squatted stance to pee on the stick for – how many seconds? She pulled the instruction sheet from the box, but the words blurred in front of her. Waves pounded along the coastline outside, the roar echoing in intensity around the tiled walls and floor of the bathroom. Or was that the roaring in her own mind? Abby jammed her hands over her ears. She willed it to stop for just a second.

A memory squashed the nausea.

Bodies colliding. The desperation, the impatience. Clothes pulled off and tossed aside. Teeth grazing her nipples followed by a flourish with his tongue. *Oh, that tongue.* And while his tongue dedicated itself to her breasts, his fingers delved and danced. Her hands had moved instinctively, intuitively, over his shoulders, down his chest and then gripping his hips, pulling him closer, willing him to be part of her. Excitement tingled through her, even now, the memory still vivid. Cody had definitely left an impression.

Had he left *more* than an impression, though? Her stomach heaved.

Abby rushed towards the stall and fell to her knees in the cubicle, the gritty cool of the tiles thrusting her back to the present. Her head spun. A wave crashed with renewed assertion against the rocks. *Don't ignore me. Don't ignore me.*

'Can you read the instructions for me?' Abby's voice was little more than a rasp. She clenched her stomach muscles, willing the whirlpool in her belly to subside. She held out the piece of paper with the instructions towards Sasha. 'Oh, God, I think I'm going to be sick.' She lurched forward; her cheeks numb as nausea swirled its ascent along her body. The roar continued.

'Five seconds, Abs,' Sasha said, not at all concerned with the sight of her friend hunched over a stainless steel public toilet. 'You've got to pee on it for five seconds.'

'Not helpful,' Abby said, swiping her hand across her mouth. She straightened slowly, testing the stability of her legs. The sickness had grown in intensity over the past few days. She clasped her hands over her breasts. Yep. Still feeling tighter and more full than usual. She squeezed gently. And maybe even a little sore? *Shit.*

'Think you can manage to pee on this and find out?' Sasha ripped the foil packet and passed it to Abby, the stick still inside.

Could she have a few more seconds of not knowing? *No!* She needed to face this. Once she had peed on the stick, she'd at least know which way to go.

Abby took the opened packet from Sasha. She closed the stall door. There were some things you didn't need to share with a best friend.

'Are you going to tell Cody?' Sasha's voice ricocheted around the walls, even over the sound of the waves.

Good question. Would she? Was it even an option *not* to tell him? 'Let me get the result and then I'll think about that.' Abby unlocked the door and held the stick out to Sasha.

'Ew,' her friend said, scrunching up her nose. 'I'm not holding your pee stick.' She ripped some paper towels from the dispenser on the wall and laid them out on the wooden seat. 'Put it down here. Have you set a timer?'

Abby tapped her phone and swiped across to the clock app. 'I have now.'

Sasha frowned. 'Abs, what are you going to do if it's positive?'

Run? Hide? 'I'll work it out,' Abby said, a little more defensively than she intended.

Sasha looked at her in an evaluating sort of way. 'You know you have choices, right?'

'I know that,' Abby spluttered. 'I'm as pro-choice as you are. But you know where I stand on this personally. If I'm pregnant – *if,*' she said, holding her hand up to stop Sasha interrupting, 'then I'm going to keep it. You know that.'

'Yeah, I know that.' Sasha gave her a half smile. 'Just checking.'

Abby wanted to grind her teeth. The frustration ate away at her. She couldn't find the words to tell Sasha about the dread. The sheer terror. It wasn't about whether she would – or could – manage a pregnancy. She could cope with being pregnant. That wasn't the issue. The issue was Joe. It was always *Joe*. If he found out she was pregnant, there was no telling what he would do. Nausea rose again, the bile burning a thick trail up her throat. 'How long's left on the timer?' she said, wrapping her arms around herself, as if that alone would protect her.

'Abs, it's on your phone,' Sasha said, not unkindly.

Abby swallowed. The phone buzzed in her hand and she jumped, despite knowing it was about to go off. She crossed the room and looked down at the plastic stick.

An unexpected grin broke across her face. For a moment, the terror subsided and she cherished the moment.

Sasha shook her head and blinked, the question in her eyes no less demanding even with the absence of actual words. 'Well?' she finally exploded, the silence not lasting.

Abby picked up the stick and held it out. There were two very distinct lines. 'Looks like I have to start thinking of names.'

CHAPTER TWENTY-TWO

SASHA ~ RECENTLY

'Fancy a drive down to Augusta, love?' Mrs M called across to Sasha.

Sasha looked up from her phone. It was a new day, and she had no plans. The hours stretched ahead of her. She was sitting on the chair outside her room, not sure what to do with herself. Mrs M had a pile of towels tucked under her arm and a streak of flour under her nose. She looked like a grey nomad with a drug habit.

'Been baking, Mrs M?'

'As a matter of fact, I have,' she said, her eyes wide. 'How did you know that? Oh, my lord, you can't smell it burning, can you?' Mrs M spun around, as if she expected to see flames leaping from the kitchen window.

Sasha tapped her finger to her top lip. 'You've got some of the evidence under your nose.' An actual smile tugged at her lips. The action felt rusty.

Mrs M swiped her hand across her face, no doubt the same action that put the flour there in the first place. 'Better?' she said. Sasha nodded. 'So, what do you say? It's only thirty minutes down the road. We can stop for a scone at The Ragged

Robin as well. They're almost as good as mine,' she said with a wink. 'If we're lucky, they might even be pumpkin ones. Oh, love, you really can't beat a good pumpkin scone,' Mrs M rolled her eyes exaggeratedly and sighed. 'I've got to pick a few things up from one of my suppliers, but that'll be done in two shakes of a rattle.'

Sasha tapped her phone while Mrs M chattered about the treasures that could be found at the pumpkin scone place. Her screen lit up with a vase of flowers. It used to be a candid shot Abby had snapped when Sam had picked her up and spun her round at the beach last summer. The photo had caught the whip of her hair, water droplets lassoing and connecting them, linking the two of them. She'd changed it last week, the happiness captured on her face too much to bear. She was no longer that person. That couple didn't exist.

Sasha sighed and looked at Mrs M. 'You know what?' she said, forcing her lips back into some semblance of a smile. 'I think I *will* come with you.'

'Just give me two ticks to drop these towels off and I'll meet you up at reception,' Mrs M beamed.

Sasha went back into her room and pulled her sneakers on. They had elasticated laces and had no need to be tied up or undone. They were the kind that pregnant women and people with arthritic hands wore. She was neither of those. Her mum had bought them for her when she'd first got out of hospital; it was a thoughtful gesture, but one that continually highlighted what she could no longer do. How long would it be before she could go back to tying her own shoelaces? Doing up the buttons on a shirt? Even pulling up the zipper on a bloody dress, for crying out loud?

And how was it that the only people wanting to spend time with her were the motel landlady and a friend of the landlady?

She tapped the screen of her phone again. Still blank. Everyone who knew her had completely stopped reaching out.

Which was what she had wanted. Wasn't it? To be left alone, in peace and solitude. To wallow, undisturbed. Oh God. Is that what she was doing – wallowing? Her stomach clenched. Witnessing people so wrapped up in their own myopic worlds was one of her pet peeves. No matter what was happening, or what people were talking about, wallowers still managed to turn the situation back to themselves. She slipped her feet into the shoes and straightened. A rush of heat up her neck made her pull at her collar. And now she had joined their ranks. No wonder no one was talking to her.

Was that why Sam hadn't reached out? Or Abby? Or even her parents? Yes, she'd told everyone to leave her alone. Maybe even *more* than told them. She cringed at the thought of how she'd raged at everyone. But since when did they actually listen to her? They'd chosen a brilliant time to start paying attention. She stuck out her bottom lip, and then pulled it in quickly, biting down on it. And now she was reduced to childish gestures. Why not start throwing toys around and stamping her feet?

The drive to Augusta had passed in a fog of one-way conversation. Mrs M seemed happy to chatter on with only the most minimal of utterances from Sasha. The pumpkin scone was indeed divine, Mrs M had collected a box of who-knew-what from the back door of a row of shops, and they were now heading south. The sign they just passed indicated a lighthouse was ahead. Which was not something they had passed on their drive *to* Augusta.

'Did you have something else to pick up?' Sasha asked. She thought they were heading straight back to Margaret River.

'Oh no, love,' Mrs M smiled as she navigated the winding road. 'I thought we'd make a quick pitstop at the water wheel.'

'The what?'

'The Cape Leeuwin Water Wheel, love. It's only five minutes out of town and one of my favourite places. And it's too nice a day to stay cooped up inside.' She smiled innocently at Sasha.

Sasha looked out of the passenger window as Mrs M turned into a carpark. She'd heard of the water wheel before, but it was one of those things that she had never gone out of her way to see. In the past, trips to the Margaret River area had centred around winery visits and maybe the odd cave tour. The last few with Sam had barely seen them leave their room, let alone drive to Augusta to visit an ancient water wheel. She shoved open the car door, pushing the memory of Sam as far away as she could.

'Shit!' Sasha yanked the door back towards her. A cyclist had appeared out of nowhere. 'Sorry,' she called through a crack, opening it slowly and making sure the cyclist was still upright. God. She needed to get out of her own head. 'Are you okay?'

'No worries.' The cyclist waved away Sasha's concern with a breezy flick of her hand. 'I shouldn't have passed so close to you. No harm done.'

Sasha stepped out of the car as Mrs M turned off the ignition. The cyclist stretched her sandaled feet to the ground, using her tiptoes to keep the bike balanced. She bore an uncanny resemblance to Abby. The girl's long hair was loose around her face, falling forward as she reached into the wicker basket at the front of the bike for a drink.

'Isn't this place incredible?' she said to no one in particular, screwing the lid back on the bottle and tossing it into the basket.

Sasha looked out to the ocean, still feeling shaky at the damage she had almost caused. One moment of inattention, and she had come dangerously close to inflicting pain and injury on an innocent person. All it took was a second of distraction. Nothing premeditated. Nothing deliberate.

Mrs M came around to Sasha's side of the car. 'What do you think, love?' she asked. 'Pretty much takes your breath away, doesn't it?' she continued, filling her lungs with the salt-laden air.

Sasha returned a wave to the cyclist, who was already heading back out towards the main road. It would be a decent ride back to the small town. She looked out to where Mrs M was facing. 'It's incredible,' she breathed, her heart rate finally slowing after the near miss.

And it truly was. What was left of the ancient water wheel stretched into the ocean, waves pounding the base. Years and years of the same repetitive force had dulled the angles of the foundation rocks, no match for the relentless force and power of the Indian Ocean. Waves reared up, reaching skyward, the sun teasing the crests, tempting them that bit higher, daring them to reach further. And at the moment they peaked, the sun's rays dusted a shimmer of light across the tips, laughing at them and then beckoning them to try again and again and again.

Sasha watched, mesmerised. There was a rhythm to the waves, although it was a rhythm that had no conductor. As soon as there was a hint of a pattern, the beat changed. The tempo switched. It surged, then abated. It raced and then stilled. It accelerated, then applied a *ritardando;* slowed. It was familiar, but also unpredictable. There was an inherent musicality to the waves.

She clenched her right fist and looked at her limp left hand. Music was everywhere. It was everything to her. What could she do without it?

Mrs M moved to her side. 'Try not to go down that rabbit hole, love,' she said, accurately reading Sasha's thoughts. 'It's not going to get you anywhere.'

'But what else do I have?' Sasha whispered. 'It's the only thing I know how to do.'

'Look at that wheel,' Mrs M said, nodding at the crumbling and weathered but still proud structure. 'How many knocks do you think it's taken? How many beatings from beyond its control?'

Sasha frowned. Was she seriously being likened to a decrepit and no-longer-functioning water wheel?

'And before you go and get all indignant at me,' Mrs M shushed Sasha, 'just stop and really look at it. Go on,' she said, nudging Sasha with her elbow. 'Tell me what you see.'

If she'd thought she could get away with it, she would have rolled her eyes. Instead, she settled for closing them briefly before looking out at the water wheel. She saw a pile of crumbling rocks and timber that had been left to rot because they were of no use to anyone. The wheel, or what was left of it, was useless. Just like her. She tried to swallow, but her throat clogged.

'Something that had a purpose, but is useless now.' Sasha forced the words past the knot.

'What else?' Mrs M said gently, refusing to be drawn in by Sasha's defeatist tone.

Sasha huffed and crossed her arms. What was the point of this? She looked out at the gnarled features. The pile of foundations holding the wooden water trough looked like lumpy body bags, destined to remain upright and never rest.

'There's part of a wheel shaped from rock, although how it ever managed to turn is beyond me. It looks like it's been welded onto the rock it's sitting on.' Sasha looked at Mrs M, who raised her eyebrows and nodded at her to continue. Was there a correct answer that would let them get in the car and go back to Margaret River?

Tufts of coastal grass wedged against every available surface like children pressing into a mother for safety and security, a few daring branches reaching tentatively towards independence. Sasha watched strands of green bob and duck in the breeze.

Three more carloads of tourists pulled into the parking lot, people spilling out and, without fail, standing tall while they filled their lungs with salty sea air. Their shoulders relaxed as they savoured the sight of the ancient wheel. Minds and bodies stilled, just for a moment.

Sasha snuck a look at Mrs M. A hint of a smile tugged at her lips, her hands clasped loosely in front of her.

Despite her protestations, Sasha understood the point. The water wheel might not be functioning in its original capacity, but it was far from useless. It still had a purpose.

A trickle of an idea began to form in her mind.

CHAPTER TWENTY-THREE

ABBY ~ RECENTLY

Abby gripped the shopping trolley tighter, hoping it would mask the shaking in her hands. Her glimpse of the figure crossing the end of the supermarket aisle had been fleeting. But it had been enough. A trail of sweat threaded its way down her inner arm. Why was Joe at *this* store? It was nowhere near where he lived. She tried to swallow, but her tongue had wedged itself in the back of her throat.

It had been an impulsive decision to dash to the store before dinner. It was a convenient time, with the lack of crowds. She'd been meaning to start stocking up on baby supplies and a sharp kick under her ribs from little Dumpling had prompted her to swerve into the carpark.

'Ma'am, are you okay?' The voice from a teenage worker stacking shelves with packets of pasta roused her.

Abby pushed her trolley to the side of the aisle, away from the centre where she had stopped abruptly. 'Sorry. Yes. I'm fine.' She nodded at him. Her voice sounded tremulous, even to her own ears.

The teen flicked stringy curls from his forehead, slipped an earbud back in place and returned to giving the pasta way more attention than was warranted.

Liar. She was anything but fine.

Her hands moved to her belly and cupped the curves that were stretching a little more each day. Little Dumpling gave a swift kick in response. It was as if he or she knew Abby needed the reassurance that all was well. Or perhaps it was a reaction to her spike in heart rate, the adrenalin surging through not just her but her unborn child, as well. Either way, feeling the movements ripple through her brought everything back into sharp focus.

She pushed the trolley and rounded the end of the aisle. Her reflection wobbled in the bank of freezers running along the far wall of the supermarket, the image distorted. She spun left and right, and then checked again. There was no sign of him. No sign of the thinning red hair that he liked to cover with a khaki-green baseball cap. *It brings out the colour of my eyes, babe.* That had been the reason he always gave for wearing it.

Abby chewed her thumbnail, her gaze still darting from one end of the store to the other. She was sure it had been Joe. It couldn't be a coincidence he was at this particular store. At this particular time. She flinched as a thread of skin tore along the side of her nail, a bead of blood oozing and framing it like a neon light.

It wasn't the first time she'd seen Joe lately, either. Or thought she'd seen him. The doubt and second-guessing he always conjured were never far from the surface.

Just last week, she'd been coming out of the doctor's surgery after her six-month antenatal check, clutching a photo of little Dumpling. She'd been grinning, bursting to get to her car and call Sasha. She couldn't wait to tell her how her godchild had a promising future as an acrobat, if the foot covering his or her face was anything to go by. She'd held the photo high in the sunlight, caught in a halo of happiness.

Until her eyes had landed on Joe. Seated on a bench at a bus stop, he'd made no move to hide. He was looking at Abby. There had been no smile. No wave. No move at all. Just his eyes locked on her. And even from across the road, she could see them shift to her swollen stomach. Feel them settle on her unborn child.

The tinny tone of the in-store speaker jolted Abby. *Clean-up in Aisle 8*. She glanced up. She was at the end of Aisle 2. The teenage shop clerk turned and headed away, presumably to whatever needed to be cleaned. Abby's body went numb. She was alone. The aisle was deserted. Was that a deliberate ploy to get rid of the clerk? Her mind raced. It wasn't out of the ordinary for there to be a spill or a breakage. Perhaps it was nothing to do with Joe at all.

Except she knew Joe.

She knew how he thought.

She pushed the trolley around to the fresh produce section. It was open and free of high shelves. Which meant fewer places for Joe to sneak around.

A man wearing a blue cap and a flannel shirt paused by the onions. Abby's hand flew to her mouth in a tight, bunched fist. She had only caught a glimpse of the figure. It could have been anyone. But her reaction had been immediate. It had to be Joe. He hadn't tried to talk to her. He hadn't acknowledged her.

Yet.

That was the thing. Joe loved to play games.

He knew she was aware of his presence.

He knew she couldn't see him.

She'd only see him when he wanted to be seen.

She paused by a bin of bananas, the smell cloying, sweet and faintly rotten. A breath of air hit the back of her neck. She spun around.

'Sorry.' The man selecting onions paused by her and ripped a plastic bag from the reel. It wasn't Joe. 'Just need another one of these.' He flapped the bag, the breeze sharp against her skin.

Her breathing slowed. It might not have been Joe. But she knew he was watching.

CHAPTER TWENTY-FOUR

SASHA ~ YESTERDAY

That evening, Sasha found Mrs M settled in the piano room, her hands tucked cosily around a mug and her eyes focused on an indistinct view outside the window. Sasha stopped at the doorway, unsure whether to disturb the lady she was quickly beginning to think of as a friend.

She watched for a moment. There was a sadness to Mrs M's features that Sasha wasn't accustomed to seeing. Had something happened since they'd got back from their daytrip?

Music circled the room, coming from a small speaker on one of the bookshelves. If she had to guess, she'd say the lyrics were Spanish. Although that was based more on the style of music than recognising any of the words. Her knowledge of music was prodigious, but the same could not be said about foreign languages, despite having toured more countries than she could remember. Three leadlight lamps bathed the room in soft light, a moth beating a frantic rhythm from under one of the shades. Sasha chewed her bottom lip. Should she say something, or slip away and leave Mrs M to her thoughts?

'Oh, hello love,' Mrs M said, making the decision for her. She patted the arm of the chair next to her. 'Come and join me.'

'Are you sure?' Sasha ran her fingers along the staff of music on her inner arm. 'I don't want to interrupt.'

'Don't be silly, love,' Mrs M scoffed. 'You'd be doing me a favour.'

Sasha crossed the room and sat in the blue-patterned, over-stuffed chair next to Mrs M. She tucked her legs under her. 'You looked deep in thought,' Sasha said, twisting a strand of hair around her finger. The least she could do was get out of her own head for a few minutes. 'Everything okay?' She didn't want to pry. She hated it when people prodded too hard. But ignoring someone's sadness was a little callous. It was a fine line.

Mrs M set the mug down on the coffee table in front of her and traced a fingertip over the pattern etched around it. The lime green base colour should have clashed horribly with the orange and mustard patterns, but somehow, they worked.

'I got this in Peru,' Mrs M said, still looking at the colourful mug.

'It's... got a distinctive pattern,' Sasha said, not quite able to say she loved it. She was not one of those people who could gush on cue, feigning genuine appreciation of something. Directness was a far more efficient way of communicating. Although she had learnt over the years to bite her tongue rather than always giving an honest opinion.

Mrs M looked up and gave a hint of a smile. 'It's not something you'd find in the stores around Perth, I'll give you that.'

'Is it an Incan design?' Sasha had always been fascinated with the ancient civilisation, but didn't know a lot of details. For all she knew, lime green could have some special significance.

'I'm not sure I'd go that far, love,' Mrs M chuckled. 'But it has that feel about it, doesn't it? Peter and I lived over there for three years,' she said, staring at the mug.

Not Gerry? Sasha tilted her head. 'Peter?'

'My first husband,' she said, a soft smile crossing her face before sighing. 'He died while we were there.' The smile vanished.

'Oh, I'm so sorry,' Sasha said, reaching across to take Mrs M's hand.

'Thanks,' Mrs M said, covering Sasha's hand with her other and giving it a gentle squeeze.

Mrs M got up, walked over to the bookshelf and pulled a carved wooden frame from the top of a pile of books. It showed a couple standing in the foreground of Machu Picchu. 'This was our last holiday,' she said, running her fingers over the glass. 'Not that we knew it at the time.'

'You look happy,' Sasha ventured, angling the frame to get a better look. She had no idea if that was the right thing to say. How had she gone through life and never had to deal directly with death? She leant forward and examined the photo. Mrs M was standing on tiptoes, her eyes sparkling, as if mischief was just around the corner. Peter had one eyebrow raised, and while his lips were yet to form a smile, you could just tell it was imminent.

'Oh, love,' Mrs M gave a small laugh. 'That man could drive a saint to distraction. He never stopped or sat still.' She shook her head fondly, memories washing across her face. 'He always had us setting off on some adventure or other.' She rubbed her thumb over his face. 'I wouldn't have had it any other way.'

'What happened?' Sasha asked, quietly.

Mrs M's lips tightened. Should she not have said anything?

'The silly fool,' Mrs M shook her head. 'If he hadn't been so damn stubborn, it all could've been avoided.'

Sasha looked at the photo. Peter was a good head taller than Mrs M. Not that she would have been *Mrs M* in the photo. She looked down at the picture again. Peter's face was alive, energy barely contained while he posed for the photo, even.

'It was blood poisoning,' Mrs M continued.

Sasha gave her a questioning look, but didn't say anything.

'He stepped in a pothole on the sidewalk when we were in Lima, the day after we took this,' Mrs M said, nodding at the photo. 'Bloody stupid man sliced the back of his heel open.' Tears pooled in her eyes. 'But do you think he'd go and have it looked at? Oh, no. Didn't have time, he said.' She closed her eyes for a second. 'You know, love, I'm so cross with myself. I should've insisted that he have it looked at then and there. But he hated a fuss being made, so I left him to it. He rinsed it off in the shower, wrapped a bandage around it and said it was good as gold. Any fool could see it needed stitches.'

'He didn't want stitches?' Sasha frowned.

'Didn't want the hassle of putting people out or making a fuss,' Mrs M said. 'I dragged him to the clinic two days later when there was still blood dripping from it. Two days! And you could see, clear as day, that it was infected. They stitched it, but it was a mess. Stupid, stupid man,' she said, suddenly angry. 'If he could've just listened, or thought of himself for once, then he'd still be here.'

Sasha was at a loss for words.

'You can't undo what's been done though,' Mrs M said, shuffling around on the chair, as if wriggling would dislodge the grief. 'He was a good man and we had some wonderful years together.' She picked up the coffee mug and smiled determinedly. 'I mean, how else would I have ended up with something as special as this?' She tipped the mug towards Sasha.

'It's definitely... unique,' Sasha agreed. 'And now you have Gerry.' Christ, was that the right thing to say? Was she sounding flippant? *Never mind! You lost your first husband but you've found another. C'est la vie!*

'I do,' Mrs M said, not at all put out. She took the frame and set it back on the bookshelf. 'How lucky am I to have had two such special men in my life? What about you, love?' Mrs M turned to Sasha. 'Anyone special in your life?'

'Mmm?' Sasha froze. 'Uhhh...' She left it hanging.

Mrs M sat back down on the chair, not giving Sasha a chance to escape. She looked at her, eyes wide and expectant. Where was a distraction when she needed it? What were the chances of a pigeon appearing in the room? Or a wombat waddling through the door? She grimaced. Not very likely, given that wombats weren't a feature in the Margaret River region.

Did she have someone special in her life? Sam had been that person. But she'd made sure he no longer was.

CHAPTER TWENTY-FIVE

SASHA ~ RECENTLY

Sasha opened her eyes and stared at the ceiling of her childhood bedroom. The glow-in-the-dark stars and music notes she had painstakingly stuck there years ago hovered above her, now a dirty yellow. She'd slept well, considering what lay ahead. As she'd crawled into bed, what she was about to do loomed over her. It was the right thing to do, the only fair thing for Sam. The knowledge hurt like absolute hell, but what choice did she have? She'd figured her chances of sleep were non-existent when she flicked off the bedside lamp that still had a tasselled crochet covering she'd made when she was fifteen. There was too much going on in her head: questions, doubts, blame, anger. But her mind was exhausted and shut down completely.

A moment of calm settled over her as consciousness tugged from the edges. She wriggled her feet to find a cool patch on the cotton sheets, her mind still. Until the stillness was shattered when she remembered what she had to do. She couldn't avoid it any longer. Her throat locked tight. Sasha flung back the covers and propelled herself from the bed, her head spinning in protest at the speed of it all.

Getting dressed was still an issue with her broken hand, yet

Sasha resisted the urge to call out to her mum for help. She needed to do things for herself. Even if it meant wearing an unflattering pair of elasticated tracksuit pants and a loose white T-shirt. When it came down to it, her wardrobe had very few choices that did not involve buttons, zips, loops to tie or hooks to secure. And anything that was tight was a nightmare to navigate. So, that ruled out fitted items and even leggings. You needed to grip fabric to manoeuvre yourself into those things. And the grip in her left hand was non-existent. So, grungy loungewear was as good as it got.

Besides, what did it matter if it looked like she'd been dragged through the vineyard after the pickers had been through? She didn't need to impress Sam. Scowling, she picked up a hairbrush and yanked it through her matted curls. Or as far as the brush would go before it dug in and refused to go any further. Christ, was that a *dreadlock*? She held the matted strand up to inspect it more closely.

Fury prickled through her. *Be positive,* everyone said. *There is so much you can still do.* She grabbed the hairbrush and hurled it across the room. An entirely unsatisfying gesture since it bumped along the bed, the blankets swallowing the rage. Sasha glared at it. She had aimed for the wall above her bed. She'd wanted a crash. An impact. To break something. Hurt something.

Downstairs, her mum handed Sasha a cup of coffee with a tentative smile. She looked exhausted. Sasha's stomach dropped. Had she done that? Had she put that look on her mum's face?

'Sleep well, love?' Her mum turned towards the sink and busied herself, wiping already clean counters.

Sasha's hand shook with the mug in it. 'Yeah. It was okay.'

Her mum put the cloth down, picked up the spotless toaster and checked it for crumbs. 'Any plans for the day?'

The conversation made Sasha want to scratch her limbs. 'Sam's coming around.' She didn't add more details. Her mum would know soon enough. And then smother her with a whole new onslaught of pity and concern.

A smile creased her mum's face. 'That'll be nice.' The words were overly upbeat.

Sasha choked back something between a laugh and a sob. *Nice* was packing a picnic lunch and finding a secluded spot by the river. *Nice* was hanging out with her boyfriend, going for a drive and exploring, hand-in-hand, with no set plans. What she was about to do was definitely not *nice*.

'Do you want me to pop a tray of muffins in the oven? Your dad wouldn't say no to a couple either. What do you think – blueberry and white chocolate?'

Oh, God. The hopefulness on her mum's face was too much. Frustration clogged her throat. 'No thanks, Mum,' Sasha forced out. 'I don't think we'll need any muffins.'

Her mum turned away. But not before Sasha saw the look of a kicked kitten slide across her face.

'Matt just called to see if we want to join him and Cass for lunch,' Sam said as Sasha walked towards him in the lounge room. He straightened beside the piano and stepped towards her, but stopped short of kissing her when she turned away. 'What do you reckon?' There was an expression of forced brightness on his face; it was an expression Sasha was becoming increasingly familiar with. An expression that infuriated her beyond all measure. 'They're at Matilda Bay. It'll be nice to catch up with them.'

Again, with *nice*. Was that all anybody could think of to say?

'Matt?' Sasha said instead. She was not in the mood to tolerate Matt's arrogant and self-aggrandising bullshit. And his girlfriend was a simpering limpet who couldn't come up with an original thought to save herself. 'Catch up with Matt and Cass?' Even if she wasn't about to end things with Sam, there was no way she could put on anything resembling a pleasant face for those two.

None of that mattered now, though. Once she ended things with Sam, he could see whoever he wanted, whenever he wanted. Still, she was powerless to stop the words. Her nerves about the upcoming conversation needed a release.

'I absolutely do *not* want to have lunch with bloody Matt and Cass,' Sasha said. A small bead of spit landed on Sam's chest. She heard him swallow. 'I'd rather stick pins in my eyes than sit and listen to that brainless idiot and his insanely boring girlfriend.' Sasha's foul mood spilled over, words pouring out of her, a balm for the dread of what she was yet to say. 'He's so full of shit and thinks everything he says is the most original thought of the century. He's an ignorant dickhead.' Sasha breathed rapidly. The clock on the mantle beside the piano added one tick for every two breaths. She took a deep breath. It was now or never.

Tick, tick.

'This isn't working.'

Tick, tick.

'I can't do this anymore.'

Tick, tick.

Sam frowned. 'You can't do what?' He took a step closer to Sasha.

She stepped sideways and held up a hand. 'This,' she said, gesturing between the two of them. 'This – whatever we are now – I can't do it anymore.' She stepped again, the dance of deflection in full swing.

The lingering smell of toast and honey from the morning diners circled the room. Sasha gulped in the air, the sweet scent sticking in her throat.

'What are you talking about?' His Adam's apple jerked up and down. 'Is this about seeing Matt and Cass?'

'No!' Sasha shouted. 'Although I really don't want to ever see the two of them again.'

'That's totally fine, honey,' Sam said in an irritatingly soothing voice. 'We don't have to see them if you don't want to.' He held both of his hands up and nodded at her, encouraging her to calm down.

Was he trying to *placate* her? For fuck's sake. Did he think he was at work and trying to talk someone unstable off a bloody ledge? And since when had she ever been a *honey*?

Sasha took a deep breath. 'You need to listen to me, Sam. This,' she said, waving her finger again between the two of them, 'isn't working.'

Sam blinked in quick succession. 'Of course it's working,' he said, desperation creeping into his tone. He closed the distance between them and lifted her good hand, weaving his fingers between hers. 'We're working through things and you're getting better. You're getting better every day. I *know* you are.' His voice sank to a whisper. 'Don't do this now, Sash.'

The fight left Sasha and every muscle and bone in her body wanted to drag her to the floor. 'Don't you see, though? Being with me isn't making you happy. And I hate that I'm the reason you're not smiling.'

'That's just bloody stupid,' Sam said, anger beginning to seep into his voice. 'You're not in your right mind.'

'Excuse me?' Sasha's spine straightened and locked. 'I'm not what?'

Tick, tick.

'You're being ridiculous.' Sam faced her squarely.

Tick, tick.

'Is that right?'

Sam slumped forward. 'You know that's not what I meant. I just meant that the pain of everything you're dealing with is clouding how you're really feeling.' He raised his head and reached out a hand to touch her cheek. 'Come on, Sash. This is you and me. Surely that's worth fighting for?'

Sasha almost cracked. The touch of his hand against her cheek, his fingers, long and firm. The anguish on Sam's face and in his voice was too much to bear. She hated hurting him. The last thing she wanted to do was cause him more pain. But she knew if he stayed with her, she would cause even more damage in the long run. Besides, how could he still love her when the one thing that was her very essence was no longer possible?

'It's for the best,' Sasha said. She wanted to pick up his hand, lean towards him and rest her head against his chest. It would be so easy to do that; to relax and feel his arms encircle her, a cocoon of safety and momentary oblivion. She breathed deeply, evoking the scent that would envelop her. Sun-dried shirts and shaving cream. The shaving cream would occasionally be different, depending on what was on special at the supermarket. But his clothes were always line-dried, sun-bleached to perfection. Oh, God. Could she go through with it?

She clenched her right fist while her left hand hung limply. Immobile. Useless. Leaning on Sam wasn't an option. She owed it to him to be stronger than that.

She owed it to herself.

'There's nothing else to talk about.' Sasha mentally pushed herself away from Sam's chest. Away from comfort and love. 'This is how it's got to be.'

'Please, Sash,' Sam said, a tremble creeping into his voice. 'Can we just take some time to think about it?'

Tick, tick.

'You're a good person, Sam.' The fight and anger left Sasha. 'Just...' She looked at him. 'Keep being you, okay?'

Sasha turned away from Sam. She couldn't stay in the same room as him any longer. Without the anger, there was only pain.

She was tired of pain.

CHAPTER TWENTY-SIX

SAM ~ NOW

After leaving Abby's place, Sam stopped at a roadside coffee van. He leaned against a barrel by the van, a group of teenagers between him and the makeshift cafe. The field behind the van stretched out to scrubby bushland and the Swan River beyond that. The rain had stopped, but rivulets of muddy water tracked through the burnt grass, the ground too baked and dry to do more than accept a superficial offering.

Sam drummed his fingers on the wooden barrel. *Not since the lad in the blue car hammered on her door and tried to rattle his way in.* He'd left Abby's place with the neighbour's words ringing in his ears. Joe drove a blue car. A blue 2021 Kia Cerato, to be exact. He'd checked as soon as he got back in his car. Joe had been driving a blue Kia when Sam first met him. But he needed to find out if that was still the case. No point getting excited if he'd bought something different in the meantime. But he hadn't. The blue Kia was still registered to Joe.

What were the chances someone else had a blue car and was frustrated enough to pound on Abby's door? Security camera footage would tell him soon enough exactly who it was. But Sam was almost certain it had been Joe. What was it Joe had wanted, though? Why had he come back a year after he'd split with Abby? Was it to do with the baby? Or something else?

A Border Collie wearing the earlier rain like a flopping, soggy coat trotted over and sniffed Sam's leg. He bent down and automatically scratched its damp ears. Sasha used to want a Border Collie. Was it something she still wanted, or had that changed as well?

Thinking of Sasha made him remember some of her concerns about Joe and his controlling behaviour. If Joe really was the controlling type, chances were, he was jealous as well. And if that was the case, exactly how would he have taken the news about Abby having a baby with someone other than him?

The dog sat by Sam's feet and looked up at him. 'What do you think, buddy?' Sam asked it. The dog cocked its head, as if considering the question. 'Was it because of the baby?' The dog's ears twitched. 'What else could it be?'

Sam stood up and looked at the collie swishing its tail against the ground. He sighed. Was it too much to hope that a dog could give him answers?

Joe – if it *had* been Joe – was clearly in an agitated state when he went to Abby's house a few days ago. Someone shaking a door when they got no answer could be perceived as a display of frustration, of anger. From what he'd heard and seen of Joe, he was sneakier and more controlled than that. He would let his jealousy play out in a more subtle and coercive way. No. There had to be something else. But what? Was he trying to get into the house to look for something? What could he possibly want after a year, though?

Sam pulled out his phone. May as well get things moving. He scrolled through his contacts, looking for the number he wanted.

'Luke, mate,' Sam said when it connected quickly. 'How's it going? How was the game on the weekend?' It had been some time since he'd seen the young IT specialist. But Sam knew he played footy for a local club.

'Sam!' The voice answered enthusiastically. 'Could have done with you, to be honest. Where the hell have you been?'

Sam wasn't part of any club, but had played his share over the years and had taken part in a few inter-station friendlies here and there. It wasn't rugby, but it was fun to have a run, every now and then.

'Keeping busy, mate. And you sure as hell don't want me and my fumbling hands,' Sam said, a mock grimace colouring his tone. He'd let an easy mark slip through his fingers the last time they'd played, and he hadn't forgotten it.

'Don't know what you're talking about. You're a bloody legend,' Luke responded easily.

Small talk out of the way, Sam dove in. 'I need your help with the case I've got at the moment.'

'Sure thing.' Luke's voice shifted quickly to brisk professionalism.

'I need some footage pulled from a couple of security cameras that are linked to a keyless entry pad on a domestic residence.'

'Yeah, I can do that. Send me the details and I'll get it to you as soon as I can. Should only take an hour or two.' Sam could already hear Luke tapping at a keyboard.

'Thanks, mate. Appreciate it. I'll catch you back at the station.' Sam disconnected.

Rain resumed in a misty fog. The collie trotted back to its owner, who was caught in the queue behind pondering teenagers. She had long curly hair and was a similar build to Sasha. His heart clenched. He knew it wasn't Sasha, yet he was irrationally annoyed by that.

Was now a good time to call her? His stomach lurched. He really needed to call Dave and June and see if they'd spoken to her yet. He slid his thumb over the smooth screen of his phone, but instead found himself remembering the soft skin of Sasha's jaw and the spot just below her earlobe. God, he missed her. He wanted to hear her voice so badly, he could taste it.

Once he called her though, there was no going back. Once he'd told her the news about Abby, he couldn't un-tell her.

He should be used to delivering bad news. It was a routine part of his job. But this wasn't just bad news. It went way beyond *bad*. This would crush Sasha. Even though Sasha hadn't wanted anything to do with Abby since the accident, there was no escaping the fact they were linked. They were family.

'Order for Sam!' The shout from the coffee van jolted him. He strode over to the counter.

'Long black with–' The coffee guy turned the cup in his hand, searching for the add-ons. 'Nope. Just a long black.'

'Thanks.' Sam took the coffee and slipped the phone back in his pocket. There were still a few things he needed to do before he talked to Sasha. He took a gulp of the coffee and winced as the scalding liquid hit his tongue.

He wanted to make one more stop before going to the station. And before he called Sasha.

CHAPTER TWENTY-SEVEN

ABBY ~ RECENTLY

Abby swiped at the tears spilling down her cheeks as she took the receipt from the doctor's receptionist. Eight months of pregnancy hormones had a lot to answer for. An elderly man tutted beside her when she reached across the counter for a handful of tissues. She wasn't sure if he was annoyed with having to wait or if the attractive mix of tears and snot on her face offended him.

She opened her mouth to inquire – politely, of course – if the *tut* was the result of an incurable and time-sensitive medical condition, but Sasha interrupted. 'Only a few more weeks and little Dumpling will be in your arms, Abs.' Sasha took hold of her elbow and gently steered her outside.

Sunlight bounced off the pavement, the heat producing a river of sweat between her swollen breasts. And down the back of her knees, all the way to her ankles. Also swollen. Abby sniffed, dragging her hand across her nose, hoping the sticky trail wasn't visible. Or *too* visible. She was rapidly realising her dignity now came in degrees. Having Sasha accompany her today was a mixed blessing. She had tried to answer the doctor's questions about mucus plugs, early breastmilk discharge and if she was still having regular bowel movements with nonchalance. But her emotions were being shaken around like the making of a martini.

Sasha let go of her elbow and produced another tissue from a tiny backpack slung over her shoulder. The now-soggy mess in her fist was only fit for a *papier-mâché* project.

'Thanks.' Abby sucked in a juddery breath that ended with a snort. 'Oh, God, Sashi. I don't know if I can do this.' She flapped her hands at her belly. She didn't normally voice her fears. Or even give them airtime. She was more than happy with her decision to have this baby on her own. Dumpling delivered a sharp kick under her ribs, as if protesting the false reason for her worry. 'Sorry, sorry.' She immediately crooned at her stomach. She'd worked so hard to keep her stress levels at a minimum and not inflict any negative emotions on her unborn child, which was easier said than done. Especially when Joe's increasing appearances were keeping her on edge.

Sasha linked her arm through Abby's and nudged her shoulder. 'I have absolutely no doubt you're going to be the best mother ever. Little Dumpling has hit the mama-jackpot with you, Abs.' Another dive into the backpack produced a mini protein bar. 'Eat this.' She tore the corner and thrust the bar at Abby. 'You're just low on energy.'

Abby nibbled the corner before popping the whole bar in her mouth. Chewing slowly reduced her heart rate. Sasha took the wrapper and tossed it back into her bag.

'Better?'

Abby chewed her bottom lip but didn't say anything. She knew her friend wanted to help. It wasn't just impending motherhood that scared her. Well, not entirely. The thought was still more than a little terrifying. No. It was more than that. It was Joe. She had no idea why he was suddenly hanging around again. Initially, she'd put it down to coincidence. She'd known he wouldn't accept their separation readily. But it had been almost a year. Surely that was enough time. And why, after so many months of nothing, was he back?

Just three nights ago, headlights had beamed through her front window, startling her. When her phone had rung at the same time with an *Unknown Caller* ID, adrenalin had coursed through her. Since she had blocked Joe's number a year ago, she'd had a feeling he had changed numbers and was using a new one to contact her. She ran her fingers along her forearm. The skin still felt tender from where she'd whacked the doorframe as she'd spun, the car headlights and the shrill tone of the phone assaulting her from all directions. Peering through the kitchen shutters, she'd seen Joe's car. She'd dismissed it, even though her heart thudded, knowing he was trying to get under her skin. Driving by her house was something he'd done many times before. Often parking up.

Waiting.

Watching.

She knew why he was doing it. He wanted the upper hand. Control. Her leaving *him* was a reality he couldn't accept.

But it was happening more and more often. The calls. Seeing his car. Was it the pregnancy? Having a baby with someone other than him was as clear a signal that she'd moved on as anything. He'd hate the fact someone else had gotten close to her.

Or was it something else? Was there another reason Joe was hanging around?

Trying to get close.

Trying to get her attention.

'Abs, are you okay?' Sasha's voice trickled through to her consciousness, bringing her back to the surface.

Her hand gripped the passenger-side door handle. Should she mention it to Sasha? She knew what her friend thought of

Joe. When they had separated, Sasha hadn't tried to hide it. *Bottom-feeding dickhead; sleazy bastard; creep.* The names resonated.

Abby opened her mouth. If she mentioned any of her concerns to Sasha, she'd want to do something. Abby wanted peace. She wanted to focus on her baby. Sure, she might be sticking her head in the sand and pretending to be an emu. Or an ostrich. Or whichever one it was that stuck their heads in the sand when confronted with danger. But she didn't want to give Joe any more attention. He craved attention. It gave him a sense of power. Control. If she acknowledged him, he was getting what he wanted.

She was done giving him what he wanted.

'Feel like some lunch?' Abby forced herself to sound upbeat. There was no need to unload her concerns to her friend. 'I need something salty. Preferably deep fried. Fancy some fish and chips on the beach?' Deflection was all she could manage at the moment.

She'd handle Joe. But she'd be careful. He was clever with words.

He always sounded so reasonable.

Until he wasn't.

CHAPTER TWENTY-EIGHT

ABBY ~ RECENTLY

The afternoon had disappeared in a blur of feeds, nappy changes and futile attempts to put Sophia down. Abby adored her baby girl, but was it not possible to have five minutes where she could adore her from the distance of her shower? Or with a hairbrush in her hand? She twisted a strand of hair around her finger and drew it to her nose. Eww. Some shampoo was definitely required. She peered a little closer. Smell aside, she didn't even want to consider what the crusty matted chunk contained.

It wasn't the cosy newborn bubble she'd imagined. Abby knew being a single mum was going to be a challenge. She'd certainly had enough well-intentioned cautions. *Make the most of the time where it's just you. Your time is never going to be your own again!* Often, it had been delivered with something of a smug or knowing tone. And, *Do you know what you're getting yourself into?* This one had her biting her tongue. A lot. Interfering busybodies who passed her at the mall and thought age gave them the prerogative to be judgemental and rude. But she had taken it in her stride, secure in her own excitement and knowing she had the support of those closest to her. That's what mattered.

Correction. That's what *had* mattered. The person closest to her was gone.

The cries grew and Abby made shushing noises, desperately hoping the sound would quieten her daughter. Wasn't doing so meant to resemble the sound of still being in the womb and reassure the baby? Clearly, that little gem of information had gotten lost somewhere in the birth canal. The second her sweet girl realised she was no longer secure in her mama's arms, her brow puckered, her lips pursed, and her belly jumped as she sucked in air to fill her lungs. Air that was promptly expelled in a wail that twanged every hormonal fibre in Abby's body. She clasped her hands to her breasts as the now-familiar feeling of milk let-down swelled and tingled. Thank God she'd thought to tuck a couple of breastfeeding shields into her bra. If she had to add another milk-soaked shirt to her already overflowing laundry pile, it might just tip her over the edge.

The cries intensified. Surely, her daughter couldn't be hungry again? It had barely been half an hour since she'd hooked her bra up from the previous feed. Where on earth was she putting it all? Her child was insatiable.

She groped for her phone as Sophia's cries continued to build. What were the chances of sending a text to Sasha before the wails had the neighbours calling noise control? Not that any of them would do that. Old Rob next door was a sweetheart, leaving small treats for her at the door like a Halloween trick-or-treater in reverse. There had been a packet of butterscotch candies propped by her door yesterday. And the day before, it had been a lamington from the local bakery. Such sweet gestures made her eyes prickle afresh each time she discovered the latest offering. Not that it took much these days. Abby couldn't decide if it was still the baby blues the midwives assured her were perfectly normal, or something more.

'Come on, beautiful girl,' Abby whispered, scooping her daughter out of the basinet next to the couch. She smoothed a thumb over Sophia's cheek before nuzzling her face into the crook of her daughter's irresistible neck. Was there anything better than the feel and smell of a newborn's neck? Despite being only a week old, the contact and murmurings were already guaranteed to soothe her precious baby girl. Abby's own shoulders dropped a few centimetres as well, the connection a momentary balm. In that moment, she was able to forget the hurt and desolation that was an ever-present shadow.

Half an hour later, Abby cradled her milk-drunk daughter in her arms. She pulled a crocheted blanket up to her baby's waist. Sasha had made it. It was one of the many baby blankets she had presented to Abby throughout the course of her pregnancy. This one was a patchwork of squares, alternating between plain grey and adorable teddy bear faces. And there was another in gumnut greens draped over the back of the couch. When Sasha had found the time to create such intricate patterns was beyond her. She shouldn't have been surprised, though. Her friend wasn't a fan of being still. If she was sitting down, she liked to keep her fingers busy. It quietened her mind, she used to say.

Abby looked at her daughter, asleep and silent beneath the blanket, her tiny lips pursed and still suckling rhythmically. Was it possible that Sasha had embedded some of those calming thoughts in the blanket and they were being transferred to her daughter? Ha. If only.

What was Sasha doing now? Abby pulled her phone out, all thoughts of a shower forgotten. She tapped out a new message. Abby's finger hovered over the arrow to send it. She pressed the blue arrow. There. It was sent. But would it be any different to the countless ones she'd already received no response to? Ones apologising over and over and over again? Why should this one be any different? Maybe it would just be another in the continuous stream of blue text bubbles with no replies.

Abby jumped at a crash outside. Was it in her driveway? Her stomach contracted and she scrunched the baby blanket in her hands. With Sophia snuggled against her like a little koala, she couldn't get off the couch easily to take a look. Abby forced herself to rock gently as Sophia's chin quivered with the change in pressure. It was probably nothing. A bin being knocked over. Or a tradie throwing something in the back of a ute. She stroked the silky strands on top of Sophia's head. Should she dismiss it, or take a look? She bit down on her bottom lip. There was more than just herself to worry about now.

Opaque blue curtains covered the windows, blocking her view. They also provided a flimsy shield. Anyone attempting to look in was not going to see anything, which was the whole point of having them closed. The lack of natural light in the small living room suited Abby just fine.

Abby eased herself off the couch. It was a lot easier to move than it was a week ago. But she wouldn't be able to run.

She paused by the window. Quick footsteps tapped along her driveway. Abby's heart raced and she clutched Sophia, pressing her tiny face against her chest. A car door closed. Trembling overtook Abby's body. What the hell was she doing holding her precious daughter this close to the window? To whoever was out there? No. Not *whoever*. She knew exactly who it was.

She turned around quickly and put her daughter in the bassinet by the couch before hurrying through to the kitchen. Any movement of the curtain by the front door would be obvious. It was a clear signal she was at home. Hiding. She crouched low by the sink and leant over a stacked pile of dirty bowls, just enough that she could see the driveway.

A blue car. Joe's car. The engine started and Abby exhaled.

Just as quickly, the engine stopped. Dread washed through Abby. She grabbed the edge of the sink and held it to steady her legs. A tiny mewl came from the lounge room. *Please stay asleep, baby girl.* The window of the car lowered. The mewl progressed to a whimper. Abby's body ached to fly back to her daughter, to soothe her. A face masked by dark aviator glasses filled the space above the car window. Abby clenched her leg muscles, willing herself to stay still. *He can't see you. He can't see you.* She repeated the words. Her hand slid across the bench, groping for the solid, cold metal of the torch she kept within easy access. It wasn't much of a weapon, but it was something. The foot-long solid metal torch had been a gift from Sasha's dad when she'd first moved in. 'Practical in more ways than one', he'd told her. Would she need to use it now?

The icy cold of the metal burned her palm. Joe's face didn't move. But Abby could picture his eyes, narrowed and calculating. Why wouldn't he give up and leave her alone?

Some teenagers nearby called to each other and Joe turned his head. The shadowy shape of his face disappeared as the car window began to close. Abby exhaled sharply.

She put the torch back on the kitchen bench. Grime from the splotched surface stuck to the palm of her hand as she drew a breath. A small groan escaped her lips and she swallowed.

Forcing her legs to function, Abby glanced at her daughter and crept across to the front door. She cracked it open. She knew he'd left, but caution dictated her actions. There was no one there.

But there was a small brown gift box sitting in the middle of the doormat. It was secured with the palest of pink ribbons. And there was a card with distinctive scrawl that sent an ice-cold chill rushing through her. *Be careful, Abby,* it said.

She snatched it from the box, her fingers shaking. There was more on the back.

You know what I want. Stop playing games.

CHAPTER TWENTY-NINE

SASHA ~ YESTERDAY

Lost in thoughts about Sam, Sasha said a hurried goodnight to Mrs M. Crossing the darkened motel grounds and heading back to her room, she remembered the power outage from the previous night.

The weathered garden solar lights stabbed haphazardly amidst the succulents were about as effective as the smattering of stars above. Pretty, but not exactly helpful. Honestly, would it hurt Gerry to prioritise adding some decent lighting as part of the motel maintenance?

Darkness enveloped her as she picked her way further along the path. Gravel crunched underfoot and the smell of pan-frying onions wafting from a nearby room made her swallow. *Excellent.* Now she was feeling hungry and uneasy in equal measures. She could see the bulky outline of her room, but there was no welcoming light beckoning from within. And why would there be? She hadn't left any lights on so there was no reason to feel trepidation about the lack of them. Still, she couldn't shake the panic from last night.

Sasha shook her head sharply, shifting the pendulum from unease to practicality. The fact that it was now as dark as the inside of a coffin was easily fixed. Pulling out her phone, she turned on the torch. Relief washed over her as the path brightened and she hurried up the stairs and into her room. She felt like she was in a weird game of cat-and-mouse. Which made no sense at all when there wasn't anyone chasing her. She jerked her head towards the door. Was there?

As the thought of games twined with the feeling of unease, a sudden memory pushed itself to the front of her mind. Her and Abby. Over a year and a half ago. At Abby's house. Locked in a garden shed.

'You see what he's doing, right?' Sasha paced around the gloomy space. Cobwebs wafted from the ceiling in the wake of her breeze. She swatted at one that attempted to linger on her cheek.

'Yes, I do.' Abby lifted her chin. 'He's looking out for me because he loves me.'

Sasha stopped and spun to face her friend. She didn't get how Abby could be so *blind*. Just this morning, Abby had cancelled their plans to go shopping, because Joe thought the crowds would be *tiring* for her. Sasha thought Abby had been joking and suggested they both take their walking frames with them. Abby hadn't been joking.

'He's trying to own you. Just like he always does.' Sasha rattled the doors of the garden shed. 'And how the hell did the door just *lock*?'

'You've got it all wrong, Sash.' Abby perched on an upturned wheelbarrow, her knees pressed together, as if unconcerned by the fact they were trapped inside a garden shed.

'How can you not see what he's doing?' Sasha shook the

doors again, the corrugated steel clanging in resistance. It felt like something was wedged against it on the outside. Which was odd, since they'd only entered less than two minutes earlier.

'How can you have such little faith in my judgement?' Abby shot back. 'In my intelligence?' She sighed, the fight leaving her voice. 'And it's not locked. It's stuck.' Uncertainty tinged her tone.

'This has nothing to do with your intelligence,' Sasha slammed her palm against the door. 'Stuck, my arse. There's something against the door, Abs.'

'I think Joe must've propped a shovel or something against the door.'

'He what?' Sasha exploded. Seriously? A shovel? What the bloody hell was he playing at? It dawned on her that Abby didn't look surprised. Goosebumps raced along her forearms. Was this something he'd done before?

'And my judgement?' Abby's voice was small.

Sasha ignored that question. Frankly, she thought Abby's judgement where Joe was concerned, sucked. 'He's not good for you, Abs. Can't you see that?

'He cares, Sashi. I've heard what you're saying. I understand what you're saying.' Abby's voice was conciliatory. 'I'll take your opinion under advisement.' But flat.

'Abby!' And *"advisement"*? If it wasn't for the small fact they were locked in a garden shed, Sasha would have said a *lot* more.

Sasha crossed to the small kitchenette and flicked the switch on the electric jug, the immediate hum filling the silence. As it turned out, Joe had arrived within a few minutes. He'd been all smiles and good humour, blustering something about not realising they were in the shed when he'd put the shovel against the door.

Which was complete bullshit.

Sasha knew he'd seen them go into the shed.

He'd done it deliberately.

CHAPTER THIRTY

ABBY ~ RECENTLY

Abby looked at the handwritten card in her hand. It quivered between her fingers and the words blurred. She read the words again. *Be careful, Abby. You know what I want. Stop playing games.* Trying to second-guess her ex was like trying to predict when a snake would strike. Anger swirled through her stomach, replacing the fear. What was he playing at? And why would he think she knew what he wanted?

Actually, that was a lie. Abby had a pretty good idea what he wanted. He wanted what he couldn't have. Her. And she had no intention of letting him have her. Her heart thudded against her ribs. He'd taken so much, but she had put a stop to it. He absolutely hated that he'd lost. Lost his relationship. Lost the power he used to have over her. Lost control. Joe hated losing more than anything.

The package sat on Abby's small dining table. It appeared to be an incongruous addition to the other baby gifts that had made their way to her over the past week. There was a profusion of pink-patterned paper and rose-coloured ribbons with soft toys and adorable onesies sitting in their midst. She hadn't opened the brown box, though. What she should have done was toss it straight in the bin and not give it – or Joe – a second thought.

But Joe had been snooping around. Abby was more convinced than ever. And his visits were becoming more and more frequent. The noises at night, the phone calls from an unknown caller ID, the feeling that she was being watched when she was out. It was all Joe. She couldn't prove it. But she just *knew* it was him. He batted people's emotions to and fro, as if they were put there for his pleasure. But she was done letting him bat *her* around.

Abby turned and yanked open the fridge to cool her face. She inhaled the stale, chilled air, her heart rate becoming steady. A few seconds of staring at two carrots, an opened tub of hummus and some pickled onions slowed her breathing.

Abby crossed to the basinet in a few quick steps. There was no way she was going to let Joe anywhere near her precious baby girl. She reached in and cupped her hand around her daughter's head. She sucked in a slow breath as she felt the silky strands of her barely-there hair against her palm. She would do whatever it took to protect her child. The knowledge was fierce and unshakeable.

Why had Joe left a gift, though? Since when would he do something nice, just for the sake of it? There had to be more to it. Thoughts looped and tangled in her head. There was no respite, no outlet. Sasha had always been her sounding board. She was the one who added logic and reason, who saw the path through a maze. A groan made its way up through her chest and escaped in a jagged breath. It was useless to wish Sasha would suddenly appear and help her make sense of what was happening. Sasha wanted nothing to do with her. Abby swatted a tear from her eye. And it was all her fault.

Just for a moment, she wondered what it would have been like if she had not snatched the keys from Sasha and insisted on driving that day. The day that changed everything. Abby tried to picture it. If it had been Sasha driving, Sasha who'd caused the accident, who looked at her phone, startled and then steered the car into a tree and left Abby's arm broken beyond repair, all would have been fine. Well, obviously not *fine*. A shattered arm was not *nothing*. But it wasn't her career, her livelihood. Her life's passion. Abby would've forgiven her friend instantly. If Sasha had been the one behind the wheel and Abby had been injured, life would have continued with barely a blip. Sasha would've been horrified that her actions had caused injury. She wasn't heartless. But their lives would have moved forward. It would never have occurred to Sasha that Abby would not forgive her.

But that wasn't the case. Abby had been driving, so Abby took Sasha's career. And with it, their friendship. She stared at her precious daughter. Sasha's goddaughter. Had their friendship really been obliterated as permanently as Sasha's career? Abby wasn't ready to believe that. She reached into her back pocket for her phone and stared at the screen. She looked at the message she'd sent. Had Sasha seen it? Read it? She willed three dots to start blinking as a sign that Sasha was responding. There was nothing.

Abby leant over and kissed her daughter's soft cheek and went back to the gift-strewn table. She couldn't tell if Sasha had seen the message but what she could do was see what was in the box. Letting it sit there like a ticking bomb, scaring her with the possibilities, was giving Joe power.

The box was the size that might contain a candle, one of the scented ones in a glass jar that dominated every gift table in pharmacies and department stores. She picked it up and sniffed. There was no obvious scent. She pushed the pink ribbon over the corners of the gift and tore the brown paper to reveal a plain white box emblazoned with the logo for a local trophy store. Abby frowned.

Sophia stirred in the bassinet, a soft little snuffle scrunching her tiny features. Abby moved back through to the kitchen. She didn't want anything from Joe remotely near her baby. She hooked her finger under the top of the box and lifted the lid.

She froze. An icy chill prickled through her, piercing her fingertips. The box slipped through her hands and crashed to the ground. Sophia startled and cried. Abby stared at the ground, at what she'd dropped.

A candle remained intact inside. A used candle. A scent-free candle Abby had used in her home last night.

Joe had indeed sent her a trophy.

CHAPTER THIRTY-ONE

SASHA ~ NOW

Wandering through the main doors of the lodge, Sasha could hear noises coming from the kitchen. It sounded like Mrs M had a bit of a kitchen concerto happening, if the assortment of clangs, bangs and scrapes was anything to go by.

Sasha used to love pottering in the kitchen. Like most things these days though, cooking was something she hadn't done since before the accident. You needed two hands to slice and dice or simmer and sauté. Not that she'd tried. She had just assumed it was something else to add to the list of "Things I Can No Longer Do". She'd assembled quite the lengthy list. She rubbed the side of her injured hand against the tattoo, feeling the faint lines. *You need to try,* she told herself.

'Hi Mrs M,' Sasha called out, determined to move forward.

'Sasha, love! I'm so glad you stopped by,' she said over her shoulder while she flipped a ball of dough over and kneaded it with practised efficiency.

'Scones?' Sasha asked.

Mrs M nodded and beckoned for Sasha to join her at the counter. 'Can't beat 'em fresh out of the oven. They're Gerry's favourite,' she said, smiling.

Sasha joined Mrs M and swept her fingers through the dry scone mixture, exposing the smooth benchtop beneath. If only she could wipe away the past six weeks with a sweep of her hand and discover a clear, unblemished past with no accidents or injuries.

Mrs M continued. 'What brings you out this morning, love?'

Sasha puffed out an exaggerated sigh. 'Just trying to get out of my head.' She stabbed at the flour with a fingertip. 'I need to work out what I can do now. Something I can do with *this*.' She fluttered her injured hand in the air.

'There's plenty you can do.' Mrs M's tone was brisk.

'I might as well be an old... microwave.' Something about Mrs M made her feel like she could blurt out the first thing that came to mind. She *did* feel like an old microwave, though. Or a broken blender. An old appliance to be discarded.

'Oh, love,' Mrs M laughed. 'You do say the funniest things. You're not an old microwave. Why on earth would you think that?'

'I might as well be,' Sasha grumbled. 'People always want the bright, shiny, new appliance. They throw away the broken ones. They want the sparkly, pretty, functioning devices. They don't want *this*!' She held out her cupped left hand.

'Do you really think that, love?' Mrs M stopped what she was doing and looked directly at Sasha. 'Sounds like a good dose of self-pity going on, if you ask me.'

Sasha wanted to poke her bottom lip out, but fought the impulse. 'I know, I know,' she conceded. Mrs M was right. It *was* self-pity. 'I tried calling Sam,' Sasha told her, changing the subject, as much to shake herself out of the mood she was in as the need to talk about Sam. 'He didn't answer.'

'Do you think he was working, love?' Mrs M replied matter-of-factly. And logically. Of course, Sasha knew he would've been working, but irrationally, she'd still wanted him to answer the call. Or text her a short message letting her know he was busy.

'Yeah, I guess. But I needed to hear his voice.'

'Does he know you're needing to hear his voice so desperately? Or is he still trying to give you the space you wanted?'

Sheesh. Again, with the logic. But Mrs M had a point. Sasha had pushed and pushed Sam away after the accident. He had respected that. Damn it.

'Are you always this sensible?' Sasha asked her friend, plucking at a piece of the scone dough.

'Why don't you help me with some of the dinner prep?' Mrs M said, winking at her in lieu of an answer.

'I can try,' Sasha said, feeling suddenly nervous and uncertain. What if she couldn't manage the prepping of a few veggies and ended up making a mess of it all? Her emotions were already as raw as the carrots and cabbage in front of her. Did she really need to shred them while they were in such an exposed state? 'What if I can't manage it?' she asked, lifting her injured hand and looking at it.

'Oh, love,' Mrs M said with an exasperated shake of her head. 'Who is really going to mind? So what if you can't peel or chop as well as you used to? You're not going to know unless you try, sweetheart,' she said, not unkindly. She nodded at the knife encouragingly. Holding the knife wasn't the issue. It was steadying the vegetable with her left hand she was having trouble with. She still couldn't straighten her fingers past a certain point or curl them into a fist. *Relax,* the therapist at the hospital had said. *Your mind's a powerful tool. Think of something that settles you.* The thought of Sam resting a hand in the middle of her lower back popped into her mind. Almost immediately, her fingers loosened fractionally. Her shoulders dropped and she could swear her whole body sighed. *Huh.* This wasn't so bad.

Without overthinking it, Sasha began chopping the red capsicum in front of her. Her left hand felt clunky, but she could tuck her fingers in enough to keep them away from the knife's blade. Uniform red cubes piled up on the wooden board. Pushing them to the corner, she reached for a stalk of celery.

The two women worked in companionable silence.

Sasha's mind wandered to what she could do, going forward. She knew she was never going to be able to play the piano again. The thought still made her stomach lurch and her heart start racing. It still caught her by surprise that she no longer had that ability. Sitting down at the piano and letting her fingers drift over the keys, playing whatever song took her fancy, had always been as natural as breathing. Music had been her language and her way of communicating. Reading a page of music was the same to her as reading the pages of a book. Actually, she would say she understood the complete message and picture being conveyed on a page of music *better* than she did within a page of prose. The nuances of phrasing, melody, timing, harmony – they all painted a picture that filled her with more emotion than words on a page ever could.

Sasha looked down. She realised she had stopped chopping and was staring out the kitchen window. She could see Gerry weaving tendrils of a tomato plant around a garden stake.

'How do you guys do it, Mrs M?' Sasha asked, putting the knife down and breaking the silence.

'Do what, love?'

'This,' she said, gesturing around her, at everything and nothing in particular. She didn't even know what she was asking.

Mrs M didn't bat an eyelid, seemingly able to interpret

Sasha's wild and erratic gestures. 'It's just living life, the best way we know how. And loving life as well,' she said, smiling as her eyes settled on her husband outside the window. 'We might not have a picture-perfect life, but we appreciate what we do have, if that makes sense?' She raised her eyebrows and nodded, as if affirming what she'd said. 'It hasn't always gone the way we wanted it to, or the way we thought it would. I don't think anyone can claim that to be the case.' A flash of pain crossed her face as she paused, her chin trembling a little. 'Gerry and I thought we'd have enough kids to fill all the rooms of this lodge. Or maybe half the rooms,' she said, pulling a tissue from her apron and offering a small smile. 'But life didn't want that for us.'

'Oh, I'm so sorry, Mrs M,' Sasha murmured.

The older woman turned and looked at Sasha. 'Don't get buried in what you think you've lost, love. Life is fragile – which *you* know better than most. Try and look at what you *can* do, rather than what you can't do.'

If this was coming from anyone else, it would have sounded like a mash-up of well-meaning motivational quotes. But coming from Mrs M, it resonated. These words were ones she clearly lived by. Mrs M turned to Sasha and reached for her hands. Sasha tried not to flinch when warm fingers grasped her left hand.

'Don't let *this* define you,' she said, shaking Sasha's hands lightly. Her left hand felt stiff, but relaxed a little at the touch. 'You love music. Music has always been your life, right?' Nodding at Sasha and agreeing with her own assessment, Mrs M continued. 'So, you need to ask yourself, how can you continue making music part of your life? Just because you can't play the piano doesn't mean you have to wipe it from your life. You know that, right?'

Sasha narrowed her eyes while she considered the words. If she couldn't perform, what was the point?

'Have you thought about teaching?' Mrs M's words put sudden pressure on a healing wound.

Teaching? She performed; she didn't teach. Well, she *used* to perform. She had never *taught*. She had never thought of herself as a teacher. Teachers required patience and, well, patience. Obviously, they needed a lot more than that, but Sasha couldn't get past that one trait. She had never been known for her love of waiting or being patient. Self-discipline and perseverance – definitely. The idea of her teaching was so far removed from anything she had ever considered doing that Mrs M may as well have suggested she become an astronaut, or a trapeze artist. She would probably consider either of those before teaching.

She reached for a slice of cheese and paused, the strong aroma making her mouth water while it simultaneously pushed a thought to the front of her mind. Her first piano teacher used to greet her at the door, creamy cheese coating her fingers and pungent tones on her breath. This was the same teacher who breezily admitted she only taught so she could pay for flying lessons. Flying-an-actual-plane lessons!

Sasha was in awe of her teachers. On some level in her young brain, she thought this woman was akin to superwoman; that if she wanted to learn how to fly, then she must have been fearless. And this fearless person could play the piano. That first impression set the mould for what she thought musicians were. And music teachers? Well, they were clearly in a league of their own. They were these masters of knowledge: wise, adventurous and inspirational.

Did she have something – anything – to offer aspiring performers? A tiny spark flared.

'You know what, Mrs M?' Sasha said, abandoning the chopping and dicing. 'It could be something I look at doing.' Her heart rate jumped from *andante* to *prestissimo*. Even as she said this aloud, she could hear the surprise and bewilderment in her voice.

'Of course, you should, love,' Mrs M said with a knowing smile. 'If you love something, then that love will come through as you pass on your knowledge.'

'I've never thought about teaching before,' Sasha said, her eyes widening in surprise at what felt like an impossibly daring thing to have voiced. But the idea was taking hold and gathering speed as it worked its way through her mind. It felt like a snowball, getting bigger and bigger, thought upon thought layering itself as it rolled around the pathways of her brain.

Before the snowball could hit a tree or find a roadblock, Sasha gave Mrs M an impulsive hug.

'Now, what's that for, love?' Mrs M laughed as she returned the hug, floury hands enveloping Sasha.

'You've given me something to look forward to. Something to think about.'

'Go on with you,' Mrs M said, a faint tinge of pink stealing up her neck. 'She looked out the window to where Gerry was trying to feed a hose through the base of a water feature in the courtyard. 'He's putting the fountain in because I saw a picture of one that reminded me of our trip to Italy about twenty years ago.' She laughed as the hose suddenly sprung out of the fountain and sprayed Gerry in the face. 'My Gerry is no plumber,' she continued, 'and that is no Trevi Fountain, but it will mean more to me than the 2,000 fountains in Rome combined.'

Sasha smiled as love and contentment washed over Mrs M's face. She wished – again – that she could talk to Sam.

Leaving Mrs M to finish up in the kitchen, Sasha headed back through to the lounge room and sat at the piano. She let both hands drift to the keyboard and rest on the keys. It was the first time she had put her left hand anywhere near piano keys in months. Whereas her right hand automatically assumed a position over the C major chord, her left hand sat in an awkward, concave shape. The only sound that would result from the keys being depressed with her left hand would be a jarring, discordant assault to the senses. She moved her right hand in a chromatic step, playing the C-sharp major chord, followed quickly by the D major chord. Moving in semitones, Sasha rapidly covered two octaves in chords, reaching the upper registers of the keyboard and breathing as quickly as if she had climbed a mountain.

The only life she had known was gone. Playing the piano, performing with orchestras and giving concerts would never again be something she could do. Panic pushed at the edges of her mind. She pushed back.

Her breathing gradually slowed as she let the idea of teaching settle over her. Up until a few weeks ago, her whole life, her whole identity, had been wrapped up in the knowledge that she was a musician; a performer. If she could no longer be the best possible pianist, was there really another way music could still be part of her life? Could there be a different direction that didn't hurt to think about?

A sense of calm circled around her. Closing the lid of the piano, she headed outside. She reached into her back pocket for her phone. The knots of blame and anger had loosened. She tapped and opened Abby's latest message.

Before she could read the words, a picture of her mother's face flashed across the screen. Her mum was calling.

CHAPTER THIRTY-TWO

SASHA ~ NOW

No! Her mind screamed the word over and over. Her mum had to be wrong.

The bike she'd blindly grabbed when she'd disconnected the call fell to the ground, handlebars splayed in aggrieved confusion. Wild blackberries prickled and clawed at the frame. Sasha held the phone between trembling fingertips, unable to look at it. Evening was falling. Dusk drew down on her shoulders. The sun had lost its earlier sting. Corellas and cockatoos competed to be more conspicuous than the others with their abrasive caws. But they were drowned out by the roaring in her head. There were no words. Just sounds. Horrible, sickening, whooshing sounds that rammed their way through her body, pounding her stomach, her head, her throat.

Sasha stared at the phone screen. The time glared back at her. It was 8.48pm.

The numbers swam in front of her with palindromic symmetry. Normally, they would have soothed her. She liked to find rhythm in numbers. A beat. A lyrical pacing. Not now.

8.48. The sharp crack of a branch shot through the air. A bird? The noise pierced her consciousness, but she remained rooted to the spot, her feet leaden. Numb. The sickly sweet scent of fallen and rotting berries clogged her throat.

8.48. Her heart raced and her breath came in shallow, frantic puffs. Waves of nausea surged in her stomach. There had to be a mistake. Her mother had to be wrong. There was no way what she said could be true.

8.49. Sasha blinked at the change in pattern on the screen. A sharp wind lashed hair loose from her ponytail, stinging her cheek. She bit down on a strand caught in the corner of her lip and spat it out.

Abby wasn't dead. She couldn't be. There had to be a mistake. The phone slipped through her fingers and landed with a soft thud in the tangle of blackberry vines. She stared at the illuminated surface, as if the sight of it alone on the ground was a mystery. The screen dimmed and then died.

Abby wasn't *dead*. She'd been sending texts to Sasha. She lunged down and thrust her hand through the thorny vines, through the pin-sharp prickles, desperate to see Abby's words, to refute what she'd just heard. Beads of blood tracked an angry pattern across her skin, each drop an exclamation point of denial. It wasn't possible.

Abby couldn't be dead. She just couldn't. It had to be a mistake. Her stomach clenched, the words curdling and churning throughout her body. It didn't make sense.

Abby had wanted to talk to Sasha, to reconstruct their relationship. They couldn't do that if Abby was *dead*. She blinked rapidly.

Sasha's thoughts tumbled and spun. She swallowed, burning bile forcing its way up her throat. Her fingers prised the phone from the tangle of thorns and it sprang back to life, blue light beaming. She clenched her jaw, her mouth acidic and her teeth chalky.

Sasha yanked her hand back through the vines, the phone

screen still alight. Alive. She inhaled and exhaled rapidly. Blood ran freely across the top of her hand, rivers of red racing to her fingertips and landing in vivid plops on the ground.

8.50. Sasha stared at her phone. Her knees gave way and she sat heavily. Why hadn't her mum called her back? Her head spun and dizziness played a disorienting dance. Her thumb hovered over the screen, desperate to hit redial and hear her mum's voice. Her laughter. Her words telling Sasha she was a funny little noodle. That's what she used to laughingly say whenever Sasha had misheard her. *Come here, you funny little noodle!* And then she'd wrap her arms around Sasha and all would be right.

But something stopped her from calling back. She didn't want to hear the words again. Sasha sucked in air, breathless despite being immobile.

When her Mum's face had flashed across her phone screen, Sasha had been in two minds about whether to answer it or not. Her mum had been good about giving her space and not calling all the time. Sasha knew she would be itching to check in with her. But she hadn't. The truth of the matter was, though, Sasha had wanted to hear her voice. She missed her mum. She missed Abby and she missed Sam as well, but right now, she needed her mum's reassurance. She'd been feeling bad about the way she had treated her parents since the accident and had been desperate to hear her mum's voice. She wanted to reconnect. And not just with her parents. She had been ready to reach out to Abby, had wanted to talk to her friend, hear about Sophia and see the two of them.

If only she hadn't answered the call from her mum. If only she had ignored it. Would it still have been real?

But she had. She had answered it without thinking, caught in the glow of wanting to move forward.

'Hey Mum,' she'd said, a smile curling her lips. 'I'm so glad you called.'

A brief pause had followed. Sasha had looked at her phone, checking the signal was still intact. 'Mum? You there? Can you hear me?' Phone service could be a little patchy in some of the rural areas around Margaret River.

'Hi, love.' Her mum's voice was flat. Choked, but clear. Sasha had checked the number of bars again, as if the lack of them might be responsible for her mum's tone. 'It's Abby,' her mum had said without preamble or small talk. 'Love,' her voice had softened to a whisper. 'Abby's dead.'

The thing you hear about time standing still or things freezing around you? That's what happened. Sasha froze, her limbs icy and weighted. There was a swirl of colours and images, merging, shifting. Sunlight pierced through vines. Sharp blackberry fronds clawed grotesquely, reaching and straining. Red dirt beneath her feet shifted and rolled. Sasha sucked in her cheeks and bit down on the tender skin. An iron tang filled her mouth. Blood. She swallowed and gagged.

She hadn't been able to find any words and her mum had kept talking. Something about Abby being found in the river. The *river?* That didn't make sense. Why would Abby be in the river? And then there was something about Sophia having been left in the vineyard. That made even less sense. Abby wouldn't have left her daughter alone. She remembered Sam's name being mentioned. He was working on the case. Fragments from the conversation bombarded her. *Police don't think... Face-down in the water... Wasn't an accident...*

The words were shrill, screaming in her head. Sasha didn't remember the phone call ending. She'd grabbed a bike propped against a wall of a nearby shed and had started pedalling. Legs pumping, right hand gripping the handlebar and her useless left hand doing absolutely nothing. Her legs burned and sweat prickled her armpits. Wind bit her cheeks. The bike path pulled at the pedals, dragging her faster and faster.

The bike had skidded on a patch of loose pebbles covering the path. Sasha had wobbled and jumped off the bike, discarding it as she dug in the pocket of her leggings for her phone.

Now, staring at the phone, her mum's words remained clear.

Abby was dead.

CHAPTER THIRTY-THREE

SAM ~ NOW

Sam grimaced as the too-hot coffee seared his tongue. Before he went back to the station, he wanted to make a quick stop at Joe's place. He hadn't seen Joe a lot during the time Abby had been with him. He didn't know much about him. All he knew had really been based on what Sasha had said. But seeing him face-to-face had pushed a memory forward. It was from one of the rare times the four of them had been together. *Double-dating,* Sasha had said, using air quotes. Sam was left under no illusion about what Sasha's opinion of Joe was.

Sasha, Abby and Sam had stopped by Joe's place to pick him up. He'd been standing outside the front of his house, deep in conversation with a pale blond-haired man. They were arguing. They all saw the shove Joe delivered to the man opposite before he suddenly saw their car and tried to segue into a clap on the shoulder.

Sam had straightened in the front seat, instinctively aware of potential unrest. The man had turned abruptly and disappeared through a finger path at the end of the street by the time Sasha had stopped the car. Joe had climbed into the back seat, all smiles and cheery greetings.

What had stuck in Sam's mind though, was what he saw when he glanced in the mirror on the sun visor. Joe had been making some mundane comment or other about the weather. But he had been agitated, clenching his thumbs in his fists, as if trying to curb the impulse to hit something.

And Abby had been visibly nervous, biting her lip and holding her hands tightly in her lap. She had laughed loudly and too brightly. Sam remembered Sasha frowning in the front.

Not long after that, Abby had called things off with Joe, and Sam hadn't given the matter any further thought. He'd never been back to Joe's house.

Until now.

Sam sat in his car outside Joe's house, drinking the coffee that was now a more bearable temperature. Rain tracked down the windscreen, blurring the world outside. But not enough to obscure the man coming from the rear of Joe's property and exiting through a side gate. Sam's pulse quickened. He recognised him. He had seen him in this exact location before.

He had unusually bright blond hair.

He also had the same furtive look as when Sam had last seen him with Joe. He was casting glances over his shoulder at the house he'd just come from and not paying attention to the car on the opposite side of the road.

Thoughts of the earlier conversation at the warehouse played through his mind. He wasn't sure what he'd hoped to achieve, but he knew Joe was hiding something. Seeing this guy coming out of Joe's place added a whole extra layer. An old white holden ute reversed out of the driveway to the left of Joe's property. A dog barked in the distance and a young mum pushed a stroller along the sidewalk. She stopped and adjusted the rain cover only a few metres from the blond-haired guy. It was enough to slow him down.

And it was enough for Sam to make a snap decision. He jumped out of his car and crossed the road, nodding at the young mum as she continued on her way.

'Sir, have you got a minute?'

The guy frowned and looked over his shoulder, as if unused to being addressed as *sir*.

'Me?' He cleared his throat and looked behind him again.

Sam stopped only a metre in front of him. Close enough that he could smell body odour mixed with weed. Close enough that he could see crusted and layered food stains on the black hoodie. Sam put his hands in his pockets. Unthreatening. He nodded, watching the man for any sudden moves.

'I'm in a bit of a hurry.' He pulled his phone out. 'Yeah. Sorry. Gotta go.'

Sam thought he probably *was* in a hurry. 'I won't keep you. You live here?'

'What?' He jerked his head back towards the house. 'Here?'

'Yeah. The house you just came from.' Sam watched him carefully.

'Nah.' He hopped from side to side, bouncing on the balls of his feet. 'Listen, man, I haven't got time for whatever shit you're selling. I've really gotta go.' He hunched his shoulders. Sam could hear the change in the guy's tone as the swagger evaporated.

The dog continued to bark in the distance. It sounded like it was coming from the property at the rear of Joe's place.

'I won't keep you long,' Sam said, agreeably. 'But you'll need to give me a minute.' He held out his hand in greeting. 'Detective Sam Tierny. And you are?'

The blond-haired guy muttered something under his breath. His jaw twitched. Sam could practically see the lack of options running through the guy's head.

'Braden... Smith.' Sam doubted that was his real name. Or his real surname, at any rate.

'Nice to meet you, Braden. Can you show me where you just came from?' Sam gave him a second before clamping a hand on his shoulder and turning him back in the direction of the gate. The rain had stopped, but the ground was muddy and slick. Mud oozed up the sides of Braden's tattered white sneakers.

Braden was slight, wrists sticking out from the cuffs of the filthy hoodie. Jeans sagged low over skinny hips. This guy would be hopeless in a rugby scrum. He was twitching as if he was connected to a misfiring electrical device.

Without warning, he twisted under Sam's arm and darted across the front yard, mud splattering up the back of his jeans. Sam watched him run. He had no desire to chase him. He would be easy enough to find. He turned and looked at the busted back door. Braden hadn't been wearing gloves and Sam would put money on his prints being in the system.

There was a screwdriver poking out from beneath the bottom step. There was every chance it was the tool that had been used to gouge at the lock. Had Braden known Joe wouldn't be at home? Sam put a call in to the station to get someone to come down and process the place.

Barking increased in volume behind the fence at the rear of the property. Sam stood at the concrete block at the base of the steps. Muddy footprints tracked up the three steps that led to the broken door. He stepped over them, being careful not to disturb anything. Since the door was already broken and ajar, there was no need for Sam to call Joe and get permission to enter. Besides, what was Joe going to say?

Sure, Detective. Go ahead and roam through my house while I'm not there and find all my dirty little secrets. I don't have a problem with that at all. Help yourself to a beer while you're at it!

Not words Sam could imagine spilling from Joe's mouth. And Joe being argumentative was not something Sam was in the mood to deal with. Joe would say no, whether he was trying to hide something or not. Pure and simple.

And he was strongly leaning towards the view that Joe *was* hiding something. Something more than being the asshole he was. No. Much easier – and useful, he had a feeling – if he continued to investigate the scene of a break-in. And there was no denying there had been a break-in.

Sam pushed the door and peered inside. The same muddy footprints continued down the hall. The house was an old 60's council estate house that hadn't seen a lot of updates since it was built. Paint peeled from the walls and dark shadows indicated frames that had once filled the space.

He crossed through the kitchen, continuing to walk alongside the muddy prints. The guy clearly wasn't worried about hiding what he'd done. Or was he really that stupid? Probably both, Sam thought.

The state of the house surprised Sam. For some reason, he'd pinned Joe as being fastidious. Anal. Sam didn't recall him ever permanently living with Abby, but he had spent a lot of time at her place. And Abby's place was nothing like this.

Sam paused in the middle of the living room. A blue floor rug curling at the corners attempted to cover the more threadbare patches of what was once – orange? – shag carpet. Now, it was a matted mess of filth and trodden grime. What had the guy been so desperate to find that he'd forced his way into Joe's place? He knew it wasn't a random break-in since he'd seen him talking to Joe a year ago. There had to be more to it.

Sam took a few more paces through the living room. The muddy prints were less distinguishable by now, but it's wasn't like there were a lot of options. The living room gave way to a narrow hallway. And the grime-filled shag led to greasy wooden floorboards. There were three doors: two closed and one open. Sam used his arm to open it wider, being careful not to touch the doorknob.

He stopped in his tracks and stared around the room. It was not at all what he had expected to find.

CHAPTER THIRTY-FOUR

SASHA ~ NOW

Sasha wanted to bash the steering wheel. Smash her palm against it and feel the sting. Small stones pierced the soft pad of her foot as she jammed it on the brake. She realised she was barefoot. It didn't matter. All that mattered was getting home.

'Love, do you think it's a good idea to be driving right now?' Mrs M clutched the rim of the car window. 'Why don't you wait until morning and get some sleep first?'

Heavy clouds rolled across the setting sun, darkening what was left of the day. The distant rumble of traffic was blurred through the thick and unkempt bush between the lodge and the main road.

'I wouldn't be able to sleep. I'll be fine.' Sasha's words were curt. There was no time to waste. She needed to get home. She'd thrown her things into her case following the second call from her mum and tossed it into the back of the car, a haphazard jumble of clothes, shoes, books, and other pointless items. What did it matter? They were just things. Stuff. None of it mattered.

'Why don't you wait a little bit and I'll get Gerry to drive you back to Perth?' Mrs M reached in and put her hand on

Sasha's shoulder. 'He's just finishing his curried sausages and can be ready in a jiffy. It'll be no trouble at all, love.'

Sasha shrugged Mrs M's hand off impatiently. It was dark and she wanted to get going. She closed her eyes briefly and moderated her voice before answering. Mrs M was just looking out for her. 'Thanks. That's really kind of you.' Sasha knew her teeth were clenched and she dropped her jaw. 'I don't want to be a bother to either of you and it's much quicker if I just go now.' Would it hurt her to be a little warmer? '...I need to find out what's happened.'

'I know you do, love.' Mrs M squeezed Sasha's shoulder before pulling her hand back. 'Just keep your eyes focused, won't you? Why don't I go and pack you a quick snack for the road? That'll help you stay awake. It'll just take me two ticks.'

'I wouldn't be able to eat anything.' Sasha ground the words out. 'But thanks.' She tried to conjure a smile to placate Mrs M, but her face refused to cooperate.

Mrs M sighed and patted the side of the car. 'Off you go then, love. Watch out for roos, won't you?'

Sasha waved and eased the car forward, resisting the urge to plant her foot and spray gravel and dirt like shards of shattering glass. She stabbed at the switch to close the window, muffling Mrs M's voice. Her mum's voice careened around her head instead.

Sasha's hands shook and she tightened her grip. Sweat pooled behind her knees. She thumped her fist against her chest and ground it against her ribcage, as if the action would slow the pounding, the sweating. Abby couldn't be dead. She just couldn't be.

Could she?

A groan filled the car, an ugly sound dragged from depths Sasha didn't know she could even feel. She wanted to run, to leap out of the car, to escape the pain. It was coiled around her, burying her, suffocating her. It was everywhere.

Headlights blinded Sasha when she turned onto the main road towards Perth. Her damaged left hand pressed against the steering wheel and she squinted until the oncoming driver dipped his lights. She stifled the impulse to pound her fist against the car horn. To infuse the sound with her anger and pain until it drained out of her.

This wasn't the way it was meant to go. She was meant to have been granted the time to be angry at Abby. Justifiably angry. Wasn't that her right? Her prerogative? Anyone would have been angry at the loss of their career and livelihood. But it wasn't meant to be permanent. The anger was meant to be a process. A path she navigated. A path that had a destination. An end point, which she'd been approaching.

Tears tracked down her cheeks and landed in the dip of her collarbone. Sasha wanted to shout, to scream. What did it matter if she did? She was alone in her car. She could yell and rage as much as she bloody well wanted. She opened her mouth, but the sound was strangled. It wouldn't bring Abby back.

Panic flared and tightened her throat, her breath quickening as her nose clogged. She pressed her foot on the accelerator and winced when pain shot up her leg. It slipped and dampness registered. Her foot was bleeding. It must have been from the sharp stones. Sasha slid it against the pedal, testing the depth of the injury, the pain. She felt skin snag and catch against the ridges of the accelerator, followed by another slice of pain and a slick of moisture. More blood.

She was tempted to grind her foot against the pedal again, to feel the simultaneous surge of speed and agony. It was a distraction. But only a fleeting diversion. As quickly as the pain in her foot registered, it detoured and took an immediate exit ramp back to her brain. The knowledge of Abby's death superseded everything.

She wound down the window and felt rushing air hit the tears on her cheeks. There were no streetlights on this stretch of road, just darkness. It had barely been an hour since she'd heard the news from her mum. Had they kept it from her deliberately? Kept her in the dark? Did they think she was so fragile and unstable that she wouldn't be able to cope with the news? Another thought punched her in the throat. Surely, they didn't think she wouldn't care? Her insides twisted and squeezed. Her jaw went numb. Now was not the time to puke.

Sasha pulled over to the side of the road, her head pounding, her breath shallow. The car's headlights penetrated the blackness. Had Abby read the text? Oh, God. Please let it have sent. She grabbed the phone from the middle console. Delivered. The tiny words blurred beneath the message Sasha had sent. But there was no reply from Abby. Had she seen it?

An oncoming car hurtled towards Sasha. She blinked and pulled down on the indicator. She needed to keep moving. She eased onto the road with deliberate care, her hands shaking, her mind swerving. Blinding lights from a truck seared her brain, shattering what remained of her composure. Tears rolled down her cheeks.

A comment from her mum flashed into Sasha's mind. *The police don't think it was an accident.*

Prickles rushed up and down her arms, her scalp, her body, wrapping her in a coarse thicket. Not an accident? That meant Abby's death was deliberate.

The air inside the car was chilled.

Knowledge punched Sasha in the gut.

Someone else *was* involved.

Air continued to rush in through the open windows. The

bloated form of a dead roo flashed in her headlights. The stench lashed at her nostrils.

Instinct screamed that Joe was involved.

Did Sam know? Her mum had said he was involved with the police investigation.

She needed to talk to him.

CHAPTER THIRTY-FIVE

SAM ~ NOW

'Sasha!' Sam pulled his door wide and wrapped his arms around her before he could think what he was doing.

She was literally on his doorstep. Right now. With no warning at all. His brain caught up and only just stopped him pressing a kiss against her lips. They were no longer together. But, shit. She was here. *She* had come to *him*. The worry that had knotted his insides since he'd realised the body in the river was Abby, loosened a fraction. Sasha was here... which probably meant that she knew.

A sheet of lightning filled the sky, framing her in his doorway. She stood there, a key clutched in her hand, her breathing shallow. He gripped her shoulders and looked at her. She knew. He hadn't been the one to tell her. But she knew.

'Is it true?' The words sounded as if they were being dragged from her.

Lightning flashed again, illuminating the entire area. Her face was as ashen as freshly poured concrete. He pulled her inside and closed the door.

'Sam?' Sasha's voice was barely more than a whisper. She crossed over to the couch, reaching out as if to steady herself after too many drinks. 'Sorry,' she said, sinking into the corner. 'I couldn't think where else to go.'

'You don't have to apologise.' He thrust his hands into the pockets of his gym shorts. If he left them out, he knew he'd need to touch her. Be close to her. 'Can I get you anything? A cup of tea?'

He didn't even drink tea, let alone have tea bags in his kitchen. Thankfully, she declined with a shake of the head.

He crossed over to the couch and sat down next to Sasha. She was huddled in the corner, her arms wrapped tightly around the one throw pillow he possessed, which had been bought by her for his previous birthday. *So you have something to snuggle when I'm not here.* She had meant when she was touring. But he had been leaning against it a lot in the recent weeks since their breakup.

She ducked her chin down to the cushion. A few seconds passed. 'It's really Abby?'

Again, Sam fought the urge to wrap his arms around her. They might no longer be a couple, but the need to help her, to comfort her, was overwhelming.

He reached across and wrapped a hand awkwardly around her ankle. 'Yes. It was her.'

Sasha's head jerked and her eyes met his. His stomach clenched. It was using the past tense. *Was.* He'd seen that reaction so many times over the course of his job. The disbelief. The shreds of hope crumbling away like rocks giving up the ability to cling to the edges of a cliff before tumbling and shattering. But he'd never been close to the situation, or to the people involved.

'How?' Sasha uttered just the one word, her eyes steady on Sam.

Sam wished he could give her an answer. Anything that would ease her pain. But he didn't have a lot.

'So far, all we know is that she was dead before she entered the water.' He tried to keep the words simple. Unemotional. Professional. But it damn near choked him. 'She sustained a blow to the back of the head, which was the cause of death.' Fuck. Now he sounded like a bloody TV cop.

Sasha's lips pressed together in a tight line, as if doing that would stop the grief pouring out. It didn't prevent the tears spilling down her cheeks. Sam reached out and brushed one side of her face, his hand moving on instinct and over-riding any resistance his brain may have put forward.

'Why was she at the–' Sasha swallowed, 'river?' She looked down at her hands, still clinging to the cushion against her stomach.

Sam could tell she knew the answer. Abby had been at the river, at the vineyard, to see Sasha. There was no sugar-coating that fact.

She leapt from the couch and ran to the bathroom. Lightning burst through the living room windows. Seconds later, thunder filled the silence, merging with the sound of Sasha retching.

CHAPTER THIRTY-SIX

SASHA ~ NOW

Sasha rolled over and found her face pressed against smooth leather. It smelt of Sam. She inhaled and pulled her knee up, wanting to drape it over his thigh. Except there was no thigh. Just her knee butting against more leather. She frowned, her eyes doing their best not to open. Of course, she was on Sam's couch. Alone.

Waves of emotion rolled through her body, hitting her with a physical intensity. It was like being immersed in hot bath water and then suddenly plunging into an ice tub. Sweat beaded on her forehead, but it did nothing to stop her shivering.

Memories crowded in. Her mum's phone call. Abby. Driving through the night back to Perth. Sam holding her at his door when her legs had collapsed. There had been no questions. Just his arms around her.

The hissing of a coffee machine filled the room. Sasha squeezed her eyes tight. She could hear soft footsteps padding close by. Was she ready to wake up? To face reality and actually talk to Sam?

A finger brushed her cheek and Sasha bolted upright, her eyes wide.

'Woah. Steady on. It's just me.'

The scent of soap filled her nostrils. Sasha blinked, her eyes adjusting to the sunlight streaming through the window. How long had she been asleep for? Sam crouched on his heels next to the couch. Damp hair was slicked back from his forehead and a bubble of shaving foam clung to his earlobe. Sasha's fingers tingled with the need to reach out and smooth it away. He held up a white-flecked pottery mug and raised his eyebrows. Steam wafted from the top.

'Thanks.' Sasha clasped her palms around the mug. Her favourite mug. Which was now the perfect shape for her injured hand. How many times had she sat here in the past, holding this very mug? She closed her eyes to stem the prickle of tears. One spilled over and rolled down her cheek. She let it slide under her jaw without wiping it away. What was the point? Abby was dead and there was nothing she could do to change it. Sam had confirmed it last night. She let her eyes settle on the rugby ball sitting on a kicking tee beside the tv and slowed her breathing. The sight was reassuring.

Sasha swung her legs off the couch and winced when her foot hit the tiled floor. She'd forgotten about the cut from the footwell of the car.

Sam lifted her foot and looked at it. 'Probably should clean that,' he said. 'Do you want a shower first?'

The taste of vomit from one of her roadside stops last night coated her cracked lips. Not to mention her clothes. But in Sam's bathroom? Was that wise? She was feeling vulnerable. Fragile. In desperate need of comfort. The thought of Sam's arms around her while warm water sluiced over her body, his hands gently sponging her shoulders, her back, was more than appealing.

'I think I'll just go and splash my face,' Sasha said, setting the mug down on the coffee table abruptly and springing up. Hot liquid sloshed over her hand. She pushed past Sam and hurried through to the bathroom. Music from a small speaker in the kitchen followed her.

Sunlight glared at her from every surface in Sam's bathroom. Sasha knew the cleanliness was not the result of a cleaner. Pain clutched her head and settled with an insistent jabbing behind her eyes. Puffy eyes framed by dark crescents stared back at her from the mirror. Sleep had been sporadic. Each time consciousness had pulled, instinct had compelled her to go and find Sam, to slip into bed with him. To sink into the comfort of his arms. She couldn't do that yet. Besides, would he even want her after the way she'd treated him? She turned the cold tap and felt the blast of pipe-chilled water spray up.

'I'm glad you came here, Sash.' Sam's voice carried through to the bathroom. Sasha splashed the chilly water over her face to douse the small flare of hope his words sparked. 'I'm so sorry, honey.'

Honey. Hearing the endearment nearly undid her. The gentleness in his voice. She didn't deserve any of it. Her arms trembled while she braced herself against the basin. She swallowed, trying to clear the sour taste in her mouth. Abby was *dead*. And what had she been doing when Abby had died? Wallowing. That's what she'd been doing. Wallowing in all she thought she'd lost. Wallowing in what had been taken from her. Had she spared even a second to think about what had been taken from Abby? Of course, she hadn't. She'd been a self-absorbed cow.

Sasha wanted to put her head under the tap and feel the water numb her scalp. Stop her *feeling*. It all hurt so much. She looked at her left hand. Just one day earlier, the pain of the accident had been all-consuming. Seemingly intolerable. Sasha took a slow wobbly breath, trying to shift the weight lodged in her chest. She'd prefer the pain of the accident to what she was feeling right now.

She grabbed a towel and buried her face in it, the scratchiness of sun-dried fabric grating against her skin. She rubbed harder. She wanted to sink onto the cold tiles and press her cheek against them. Once she walked back into the living room and faced Sam, reality began. She would hear Abby's name and details of her death. She swept her foot across the smooth floor. Could she maybe just sit on the tiles for a moment?

No. She dug her toes against the unforgiving surface. She needed to be stronger than that. She owed it to Abby. Sasha took a breath and placed the towel neatly back on the rail. Now was not the time to be weak. She needed to find out what had happened to her friend. Her best friend. And her baby daughter. Oh, God! Abby's daughter! Sasha rushed out of the bathroom before despair claimed her completely.

'How are you feeling?' Sam was in the kitchen, breaking eggs into a pan. 'Want some breakfast?' The fluid tones of George Ezra drifted from the small speaker on the kitchen bench.

Sasha's stomach growled, but she wasn't sure she'd be able to swallow anything. The knowledge of Abby's death was lodged in her throat. She picked up the mug. The coffee was still warm. 'I'll stick with this,' she said, lifting the mug to her lips.

'So, you really don't think it was an accident?' Sasha twisted and faced Sam on the couch. 'And you believe Joe is somehow involved?'

'I've been out to talk to him and he knows something. I went to his house as well.'

'God, I hate that guy. How the hell did Abby get taken in by someone like him?' Sasha jammed her fist into the couch cushion. 'He was such a bastard to her. And I know she didn't tell me even half of what went on. Why didn't I make her tell me more?'

'You were respecting her space. You knew she'd tell you if she wanted to.'

Sasha chewed the corner of her lip. 'Or was she too scared to?'

'Sash, she left Joe. She moved on. Maybe talking about it was something she wasn't ready for.'

'So, why do you think he was involved in her death if they broke up a year ago?' Sasha frowned. 'Abby didn't say anything about him contacting her or trying to talk to her.' Or had she tried to? Sasha squeezed her knees together. She hadn't let Abby talk to her since the accident. The knowledge made her squirm.

'He lied about seeing Abby when I went to talk to him at the warehouse. How else would he have known about the baby?' Sam left the couch and paced around the living room. 'And the tech setup at his house was unusual, to say the least. He was monitoring dozens of cameras. Not that I could look at any of it. The warrant should come through this morning.'

'Do you think he was watching Abby?' Sasha jumped up off the couch. 'Wouldn't she have noticed a camera?'

'Not necessarily. Soon as we have the warrant, I'll know more.' Sam grabbed the empty mugs and took them back to the kitchen. 'Sash, there's every chance he was watching you as well. You weren't his favourite person.'

Sasha snorted before she could stop herself. 'Uh, no.' Disgust coated each syllable. 'And the feeling was mutual. But why would he watch me?'

Sam sucked in a breath. Sasha was used to his pauses, the way he considered everything he said. 'He couldn't control you. And he probably blames you for Abby breaking up with him.'

'Me?' Sasha exploded. 'I didn't break up with him.'

'No. But he saw you living your life, being independent, making your own decisions, that kind of thing. He would've seen you as influencing Abby. Could be he blames you for them breaking up.'

Sasha exhaled sharply. 'Abby leaving that dickhead was the best thing she could've done. But I had nothing to do with it.'

Sam raised his eyebrows.

'I didn't!' Sasha said. 'She made the decision. She was the one who told him. Was I happy? Of course, I was.' She paced in circles around the small kitchen. 'The guy's a jerk who didn't deserve someone like Abby.'

Sam nodded. 'Sash, you didn't have to say anything for Joe to blame you. And you're right. I'm happy she left him, too. But it doesn't change the fact that a control freak like him would see you as responsible. And if that's the case, he'll want you to pay. One way or another.'

'So, what am I meant to do?' Sasha scowled. 'I'm not going to hide from him or something stupid like that.'

Sam changed the subject. 'Have you noticed anything out of the ordinary while you've been away?'

Sasha sank onto the couch, dipping her head to her knees. Had she seen anything out of the ordinary? She wanted to cry and have fat hot splodgy tears carry the shame of her selfishness out of her body. No. She hadn't seen anything out of the ordinary. She'd been so wrapped up in her own myopic misery that she hadn't responded to any of Abby's texts or calls.

She lifted her eyes to Sam, about to admit her total selfishness, when her phone pinged. She pulled it from the pocket of her jeans.

'What the hell?' Sasha exhaled sharply and held the phone out.

George Ezra's voice filled the space and Sasha's heart raced in triple time to the song's beat. Clouds pushed their way in front of the sun, removing the warmth from the room. A spark of something flared in her chest.

'Why have I just got a message from Abby?'

CHAPTER THIRTY-SEVEN

SAM ~ NOW

Sam stared at the words on the screen. Sasha sat next to him on the couch, the phone still clutched in her hand.

I need to see you.

'You're sure it came from Abby's phone?'

Sasha rubbed the corner of her eye. 'I don't have any other contacts in my phone listed as *Abby*.' Her voice was sharp. 'Sorry,' she said. 'I didn't mean it like that.' She dropped her arm and Sam reached for the phone.

'Do you mind if I...?' Sam nodded at the phone. He needed to double check the number really was Abby's.

Sasha shrugged helplessly. 'What's going on, Sam? Why am I getting a text from her?'

Sam could hear the confusion in Sasha's voice. And he knew if he looked up and saw the same expression in her eyes, he wouldn't be able to think at all. He tapped Abby's name at the top of the message, pulling up the sender details. They matched the number he had in his phone for Abby. The message had indeed come from her phone. What the hell was going on?'

'Should I send something back?' Sasha leant towards Sam, all but bouncing on the spot. 'You know, in case there's been some mix-up and the message really has come from Abby?' Her voice dropped in volume. 'In case there's been a mistake and she's not really, you know, *dead*?'

Sam closed his eyes briefly before turning to Sasha. The hope in her voice twisted his stomach. 'Sash. Honey. There's been no mistake.' He wished he could tell her otherwise, that he could scrub away the look of despair.

'You don't know that! What if the woman you found was someone who just looked a lot like Abby? Maybe that's what happened.' Sasha sprang off the couch. 'Actually, let's go down to the morgue or the mortuary, or wherever it is you keep bodies, and let me look. I bet you anything there's been a mix-up.' She spun around, grabbing for her keys from the coffee table.

The desperation in her voice tore through Sam. There was no way he was going to let Sasha anywhere near Abby's body. He snatched the keys from Sasha.

'Sash,' he said, picking up her hands. 'Look at me. It really is Abby. I've checked and it's been confirmed. I'm so sorry, honey.' The term of endearment slipped out again, but she didn't seem to mind. Without thinking, he pulled her towards him and wrapped his arms around her. She stiffened for a second, but then collapsed against him.

'I'm sorry.' Sasha's voice was muffled against his chest. Sam felt her body sag against his and he tightened his arms, resisting the urge to kiss the top of her head. 'So, who's sending me the message?' She broke the contact, pushing away and leaving Sam with a rush of cool air filling the space between them. 'Wait,' she said, frowning. 'Do you think whoever sent it had something to do with her death?' She dragged an impatient hand through her hair, eyes wide. 'Sam, you've got to track her phone and work out where it is!'

'Sash–'

'Plus, whoever sent it said they *need* to see me.' Sasha interrupted Sam. 'Give me the phone and I'll text back and arrange it.' She thrust her hand out.

'Hold on, Sasha.' Sam's words were clipped. 'We need a moment to think about it.' His eyes scanned the message again. There was no doubt the message had come from Abby's phone. He flicked his thumb over the screen and the previous messages scrolled down. All looked to be from Abby; it looked to be an unbroken chain with no replies from Sasha apart from one she'd sent yesterday. He glanced up at her pacing back and forth in the living room like a caged animal. The previous messages Abby had sent all ended with their customary *xxx*. In stark contrast, the latest message had none.

'Come on, Sam.' Sasha sank onto the couch, her body limp. 'We've got to do something.' Her voice trembled on the last word.

Sam nodded slowly. 'Yeah. We do.' He reached out to pick up her hand, but again, stopped himself. Instinct was difficult to subdue. 'You both have iPhones?' He turned the phone over in his hand.

Sasha nodded. 'We got them about the same time, just over a year ago.'

'You didn't happen to have the "Find My" function synced?'

Sasha scowled. 'We talked about it, but she had it turned off. She didn't want Joe knowing where she was all the time.'

'Yeah, I can see that.' Sam rolled his shoulders and leant back in the couch. 'Smart move from her, but not so helpful to us right now.' He focused on the coffee mug on the table in front of him, thinking.

If only he'd paid more attention to what was going on when

Abby split with Joe. Would it have helped? Changed anything? He hadn't thought too much of the breakup at the time. Just that Sasha was pleased to see the back of Joe and have him out of Abby's life. That had been enough. He rubbed his palms along his thighs, as if the action would produce an answer. He'd barely known the guy, but there had been something about him that Sam had found unsettling. He should've paid more attention. A shadow passed and he looked up at Sasha standing in front of the window. She was restless, moving from one location to the next. A sudden thought occurred to him.

'Did you and Abby use the "share location" feature?'

Sasha's eyes widened, comprehension flooding them.

'We did.' She hurried back to the couch, knocking the coffee table. 'Oh my God, Sam! We can use that to track the phone, right?'

'Only if it's still turned on.'

'I only just got the message, didn't I?' Her eyes were wide, her lips pressed together tightly.

Sasha held her hand out in a silent demand for the phone.

Sam knew that once he passed the phone over to Sasha, she would act, driven by instinct. What were the chances of her accepting his reason, his logic? He looked at Sasha's upturned palm. He weighed the options in rapid succession. Wait and see if another message came through? Or instigate some action and take control?

Was there even a question about what he'd do?

CHAPTER THIRTY-EIGHT

SASHA ~ NOW

Sasha rounded the bend in the trail. Abby's phone was in the nature reserve less than two blocks from Sam's place. It was *on*. That had to mean something, surely. As soon as Sam had handed her the phone, she'd flown out of the door and headed straight for it.

A black cockatoo startled and took flight, spreading its white-banded tail feathers and squawking. She stumbled in the loose gravel. The puff of air from the bird's wings grazed her cheek. She blinked at the span of indignant feathers obscuring her sight. Her heart stuttered before racing, desperate to escape the caged confines of her ribs. It was as if it thought it could follow the trajectory of the bird.

She jumped when a hand landed on her shoulder. Sam. It was just Sam.

'Can you see anyone?' Sasha gasped. She crouched over and hooked her finger into the back of her sneaker, which had come loose. 'Abby's phone was right here.' She jerked her head each way, scanning the surrounds.

She knew the area reasonably well. She and Sam had often taken advantage of the proximity of the nature reserve, wandering through it in the evenings or at weekends when she'd stayed at his place. Trails criss-crossed through the banksia tree wetlands, a maze of paths showcasing native vegetation and wildlife. Why would someone bring Abby's phone here? And if they wanted Sasha to see them, why were they moving?

'Sash, we need to slow down.'

'We need to see who has the phone.' The fact that Sam had confirmed Abby was dead wouldn't sink in. There was still a tiny pebble of hope skimming along the surface of her mind. It refused to sink beneath the depths. 'Come on. We have to keep moving.' She lunged forward, arms pumping, heart still pushing against her ribs.

She could hear Sam's footsteps behind her. Steady. Rhythmic. Sasha knew he could outrun her. Why wasn't he moving faster? Why wasn't he trying to reach the phone? She sucked in air, the scent of wild freesias invading her lungs.

A flash of black caught her attention on a narrow dirt trail to her right. It was nothing more than a shortcut carved through the scrub. Possibly a path used by animals. She stabbed at her phone screen, bringing it to life. Lines on the electronic map swam in front of her. Abby's Bitmoji face pulsed in the middle. She shook her head, trying to get her bearings. She couldn't tell which of the stupid little lines matched the trails they were on. She swung back to Sam.

'Do you think the phone is in this direction?' She pointed along the trail, disappearing into undergrowth.

She didn't wait for an answer. She needed to find the phone, find whoever had the phone. Finding it meant getting answers. She knew the likelihood of it being Abby was slim to non-existent, but she still needed to see.

Without looking back or checking to see if Sam was behind her, Sasha pushed along the narrow trail. It was only wide enough for a single foot, which meant she had to look down. It slowed her pace. She had to stop, look up and check if she could see movement ahead of her. Spindly needles from encroaching foliage poked tiny pricks along her forearms. Movement rustled to her left. Not a person. Maybe a bird. Or a quenda. The rat-like creatures liked this habitat. Hopefully not a snake. No. The sound was too jerky to be a snake. She forced a breath out, slowly. Deliberately. She needed to focus. She wouldn't find Abby – Abby's *phone* – if she kept darting around like she was in a pinball machine. The thought of seeing Abby remained irrationally present.

She understood what Sam had told her. What her mum had told her. That Abby was *gone*. But her brain refused to accept it. In her mind, she could see Abby's laughing eyes; the way she sat, twirling her hair, deep in thought and often chewing the corner of her lip. How was it possible she would never see that again?

She stretched and took another breath to slow her heart rate, her hands in fists on her hips. There was nothing in front of her apart from tangles of scrubby foliage. Grass trees claimed space, distinctive with their green sprouting tops and thick squat trunks. She knew they had a more Latin sounding name than *grass tree*. Something starting with "x". The distraction was a brief balm, allowing her to think.

If it wasn't Abby who had sent the text, then who was it? Who was twisted enough to send a message from a dead woman's phone?

Awareness crept down Sasha's spine. Her scalp prickled as a rush of thoughts crowded her mind. Her breathing quickened again, her mind not yet ready to unscramble what was struggling to surface. The narrow trail disappeared into a shadow of nothingness. She turned and covered the short distance back to Sam.

'It was nothing,' she said, only glancing at Sam before

pulling her phone from her pocket. 'Abby's phone is still on. And it's still in the reserve.' She thrust it towards Sam, almost defiantly. She needed his help. He knew the area a lot better than her. But she was irrationally annoyed that he didn't share the same urgency. *He knows it won't be Abby holding the phone.* The voice in her head whispered the logical words. She squashed her lips together. 'Which way should we go?'

'Looks like its midway along the Jarrah Trail,' Sam said, pointing ahead. 'We stay on this track and turn right at the next one.' He strode ahead, not running. But he was walking with intent.

It was all Sasha needed to hear. She raced ahead of Sam, coarse dirt spraying out behind her. Tree limbs stretched overhead, straining to meet their mate on the other side, creating a canopy across the trail. Sunlight struggled to find its way through. Shadows obscured her vision.

She could hear the scrape of footsteps up ahead and quickened her pace, urging her legs to go faster, harder. There was a flash of movement between the branches. She flew around a tight corner, yanking her arm as fingers of reaching vine snagged against her forearm. But she kept her eyes ahead, putting one foot in front of the other. Ahead of her, branches swayed. Was it from the wind or human movement? She darted through the scrub, determined to close the gap. She could hear Sam behind her, but kept her attention on what lay ahead. Would he follow her?

She landed her foot awkwardly on a loose rock and crashed to the ground. Her knee grated against the gravel, blood immediately oozing. Her mouth was gritty and dirt coated her lips. She lifted her head, disoriented.

Feet appeared in front of her and then retreated. She looked up expecting to see Sam's hand.

'Give me a hand, Sa–' His name died on her lips. It wasn't Sam.

The pebble of hope plummeted, swallowed beneath the surface, dragged into the depths. It wasn't Sam. And it wasn't Abby with the phone.

The figure with the black shirt was partially obscured by a paperbark tree. Ribbons of bark looked as if they'd melted from the trunk, shreds torn and dangling like decaying bandages in an ancient crypt. That prickle of awareness materialised. Disgust raked her limbs and slithered up her back. It was a sensation he never failed to produce in her.

'Joe?' The word was sour on her tongue. Of course, it was Joe. Who else would be calculating enough to use Abby's phone? She found her voice. 'Joe.' His name fired out of her. A curtain of corellas shot up from the branches, shrill white pearls scattering in every direction.

Joe stood in front of her. 'You took your time.'

CHAPTER THIRTY-NINE

SASHA ~ NOW

'Looking for this?' Joe loomed over Sasha where she'd fallen on the trail, waving Abby's phone in front of her face.

'Wha–?' Sasha stammered, her words lost. Dirt and dust caked her eyes. She got to her knees. That scalp-prickling awareness from only moments earlier flooded her again, no longer hidden. It had been Joe all along. He'd been the one who had sent the message. Not Abby. Abby was dead. Oh God. Abby really was dead.

She needed to gather her wits, to focus. If Joe had the phone and had sent the message, did that mean he was involved in Abby's death? Did *Joe* kill Abby? But why? The wind swirled dust around her knees. She clenched her jaw and winced at the crunch of dirt still in her mouth. Joe was a jealous, possessive, self-absorbed creep, but had he *really* been driven to kill? Abby left him over a year ago. Why would he wait this long to act? There must have been something else, something she was missing.

Thoughts swirled through Sasha's mind, rushing at her from all directions. Why had Joe texted *her*? She pushed against the ground, struggling to get up as questions gathered momentum at a dizzying rate. Hair whipped across her face. She swiped the strands away as Joe advanced, his arm swinging towards her a beat before the phone smashed against the side of her head. Buzzing filled her skull, a shrill ring sparking bursts of light behind her eyes. She reeled, the force sending her flat against the ground. She scrambled backwards, fingers scrabbling in the dirt as she tried to push herself upright. Blackness seeped into her vision. She blinked rapidly. She needed air. If she passed out, there was no telling what Joe would do. She had to get some distance between them.

Sam couldn't be far away. He mustn't have seen her take the sudden turn. But if she called out, surely he would find them.

'Sam!' Her voice came out a croak. She swallowed, about to try again.

'Don't even think about it.' Joe moved closer. 'You call out to your cop boyfriend and I'll do more than smack you across the head.'

Sasha's head pounded and the ground swayed uncomfortably. Could she even stand?

'What do you want, Joe?' She swallowed and kept her voice quiet, despite the urge to yell and scream.

Joe reached over and yanked her up off the ground. Sasha groaned.

'What do I want? Don't play dumb. Just fucking give it to me.' He spoke through clenched teeth.

Give *what* to him? None of it made sense.

'You and my idiot ex-girlfriend think you're so bloody clever.' His lip curled. 'How's that working out for you?'

Joe shoved her in the middle of the back and she stumbled. Her foot scuffed the gravel, but she stayed upright.

A rustle a few metres ahead snagged Joe's attention. He clamped a hand over Sasha's shoulder and hissed in her ear. 'Don't make a fucking sound.'

Sasha kept her eyes on the ground and glanced sideways. It was a common area for snakes, especially deadly dugites. What were the chances of Joe being bitten right about now? She shivered. She needed to watch her step.

Sasha bit down on her lip. His breath was sour in her face and she fought the urge to gag. His fingers hooked painfully over her collarbone.

They weren't on one of the marked tracks. If you could even call it a track. She concentrated on breathing evenly. Joe's fingers dug deeper into her flesh and she tried not to flinch. She didn't want to give him the satisfaction.

The wind picked up again, flinging grit against her ankles and stinging her eyes. But she stayed still. The sound rifled through the leaves, moving closer. Joe froze and reached behind him. Shit! Did he have a *gun*? The sound was of something dragging along the ground, steadily advancing. Sasha's eyes grew wide and she braced herself. This could be her only chance. With Joe focused on the sound, perhaps she could get away.

She wanted to wrench free from Joe. She was desperate to shove her elbow back, deep into his solar plexus. She wanted to drop suddenly, to twist and knee him in the groin. She wanted to turn and thrust the heel of her palm at his nose, breaking it in one smooth, fluid and bloody action. She knew what she needed to do. She was ready. Sunlight swept through the branches, a spotlight of anticipation. Every muscle and sinew in her body tensed.

Except it wasn't Sam.

A cat slunk out from the bushes.

'For fuck's sake!' Joe aimed a vicious kick at the black and white animal, who side-stepped as if it knew it was coming. It looked over its shoulder, eyes trained intently on Joe before ducking through the undergrowth and out of sight.

Joe's breathing was rapid. The cat had rattled him. Good. She could use that to her advantage. The desire to wrench free and inflict pain coursed through her, a force compelling her to act, to do something. Anything. But she held back. There was no doubt in her mind that Joe was dangerous. And she was now convinced he'd been involved with Abby's death. But Joe also knew she would grasp even the slightest possibility that Abby might not be dead. Why else would he have contacted her? He was gaslighting her, pure and simple.

No. She needed to be patient. See where he took her. See what he wanted. But was she walking straight into danger? She slowed her pace. Leaves washed around her feet in a scrubby wave. There was no path, no discernible trail.

Joe seemed to know where he was going. Would Sam hear them moving? Or would he still be on the main trails that were well-worn by the public? Wherever Joe was taking her was not somewhere accessed by regular trail walkers.

Joe moved to her side and elbowed her forward. She tried to get her bearings. Trails criss-crossed the area, but the wetlands and surrounding bushland was dense. Seemingly impenetrable.

They kept walking, Joe shoving her ahead of him. His hand gripped the fabric of her shirt, balled it into a fist. Overgrown scrub scratched her arms, her neck, her cheeks. Noises swirled around her. Birdsong that sounded like voices. Sam?

Joe stopped, yanking Sasha backwards. It would be so easy to drive her elbow back into him. She steadied her breath. She needed to get proof that he was responsible for Abby's death. And she couldn't do that if she acted too soon. But, oh boy, did she want to hurt him.

'Through here,' Joe said, adding another vicious shove in Sasha's back.

She ducked under the branches of a wattle tree, heavy with swollen balls of yellow pollen. Damp bush debris swallowed her feet, but she stepped forward, moisture leeching into the sides of her sneakers. They were on the edges of the swampy wetland reserve. She looked up. Barely visible just metres in front of her was a makeshift shack. A few pieces of corrugated iron, rusted and weathered, were streaked with sludgy mildew. Limbs from surrounding trees tangled around it, bark ripping, dripping, ghoulish and protective.

Sasha turned back to look at Joe.

Joe said nothing. He reached again into his back pocket. Was it a gun? Clouds crossed thickly in front of the sun, shuttering the light.

Sasha drew a breath and braced herself, knees slightly bent, arms poised, ready for him to shoot.

CHAPTER FORTY

SAM ~ NOW

'Sasha!' Sam's voice was sharp.

Where the bloody hell had she gone? Sam picked up his pace. The trail was uneven; it was soft in patches from dirt dumped by the local council and waiting to be graded. He moved to the edge and made himself stop. Listen. Magpies trilled. Branches scratched and creaked in the wind. There were no voices, no footsteps. Had she found Abby's phone? Or had the person with it found her?

Sasha was so damn infuriating. Why couldn't she just have waited for him, instead of haring off ahead, expecting him to read her mind and know where she was going?

'Sasha?' He called out again, his voice carrying in the wind. Nothing. The trail ahead was deserted. He looked around. He could hear voices behind him, but they were from a group of elderly walkers he'd passed only moments before. One had raised his walking pole in greeting and would have impaled Sam, if it hadn't been for some fancy footwork.

Sasha must have seen something to make her leave the main trail. Dammit. Would it have been too much for her to wait two seconds for him?

He turned, his eyes scanning for the green fabric of her shirt. A difficult colour to see in the dense bushland surrounds. Why couldn't she have been wearing something red? Pink? He almost snorted. Sasha in pink was about as likely as a dolphin appearing in the swamp water. He stared at the stagnant patch to his right. There was no way anyone could pass through that. Not without some serious wading gear. And who knew how far you'd sink in the claggy mud.

Where the hell are you, Sash?

Sam thought about the conversation he'd had with Joe. He'd said he hadn't been in contact with Abby since they parted ways a year ago, which was a complete lie. And Sam hadn't been fooled by the disingenuous display of surprise when he'd told him Abby was dead. He thought about the computer monitoring gear he'd seen in Joe's house, the cameras watching everything. He thought about the text message Sasha got from Abby's phone. The phone hadn't been found on Abby's body or even in her house. Had Joe had it all along? Certainty spiked through Sam. Of course, it was Joe. And now Sasha was chasing him.

His eyes settled on a small path ahead on his left, almost obscured by tall grass. It wasn't one of the marked trails. He stepped towards it. The ground was firm. Dry. Separated from the swamp. Easy to move along. It had to be where Sasha had gone. He swept a cursory glance along the ground for snakes and pushed through the knee-high strands. There was no dirt visible. Flattened grass was the only sign that it was a track. It was flattened enough that Sam could tell it had been used occasionally, but not routinely. He surged ahead.

A sound caught his attention. A snap. He listened for a second, and looked. Was that movement between the branches? The rustle of wind through the trees was a backdrop for the raucous call of corellas above. He focused his attention to ground level. He heard it again.

A crunch of dry leaves. Uneven. Syncopated.

He stopped. A magpie strutted along the flattened grass, its sharp beak prodding insistently between the fallen blades and twigs. Was it the bird making the noise?

He screened out the surrounding sounds, listening intently.

And there it was. The soft stutter of uneven footfalls. Like a series of slow-motion side-steps on the rugby field. Undeniably human. And not rapid. He remained still, frozen to the spot, eyes scanning the dense foliage for any sign of movement between minute spaces. Was it Sasha? The spacing of the sounds suggested there was more than one person. His pulse quickened. She must have found whoever had the phone. Joe?

Sam stayed still. The sound disappeared. Had they stopped? He squinted, hoping to hear something, anything, that would indicate Sasha's location.

He walked a few more steps. Cautiously. Quietly. He walked until he could see daylight through the leaves, being careful to make as little sound as possible. Wind whistled through the gaps in the trees, tunnelling along the narrow space.

The track thickened again and evidence of it being anything other than undisturbed bushland faded. Sam twisted and wove his way between the needle-sharp fronds of spinifex. He winced when one spiked him under his thumbnail.

Voices filtered through the scrub, more distinct now. It was Sasha.

And she wasn't alone. She was with Joe.

Sam felt his phone vibrate in his pocket. Was Sasha trying to tell him something? He pulled it out. Adrenaline surged through his chest. The message flashed to life on the screen. It wasn't Sasha.

CHAPTER FORTY-ONE

SASHA ~ NOW

Was it a gun? Another weapon? Possibilities flashed through Sasha's mind like fireworks. Joe reached behind him, his eyes small and squinty and trained on Sasha. His shoulders were hunched and his chin squashed against his chest like a rotten plum. How had she never known this hut was in the reserve? It sagged low, weeds and creeping vines crawling the walls as if to smother its very existence.

'Shut your mouth and don't make a sound.' Spit sat in the corner of his mouth. A fly buzzed around his head, zeroing in on the moisture.

Sasha kept her eyes on Joe. She clenched her good hand and braced her injured one. Her head throbbed from the earlier blow, but the dizziness wasn't so bad. The burnt orange bulb of a Grand Banksia hovered above Joe's head, as though ready to drop down on Sasha's command. If only it were that easy. She watched him carefully while his hand delved in and out of his back pocket. Not a gun, if he was having that much trouble locating it. Seconds ticked by, marked by the rhythmic clicking of a nearby grasshopper.

'What do you want, Joe?' Sasha kept her voice low. Neutral.

All she wanted to do was scream at him. Hurl words and demand answers. *What did you do to Abby, you disgusting piece of shit?* She was more convinced than ever he'd been involved in her death. But she needed proof. Which was why she had to be patient. See what he wanted and get the answers. She wanted to hurt him. So, *so* badly. But if she did, there would be no answers. No proof of what he did to Abby.

There had to be answers in the hut. Something important. It was the only reason why Joe would have taken her here. Despite being a suburban wetland reserve, the hut was well hidden. Away from the public eye.

She looked straight at him, not cowering. 'Why did you *need* to see me?'

'She gave it to you,' Joe said. His hand was still behind him, digging around in his pocket. 'Just hand it over.'

Sasha had no idea what Joe was talking about. No idea whatsoever. Should she play along? Pretend she knew what he was talking about? It might give her a hint as to what Joe had done to Abby. It would also buy some time in which Sam could find them. She knew he wasn't far away. She was certain it had been his voice calling out just moments earlier.

'Not until you tell me what you did to Abby.' Sasha forced the words out. She couldn't afford to let any emotion show. He fed off weakness.

Joe's face slid into a smirk. 'It's eating you up, isn't it? Poor little Sasha doesn't have all the answers.' He used a sing-song voice to taunt her.

Fine. He wanted to play games? It took two to play. She wouldn't give him the satisfaction of setting the rules. There was no doubt in her mind now that Joe had hurt Abby. One way or another, she was going to make him admit it.

'How about you answer this, then.' Sasha breathed slowly, outwardly calm. Inside, she was like a shaken can of drink, about to explode. She cast her mind back. 'When Abby and I had a massage about a year ago, you knew exactly where we were.' It wasn't a question.

Confusion rippled across Joe's face. 'So?'

'So...' Sasha dragged the word out, watching Joe's face. 'How did you know?' The question felt silly, even to her own ears. But she wanted to buy some time. Give Sam a chance to find them. She ploughed on. 'It was a spur-of-the-moment decision to go there. But you knew Abby was there. How?'

Joe's smirk grew. 'Gee, and I thought you were smart. Actually, no. *You* think you're so smart. I know better, don't I, Sasha?'

He was deliberately taunting her. Trying to get the upper hand. She knew that. But fuck, it hurt. She willed her racing heart to steady a fraction.

'How smart was it for you to ignore her after the accident?' The words punched Sasha in the gut. 'Yeah, yeah,' Joe said, holding up a hand even though Sasha hadn't said anything. 'It was her fault. Bloody hell. Who fucking swerves for a *possum?*' He shook his head and finger, as if berating a child. 'Abby, Abby, Abby. She always was a pretty pathetic driver. But still.' He paused and rolled his eyes with exaggerated theatrics, as if narrating to an audience. 'Not smart, Sasha.'

Sasha's skin prickled, like shards of glass were being ground into her arms. Breathe in. Breathe out. She didn't blink.

Joe continued. 'How smart was it to not answer her last text?'

The words knifed through her. But she let him keep going.

'How smart was it to let your best friend die alone?'

He twisted the knife brutally, and with precision. Sasha couldn't let him see her pain, though. She wouldn't.

'So, you're admitting you killed Abby.' Her voice was monotone. Devoid of emotion.

Joe looked at her and shook his head sharply. 'You'd like that, wouldn't you?' He jammed his hand once again into his back pocket and dug around. 'You're such a fucking arrogant piece of shit.' He finally wrenched a key from his pocket. 'Stupid bitch.' The words were casual. 'All she had to do was tell me what she'd done with it.'

What the hell was Joe talking about? What was he after? Despite the wind, the air was heavy. Beads of moisture pushed out along the top of Sasha's lip, but she kept her tone level. 'Still not helpful, Joe.'

She could see her words annoyed him. He hated people answering back. 'Cut the fucking crap. She told you everything, the whiny little cow.'

The wind picked up. A machine-burst of sound cracked through the air as a shower of gumnuts fell on the metallic roof behind Sasha. Joe jumped.

Sasha was used to the sounds of the reserve. She held her stance, even straightened a fraction. She had no idea what Joe wanted. But she knew what *she* wanted. *Needed.*

'What did you do to Abby? Why have you got her phone?'

Joe glanced around, his eyes darting in all directions. A black cockatoo swooped low over him and then up to the roof of the hut.

Sasha tried to make her face bland, expressionless. But inside her strength solidified. Joe was unsettled. Good. It was a look she hadn't seen on him before. She could use it to her advantage. She needed to keep her composure. It was the only way she'd get any answers.

'Forget the bloody phone. Just hand it over.' Joe advanced a step. 'I know she gave it to you.'

Sasha held her ground, refusing to step back. 'Joe,' she said, as if placating a moody toddler. 'Abby didn't give me anything.'

Joe raked a hand through greasy hair. He stepped again, his

foot slapping against the ground. 'If it wasn't for you, none of this would've happened.' The same fly buzzed around his ear and he smacked the side of his head. He screwed up his face, the force clearly more than he'd intended to use.

Sasha bit down on the corner of her lip. None of this was funny, but the look on Joe's face was levelling.

'What wouldn't have happened?' Sasha flexed her fingers, poised to engage. 'None of what, Joe?'

'You know it's your fault Abby's dead, right?' He jutted his bulbous chin at her. A cobweb of bloodied veins criss-crossed his nose.

Sasha's stomach twisted. His words stung, hitting raw strips of her soul. She couldn't let him see. There would be time later for blame and self-recriminations. She raised an eyebrow coolly, finding a sliver of strength to squash her feelings. She straightened her spine further. 'I don't think so, Joe.' She inhaled, steadying herself. 'Abby hated you.'

Joe's nostrils flared, the veins wriggling like trapped worms on a fish hook.

'She hated you and couldn't wait to get away from you.' Sasha knew she was moving into dangerous territory. How far could she provoke Joe before he snapped? 'She said leaving you was the best thing she'd ever done.'

And there it was. That pop. The moment that Joe snapped.

CHAPTER FORTY-TWO

SASHA ~ NOW

Joe lunged towards Sasha. She side-stepped him easily. He stumbled and landed heavily, sprawled on the ground. Sausage-like fingers splayed in the dirt.

'Fucking bitch.' The words exploded out of Joe. 'You had to make things difficult, didn't you?'

Sasha took a step towards him. It would be so easy to squash him. Right now. Squash him like the bottom-feeding scum he was. She might have an injured hand, but one sharp knife-edged kick against his windpipe while he was on the ground would silence him. The impulse to stop him – *right now* – burned through her. But no. Not yet.

She needed to wait and get just a little more information. *Then* she would act.

'You're as dumb as she was.' Joe spat the words. He stood and scrubbed at some dirt on his chest. 'You think you're so fucking clever, but you're just a trumped-up little show pony.' Fury replaced his smugness from only a few seconds ago. He waggled plump fingers along an imaginary keyboard. 'Now hand it over.'

Anger sparked through Sasha. She clenched her good fist.

'Joe,' she said, keeping the anger under wraps. Now was not the time to lose control. 'I honestly have no idea what you're talking about. What do you want me to hand over?'

Joe narrowed his eyes until they were fleshy little slits. 'The thumb drive.' He hissed the words. 'She gave it to you. I know she did.'

Sasha's mind whirled. A thumb drive? That's what this was about? Abby hadn't given her a thumb drive. But Joe clearly thought she had. If she played along for a little longer, she knew she'd be able to get answers.

'The thumb drive?' Sasha cocked an eyebrow at Joe. She kept her tone ambiguous. There was no way she was going to let him know she didn't have it. Not yet, anyway. 'Well, why didn't you just say so?'

'Stop being so fucking dumb.' Joe screwed fleshy fingers into a fist and advanced towards Sasha. 'Hand it over and you can go running back to your boyfriend. Useless bloody cop that he is. Where the fuck is he now? Couldn't even keep up with you.' He threw a cruel smile in her direction.

The wind caught Sasha's curls and dropped cool fingers of breeze along her neck. Joe was still trying to goad her with such blatant transparency that she almost laughed. She reined the impulse in and instead raised an eyebrow. 'What's so important about the thumb drive?' She delved into her pocket, as if to pull something out. Joe's eyes followed her hand. 'What's so important about it that you had to hurt Abby?' The question was heavy on her tongue. She felt like it would choke her if she swallowed. 'What did you do to Abby?'

'Do to her?' Joe barked a laugh and then narrowed his eyes, assessing Sasha. 'What's up, *Sashi*? Were things not right with the two of you?'

Sasha flinched at the use of her name's diminutive. Abby was the only one who had ever used it. She stood her ground and lifted her chin. If Joe knew her and Abby hadn't been talking, he'd obviously been lurking around. Watching Abby. Watching her, as well?

'Not important, Joe.' The words stuck in her throat, like a stick wedged sideways. Of course, it was important. Ignoring Abby after the accident was a pain she would bear forever. She wouldn't let this pathetic excuse of a human see it, though. She wouldn't let him get the upper hand. 'What's so important about the thumb drive that you'd kill Abby over it?' She clenched her fist in her pocket, as if gripping something. Joe wasn't to know her fist was empty.

'Cut the crap and just fucking give it to me.' Spit flew from his mouth, little darts of impotent rage.

'Here's the thing.' Sasha paused, as if the act of making conversation was the only thing she had to concern herself with. As if she wasn't desperate to shove him to the ground and make him beg and grovel. 'You're not going to get what you want until you tell me what happened to Abby.' She shrugged, feigning indifference, when every fibre of her body screamed to scratch his eyes out until they were nothing more than bloodied sockets.

Tension radiated from Joe. 'Nothing to tell.' He looked at the key in his hand. 'Nosy little bitch couldn't stay out of things. Not my fault she was... clumsy.' The sneer at the last word curdled Sasha's stomach.

The banksia bulb above Joe bobbed and drew Sasha's eyes towards it. She caught a flash of movement that stilled just as quickly. She blinked. Sam! It was Sam. Relief washed over her in a cool wave. Her legs almost buckled, but she tensed her thighs. He raised a finger to his lips and remained still. Even though she knew she could deal with Joe, Sam's presence brought a surge of relief.

Joe took a quick step towards the hut and grabbed the top of Sasha's left arm, his fingers digging roughly into her flesh. It was her injured hand. Which left her uninjured one free to react. Sasha's eyes flicked towards Sam. He shook his head. He wasn't going to act. Yet. And Sasha didn't want him to. She needed to see what was in the hut, to find out why Joe wanted a thumb drive he thought she had.

And why he had hurt Abby.

Blunt fingers dug into the soft skin at the top of Sasha's arm, but she refused to flinch. There was no way she'd give him the satisfaction. But the feel of his hand on her shoulder burned. She drew in a long breath to steady herself while Joe fumbled with a padlock on the door. The sheen of the lock was at odds with the grime and rot of the rest of the hut.

Sasha's back was to Sam, but she knew he was close. There was no sound. Nothing to give him away. Dripping paperbark from surrounding gums rippled in the wind. Sam would use the movement to his advantage. Slowly. Steadily. Sasha allowed herself a fleeting moment to acknowledge their synchronicity; she knew what he would do, how he would think and react.

The lock clicked as Joe finally turned the key.

'Get in.' His elbow jabbed her in the middle of her back.

Sasha stumbled forward. Darkness swallowed her and sucked the outside light to nothingness. The floor wasn't where it should have been. Her stomach whooshed as her mind recalibrated the space. She blinked and steadied herself, desperate for her eyes to adjust.

And then they did.

CHAPTER FORTY-THREE

SAM ~ NOW

The phone screen glared at Sam in the shadows. It was an incoming message. He squatted low and tucked himself behind a tree. He didn't want Joe to see him. Yet.

The ground was damp from the nearby swamp, so it muffled any small sounds. *Almost* muffled them. The flattened grass had been easy enough to follow, once he realised it was there. He'd heard Sasha and could see Joe with her. But Joe didn't know he was being followed. The guy was either ignorant or arrogant. Or a combination of both. Sam was fine with that. With any luck, Joe thought it was just Sasha out here and would stay focused on her.

Sam pressed himself against the damp tree trunk and swiped his thumb up the screen. The message was from Tom in IT at the station. Sam had asked him to access the computers and cameras at Joe's place once the warrant came through and get back to him.

> Call ASAP, mate. Dodgy as shit stuff going down.

Tom was new and enthusiastic. Probably watched too much

Hawaii Five-O or *Rookie Blue*. Sam glanced up again. Joe had his back to Sam, but it wouldn't take much to get Sasha's attention. He scanned the rest of the message.

> Cameras monitoring owner's residence, a
> warehouse in Malaga and a direct feed from a
> private residence. All recent files accessed
> have been via USB, so nothing I can read.

The hairs on the back of Sam's neck prickled at the next words.

> Only thing visible is a folder on desktop with
> photos of a baby and woman.

It had to be Abby and her daughter.

Why was Joe keeping photos of them? More to the point, why did he have them in the first place? Abby had moved on and she'd thought Joe had too. It'd been her choice, but maybe it was a choice Joe hadn't accepted. Had he simply been biding his time?

Something must have happened to have made Joe act, though.

Sam's thighs twitched in their cramped stance. Men like Joe were disgusting. Their subtle scorn, derogatory comments and hidden abuse covered weak, pathetic excuses for human beings.

Insects clicked in the dense shrub around him, invisible but claustrophobic. There was movement by the hut and Sam straightened his back, his heart rate spiking as he watched Sasha confronting Joe. It was unnerving to sit back and watch her poke and prod, needling away at him.

Sam tapped out a quick message to the station and slid the phone back in his pocket. The sight of the ramshackle hut behind Sasha surprised him. All these years he'd lived in the area and run kilometres through the reserve and he'd had no idea it existed. True, it was well hidden and completely off the beaten path. There had been no reason to suspect something was tucked away, especially in the boggy swamp area. How long it'd been there was anyone's guess. It certainly didn't look as if it had been a recent addition, given the weather encrusted exterior.

Sam listened carefully to Sasha's voice. She was talking to Joe. He had a decent view of them, but couldn't hear the words clearly. Something about a thumb drive? Not far from him, a corella shrieked, sharp and shrill. Joe flinched, but Sasha remained composed. The comment from Tom about files being accessed via USB suddenly made sense. That had to be what Joe was after. He clearly thought Sasha had it.

He looked through gaps in the scrub to where Sasha was standing. He winced at the sight of blood on her cheek. The bastard had hurt her. The impulse to propel himself at the slimy creep almost overwhelmed him. Every muscle in his body tensed, ready to pounce. Whatever had happened to Sasha though, it hadn't stopped her. He still couldn't hear all the words, but he knew her body language. She was trying to get Joe to talk.

Sam turned and adjusted his position, trying to hear more. Long grass scratched his neck, pricking his nerve endings. Every fibre of his body screamed to act.

Almost as if he'd willed her to do so, Sasha's eyes landed on him. He raised a finger to his lips. She gave nothing away. He knew she could take care of herself. But Joe was unpredictable.

Sam listened. The rustle of the wind through the paperbark gums drowned out most sounds. He wasn't sure what Joe would admit to. He was hardly going to casually drop into a conversation that he'd murdered Abby.

Sam braced himself when Joe grabbed Sasha roughly by the shoulder and shoved her towards the hut. Dizziness swept around his head as he squashed the need to rip Joe's hands from Sasha. Wind threw sharp needles of spinifex against his arms, his back, his face.

Not yet. He needed to stay still.

Joe was trying to open the hut door. Sam rubbed a hand across his eyes and squinted through the grass. If the bastard didn't get his hands off Sasha, Sam was going to tear them off. He swallowed.

And waited.

The lock clicked and the door opened.

Sasha stumbled into the darkness.

Sam lunged towards the hut.

CHAPTER FORTY-FOUR

SASHA ~ NOW

Sasha steadied herself. That sickening sensation of falling through space gripped her stomach. It had barely been a drop of half a step, but she hadn't been expecting it. Darkness swallowed her, even though the door was open. Sunlight struggled to find its way in, as if being repelled by a fug of dank despair.

'Move.' Joe shoved her between the shoulder blades.

Sasha felt the air being forced out of her lungs. She stumbled forward. The foul smell of urine and shit slammed against the back of her throat. She gagged. Where was she? What *was* this place? Her heart pounded in her ears, reverberating around the putrid space. The air was soupy; damp and thick. Hot puffs of Joe's breath hit the back of her neck, wrapping around her throat, constricting her airways further. She shuddered. He was too close.

Sunlight inched its way into the cramped room and Sasha took a small step, increasing the distance between her and Joe. She needed to get as much information from him as she could. She still needed to find out exactly what he'd done to Abby.

The surface of the ground was slippery. Sasha slid her foot along the floor, being careful to keep her balance. There was no sound or movement from Joe. He stayed where he was in the doorway. *Blocking* the doorway. She needed to get more space between her and Joe, to be out of his immediate reach. But if she did that, was she moving away from her only means of escape?

Water dripped from somewhere in the space, rhythmic soft thuds. It dawned on Sasha that it wasn't the sharp splash of drops against a concrete floor or hard surface. But the floor was clearly wet. She reached her good hand out fractionally, her fingers splayed.

Splat. Splat. Splat.

Her hand connected with coarse fabric. She recoiled. A chill ran down her spine. What had she walked into?

Splat. Splat. Splat.

She sucked in a sharp breath, ignoring the acrid burn at the back of her throat. Weak bands of light wove their way into the room. They circled and landed on a slumped form. An undeniably human form.

Splat. Splat. Splat.

Sasha's brain scrambled to make sense of the scene. Why did Joe have someone in this remote hut? Who was it? Were they even alive? Her eyes adjusted enough to scramble to the other side of the room. It was someone sitting on a chair, their hands bound behind them, their head dangling forward. Bile churned its way up her throat. Grimy cloth coiled around his neck.

The shriek of wind outside the hut jolted Sasha. It sounded like Abby calling out to her. She looked up at Joe. It wouldn't be Abby. It was never going to be Abby.

'What the hell, Joe?' Sasha swallowed and her eyes narrowed. Fear threaded its way along her spine. 'Who's this?'

She looked down at the body in the chair. Matted tufts of pale blond hair poked through a cap. A niggle of recognition wormed its way through her mind as she took in the dust-caked skin and parched, cracked lips.

A groan slipped out. 'Don't...'

A splintering crash and a wail of birds erupted.

CHAPTER FORTY-FIVE

SAM ~ NOW

Sam covered the distance from the tree line to the hut in seconds. His breath was thunderous in his ears. His heart pounded against his ribs like a caged animal, desperate to escape.

The door to the hut had ricocheted against the frame and then settled ajar after Joe had shoved Sasha inside. The wind scraped and pulled at surrounding tree branches. Without pausing, Sam wrenched the door wide open. It splintered from the hinges. An avalanche of screeches erupted in protest from nearby birdlife. He needed to get to Sasha. Joe had shoved her in there for a reason. He just hoped he wasn't too late.

Joe spun towards the door. Sasha was on the far side of the cramped space. And right in the middle was a man bound to a chair. His head bobbed about like a dashboard toy, completely at the whim of momentum and gravity.

'Sasha!' Sam shouted her name, even though she was barely two metres from him.

She looked up and jerked her head in Joe's direction. Sam understood immediately. She wanted him to focus on Joe.

Joe hesitated, then lunged towards the door. Sam blocked

the space easily. Sasha moved towards the chair and crouched beside it. Water dripped from a crack in the roof.

'What's going on, Joe?' Sam kept his voice measured. What he really wanted to do was feel his fist crack against the creep's jaw. He'd messaged for back-up, but it would be a few minutes until anyone appeared. And he knew Sasha wanted information. But it was a fine line.

Joe's foot slipped along the slimy surface, bringing him to an awkward stop in front of Sam. 'Get outta my way.'

Sam stayed where he was in the doorway. 'I don't think so.' He rubbed his chin, feigning contemplation. 'Seems to me we need to work out what's going on here.'

A groan came from the guy in the chair. 'Don't give it to him.' His voice was tortured, as if being dragged along a gravel road.

'Shut up, you fucking idiot!' The words fired out of Joe.

'What?' Sasha moved her head, trying to track the sunken eyes of the man in the chair. 'Don't give him what?' She looked up at Joe. His face was an ugly pattern of blood vessels and anger. 'The thumb drive? Is that what all this is about?'

She leapt up and planted herself in front of Joe. Sam tensed, ready to act.

'What's so important about the thumb drive?' Sasha's voice raised in intensity with each word. Each syllable bounced around the cramped, dank space.

Joe raised his hand, fist balled. Sam wrenched it behind his back before the idiot could even blink. The pathetic whimper from Joe shot a small degree of satisfaction through him.

'Is that why you were after Abby?' Sasha stood toe-to-toe with him. The room was strangely quiet. No bird sounds. No wind.

Joe grunted as Sam twisted his arm another fraction. He didn't answer.

A shuffle came from the middle of the room. 'It's all on there.' The voice scratched through the gloom, pain constricting the sound.

'Shut the fuck up.' Joe. Again. This time, the words were more of a desperate pant than the earlier snarl.

Sasha darted back to the chair and moved to untie the hands bound at the back. The man held captive was a silhouette of battered and bloodied body parts.

Joe moved suddenly and kicked Sam's shin, a vicious blow that made him loosen his grip on Joe's arm. Joe twisted and slithered from Sam towards the door.

'No!' Sasha screamed.

CHAPTER FORTY-SIX

SASHA ~ NOW

'Go!' The word ripped through Sasha and shot through the heavy air. 'Don't let him get away.'

Sam threw a look in her direction. Sasha knew he wouldn't want to leave her, but she needed him to follow Joe.

'I'm fine.' Sasha widened her eyes. 'Just get him.'

They couldn't let Joe escape. Not when they were so close to getting answers. If he escaped now, Abby's death would be in vain. He'd held whoever this was for a reason. She needed to find out why. The wind picked up in intensity again. It sliced through the trees and pushed sounds through the door of the hut. The walls rattled. The roof groaned. Or had the sound come from the body in front of her?

I'm so close, Abby. I'll get there. Sasha whispered the words in her head. If only she had been close by. If only she'd been at the river to help her friend. But she hadn't. She'd been so wrapped up in her own sense of injustice that she'd missed the desperate struggle her friend was going through, the danger she was in.

She blinked sweat from her eyes and focused on the knots, trying to steady her hands. Which was easier said than done when only one had any dexterity. Slimy leaves huddled against the chair legs like soggy pant-protectors.

'Why's Joe got you here?' Sasha seized the chance to ask questions. The knots binding the guy's wrists were grimy and tight. Whether it was from Joe's knots or because of his victim straining against them, Sasha could only guess. A knife would quicken the task, but she didn't have one. Raw welts formed painful looking grooves around his wrists.

Consciousness held a tenuous grip on the captive. Each expelled breath sounded like it was being yanked from deep within. Sasha shook his hands, trying to jostle him into staying awake, staying alive. There was something so familiar about him. But as quickly as she tried to grasp the knowledge, it slithered away.

'Was it to do with Abby? Did you know Abby?' The questions flew out of Sasha. Adrenaline washed through her, making her heart pound.

From inside the hut, Sasha could hear faint shouts over the howling wind. She knew Sam could look after himself. But Joe was cornered and dangerous. If he thought she still had the USB, would he hurt Sam and circle back for her?

'Shit!' Her thumbnail tore to the bed of her finger as she dragged threads loose from the rope binding the guy's wrists. Blood ran along her thumb and pooled in her palm. She needed to hurry up and get his hands free.

She needed to get them both out of the hut.

CHAPTER FORTY-SEVEN

SAM ~ NOW

Sam cast a look back at Sasha, pressed his lips together and started running. His chest pounded in time with his steps. Energy poured from his core, pushing him forward. The sooner he caught the bastard, the sooner he could get back to Sasha.

He backtracked along the barely-there trail and onto the main thoroughfare. Damp swampy earth gave way to tinder-dry ground cover and spinifex grass. Which way had Joe gone? A dog barked to the left. Sam turned towards it and started running. The sun was high, its heat piercing. Muffled voices reached him. People were out walking, oblivious to what was happening. He side-stepped a teenage couple with a wiry Jack Russell. It was straining at its lead. Could it sense the danger? Smell the sour stench of Joe? Sam glanced back at the dog to see which direction it was pulling in.

'Marge! Heel!' The teenage girl gave a distracted tug on the lead. 'Sorry,' she offered to Sam. The dog was veering to the right, to a small trail that deviated from the main one.

He started running again. The wind tunnelled along the trail, stinging his eyes. He had no doubt the dog was reacting to

Joe. He increased his pace, his steps getting faster and faster. Joe couldn't be that far ahead of him.

Sam reached a small clearing and hesitated, his foot skidding across the smooth gravel surface. The exit to the reserve wasn't far away. Was that where Joe was heading?

A snap of sound made Sam spin around. Joe. He was standing in the shade of a eucalyptus. Waiting. The sound had been deliberate.

'Took you long enough, mate.'

CHAPTER FORTY-EIGHT

SASHA ~ NOW

Sasha watched Sam thrash through the scrub. She had no doubt he would find Joe. Right now, though, she needed answers from the person Joe had kidnapped. And beaten, by the looks of the amount of crusted blood under his nose and around his eyes. Had Joe intended him to meet the same fate as Abby? Sasha sucked in the thick air and shuddered. Whatever was on the USB was making Joe desperate.

'Can you talk?' Sasha finished pulling the rope from the man's bloodied wrists. They dropped and dangled by his side, no sign of life or a sense of relief.

She darted around to face him and pressed her fingers to his neck. There was still a pulse, but not much of one. His head bobbed, as if he were straining to surface from the murky depths of a nightmare. She looked around the dank hut, searching for signs of anything that might be useful. He needed help right now. But if Joe had gone to the trouble of bringing whoever this was out here and leaving him for dead, then he was hardly likely to have left a convenient stash of water bottles and snacks.

'Why did Joe bring you here?' A shiver of recognition again

inched its way down the back of her neck. She'd seen him before. She could feel it. But where? 'Did you know Abby?'

His eyelids flickered, trying to open. Clouds pushed past the sun, light suddenly flooding the dark interior.

Sasha recoiled. The beating had clearly been extensive. What was it Joe needed so badly that he'd killed Abby and then left this guy for dead?

She grabbed his forearms and shook him gently. 'Is this about a USB? Is that why Joe has you here?'

At this, he stirred. His eyes strained to open and he squinted in the sunlight. 'Records.' The word was a rasp. He swallowed and winced. 'On the USB. Thinks you have it.' His head jerked to the side, the effort to keep it upright too painful.

Sasha stared at him. It really *was* about a USB? 'But I don't have it.'

'Thinks Abby gave it to you.' He tried to straighten in the chair, but groaned and slumped forward.

Recognition suddenly pinged through Sasha. She knew where she'd seen him before.

'You've been at Joe's house! When Abby and Joe were still together. ' She frowned. 'But you ran away. Why was that?' Sasha thought back to the time they had pulled up at Joe's house, Sam and Abby in the car as well. Joe had been talking to him. The bloodied mess tied to the chair was barely recognisable but she was sure it was him.

'Tried to warn her,' his breathing was ragged, 'that Joe is bad news.' If he didn't get help or water soon, it might be too late.

'Why's Joe got you here?'

'Been hiding from him. But the bastard found me.' He tried to swallow, but choked instead. 'I know what he's been doing. Tried to find proof yesterday, at his house. He doesn't want any loose ends.' He finished with a gasp.

'And Abby was a loose end?' It was a question, but Sasha knew the answer.

The distant whine of sirens carried through the hut door. The sharp staccato breaths from the chair were regular. He was alive. She was sure he'd survive until help reached him. His head slumped forward again. She was *pretty* sure.

She moved to the door. 'I'm sorry.' She glanced over her shoulder at the slumped body in the chair. 'Help's on the way.'

She needed to find Sam.

CHAPTER FORTY-NINE

Sam looked at Joe. At his splodgy face. At the sweat soaking the neckline of his shirt. At the fist clenched by his side while the other gripped something.

Sam took a step towards him. He didn't want to make the mistake of moving too quickly. Joe had stopped for a reason. But why?

'You know I'm going to have to take you to the station, right?'

'Yeah,' Joe dragged the word out. 'Nah. That's not gonna work for me, mate.'

What the hell game was Joe playing at? Sam felt the hairs on his forearms lift. Joe had managed to get Sasha to the hut, presumably to get a USB from her. But Sasha didn't have it. Which made Joe... what? More dangerous? They already knew he was dangerous. Unpredictable? They knew that too. Dangerous and unpredictable was not a great combination. Support was on its way, and his location would be easy for the officers to track. Would it come soon enough?

'How do you see it working?' Sam needed to find out what Joe was going to do.

'Working?' Joe barked a laugh. 'That's the thing. It was meant to mean *less* work. For me, at any rate.'

'How was hurting Abby going to mean less work?'

'Fuck, you're thick, mate. Do you cops ever think?' Joe jabbed his finger against the side of his head. 'She had the records of all my *transactions*. If that got into the wrong hands – *your* hands, in case you're wondering, mate – then the whole shebang would be over.' He exploded his fingers wide. 'I'd have a lot of very unhappy people if that happened.'

So, Joe was trying to hide a trail of illegal acquisitions? It suddenly made sense. The dots slid into place like ants finding their place in an invisible line. The warehouse where Joe worked was the perfect place to ship and receive things. And it would have been easy for him to adjust the records. Clearly though, he had to keep some kind of record of the stock – whatever that might be – that he was moving. The USB. Which was what he thought Abby had. What he thought Sasha now had. He briefly wondered what it was Joe was shipping or receiving. Did it really matter, though? It'd clearly been important enough for him to threaten and hurt Abby. *Kill* Abby. Sam stepped closer.

'Uh, uh.' Joe wagged his index finger at Sam. 'You're gonna have to stay where you are, mate. Can't have you sneaking up on me, can we?' He opened his fist and looked at the object sitting in the middle of his palm. 'I mean, who knows what would happen if I was to, you know, *accidentally* flick this?'

A blue plastic BIC lighter. Sam froze, his breath catching in his chest. What was Joe planning to do? Set fire to the whole reserve? He looked around at the area where they stood. Wind whipped dust around his ankles. Parts of the reserve were swampy wetlands, but most was native scrub. *Parched* native scrub that hadn't seen rain in a long time. Even the electrical storm last night had been nothing but an expulsion of energy.

Between the tinder dry bush and the gusty wind, a fire would roar through the area, decimating everything.

'Would you look at that!' Joe clapped his hands together.

Clap.

'It looks like there *is* something happening up there.' Joe nodded at Sam's head.

Clap.

'Full marks to the detective.'

Clap.

'You don't need to do that, Joe.' Sam nodded at the lighter.

'That's where you're wrong, Detective. I really do. You can't save your precious girlfriend *and* stop me, can you?'

He was forcing Sam to let him get away.

'All I needed was the fucking USB. But if I can't have that, then I need time to get away from you lot.' Joe shrugged his shoulders. 'It's the smart thing to do, ya know?' He turned, as if to leave, but stopped and looked at Sam. 'Oh yeah, in case you think you can pull any hero-cop-macho-bullshit, I pre-empted your girlfriend messing things up for me. Before I sent the text *inviting* her to join me, I took a little stroll. Ya know, it's amazing how far you can get with a leaky gerry can full of petrol before it's empty.'

Joe paused and flicked the lighter, the flame leaping sideways in the wind. 'Would you believe I got *all* the way around the reserve?' His lips stretched into a mockery of a smile.

Sam's breath caught in his chest. Joe was insane. He had the blue lighter gripped tightly in his hand, his thumb still jerking over the small igniter. He had no doubt Joe would use it. And with petrol ringing the perimeter? It was a death sentence for everyone in the reserve. The elderly walkers, the teenagers.

Sasha.

Realisation bubbled up in Sam. Joe wanted power. He craved it. Over people. Over events. Over what was happening at this very moment. This was as much about power as it was about the USB.

A smile flashed across Joe's face. Jubilant.

'You drop that now and you're caught up in it as well.' Sam shifted his weight and leant forward. 'You know that, right?'

Joe blew air out between his teeth. 'You really need to give me a little more credit, Detective. Christ, I'm not a fucking monster. No. What I'm going to do is give you a chance. Would a monster do that?'

Sam looked at the lighter in the other man's hand. He had no intention of giving anyone a chance.

CHAPTER FIFTY

SASHA ~ NOW

Sasha threw a last look over her shoulder at the hut and started running. She headed through the swampy scrub and onto the main trail.

Despite the sun, the weather was harsh. The wind gusted; there were angry surges of air throwing gritty dust at her face, her neck, her ankles. Adrenaline surged through her, propelling her forward. If Joe still thought she had the USB, what would he do to Sam? There was no way she could let Joe hurt him, or take anything else from her. He'd taken Abby and left her daughter without a mother. There was no coming back from that; nothing she could do would change that outcome.

But she could make sure it ended here. She could act now. Ignoring Abby and turning inwards to process her own loss had cost her way too much.

She *would* act now.

A Jack Russell terrier barked ahead. It was the kind of frantic barking that meant it wanted to chase something. Weren't Jack Russells instinctive hunters? The thought galvanised her.

Without pausing to think, she followed the direction in

which it was pulling. Fear scrambled her stomach, making her legs feel weak. She didn't want to call out. That would alert Joe and make him do something reactive. No. She had to find them. Quickly.

She was about to lose hope when, through swaying branches, she saw them. Joe had his back to her and Sam was standing only a few metres away from him. But he wasn't moving.

Sasha crept forward, inching her way through tangled fronds of grass and scrub. Her eyes connected with Sam's, but he gave no indication he'd seen her. At least, no indication to *Joe* that he'd seen her.

She stopped abruptly, the colour draining from her face. Patterns in the dirt spanned the space between Sam and Joe. Curved lines like those of a soundwave. She widened her eyes and gestured frantically at Sam, drawing jerky waves in the air with her index finger. That regular, undulating pattern in the dirt could only have been caused by one thing.

A snake.

CHAPTER FIFTY-ONE

SAM ~ NOW

Sam kept his eyes on Joe, all the while aware of Sasha waving her hand up and down. Even from this distance, he could feel the fear pulsing off her. She jabbed her hand towards the ground in front of him, her eyes wide. Keeping his face neutral, he glanced down.

Shit. He breathed in sharply. They were snake tracks. *Recent* snake markings that had yet to be disturbed. Which meant it was close by. Had Sasha seen it? He darted looks to either side of his feet. Then stepped forward a fraction and turned to look behind him. Nothing. He breathed out slowly.

'That's far enough, mate.' Joe continued to scroll his thumb down the grooved wheels of the disposable lighter in an even rhythm. As if it were a kind of stress toy and he was meditating.

Sam looked across at the man who had caused so much pain and intended to cause so much more. A vein pulsed down the middle of his forehead, spewing venom from his brain. He'd taken so much, caused so much pain.

'What's the matter, Detective? You're looking a bit nervous, mate.' Joe's lip curled up at the corner. 'In a hurry to get back to your girlfriend?' He looked at the flame dancing in front of him.

'Ya know, I'm not stopping you. Probably time you got moving...' He tapped the side of his head. 'If ya know what I mean? I told you. I'm not a monster.'

Sam's eyes settled on a low shrub, rocks dotted around it and littered with charred branches from an earlier fire. Camouflaged amidst the blackened sticks, but at odds with the rigid angles, was a coiled mass. A dugite, if he had to guess. It was barely a metre from Joe's foot. From his exposed ankle and lower leg. Should he warn Joe? He knew Joe wouldn't have afforded him the same courtesy. If he said nothing, wasn't he just as bad?

'You might want to move away from the snake behind you mate.' Sam couldn't help it.

'Fuck, you really think I'm gonna fall for that?' Joe barked a harsh laugh and kicked the ground in front of him. 'What kind of loser do you think I am?'

Sensitive to the slightest movement or vibration, the snake's survival instinct kicked in as Joe kicked out. With whip-like speed and accuracy, the coils were released.

Straight at Joe's ankle.

CHAPTER FIFTY-TWO

The snake sprang towards Joe like a toy being released from a spring-loaded can. Except this wasn't a toy. From her vantage point, Sasha watched the snake rear upwards in a tight S-shape, its hiss loud and indignant. And then it struck. Joe's bare pasty calf was a perfect target.

He jerked and looked down. 'Fuck!' He threw the lighter at the snake. It hit the ground and was swallowed by a dusty carpet of leaf litter. The snake slithered to the safety of some nearby branches and disappeared. The colour drained from Joe's face.

Instinct propelled Sasha forward. Sam. It was Sam she had to reach. Sam was her priority.

'Stay back!' Sam shouted.

'You're okay?' She looked at him, her eyes raking over every inch of him. She could tell he was fine, that he wasn't hurt. But the fear that churned through her was powerful. She'd lost too much. She couldn't lose Sam. She whirled around to Joe.

'Sash, keep away from the snake.'

She had the sudden urge to laugh. Which snake? The actual reptile? Or Joe?

'It bit me!' Joe's face contorted, his eyes bulging. 'You've gotta help me.'

For a moment, Sasha stared at him. This person had caused so much pain. And now he wanted *her* help. She waited for a feeling of power to wash over her, satisfaction in knowing she had control of the situation. Joe had lost. He wasn't going to escape. And he didn't have what he wanted. But then, neither did she. Not really.

'Not until you admit what you did to Abby.' The words spilled out of Sasha. She needed him to be accountable for what he did. She would face her own shortcomings soon enough. But right now, she needed this for Abby.

'Are you out of your fucking mind?' Joe screamed, his face the colour of a squashed beetroot. 'I've been bitten! I need help!' He gestured wildly, his arms spinning like blades on a windmill.

Keep doing that. Let the venom circulate nice and quickly. Sasha watched him thrashing around.

'You'll get help when you tell me what happened to Abby.' Sasha moved towards Joe. Her voice was strong. Determined.

'Are you gonna let your fucking girlfriend call the shots?' Joe doubled over and clutched his leg. 'The fucking snake bit me!' His voice was a screech that sent nearby black cockatoos lifting skywards.

Sam held his hands up. 'I don't tell her what to do. I'd answer her, if I were you. *Mate.*' He crossed over to the pile of leaves and fished out the lighter.

The distant drone of sirens circled the reserve.

Sasha cocked her head to the side and cupped her ear theatrically. 'Sounds like help's on the way. They'd get to you a lot faster if we told them where you were.' She sighed and shrugged. 'Your choice.'

Joe started shivering. Possibly from shock. And possibly from the venom. Although there was every chance it was a dry bite – most snake bites were – and no venom had been released. Sasha wasn't about to share that with Joe, though. Let him think he was about to die. Let him think his life was in danger. Let *him* be the one to beg for help.

'Let me get you started.' Sasha moved towards Joe and crouched down, as if she was talking to a toddler. The image of him cowering and quivering on the ground was one she'd file away and revisit later. Right now, she needed to stay focused. 'Abby came to the vineyard. You were there. You threatened her.' She snapped up a finger on her good hand with each statement. 'She had Sophia with her, and there's no way she wanted you anywhere near her daughter.'

Joe convulsed and heaved, as if he were about to empty the contents of his stomach.

'Ooh. Looks like the venom's working its way through you.' She glanced over her shoulder at Sam. 'What do you think? Is he going to puke? I think he is.'

'Mate, you can't just stand there and let her do this. It's bloody torture! My leg's fucking killing me.' Joe pleaded directly to Sam.

'Quickest way is to answer,' Sam paused, 'or not. I think I need to get back and check on our mate in the hut. See how he's doing. The medics are going to need to check him over pretty thoroughly. Who knows how long that'll take.'

Sasha bit her lip. She knew Sam would never delay help getting through. And she knew he would stay right there. Joe didn't know that, though. Saliva dribbled down his chin as his jaw went slack.

And, finally, Joe talked.

CHAPTER FIFTY-THREE

ABBY ~ RECENTLY

Abby crouched down between the vines and ran her hand over Sophia's silky hair, marvelling once again at the sheer perfection of her daughter. She glanced up. The sky was the kind of blue that startled her eyes. Her daughter stirred at her touch, her mouth pursing in a perfect little rosebud. She had dressed her in a black romper with a striped shirt underneath and tiny gold, soft-soled ballet slippers. She was ridiculously adorable. How was it possible that this miracle belonged to her?

'What do you say, baby girl?' Spears of sunlight shot through the vines and Abby pulled a light cotton sheet over her daughter's legs. Protecting her was instinctive.

Despite the warmth, Abby resisted the urge to shiver. She turned her face towards the sun and willed the rays to chase away her sense of unease. Joe was after her. She had the sense he thought she had some kind of information. She'd deal with that later. Her priority was connecting with Sasha, reconnecting with her best friend. Sasha had to know how truly sorry she was.

She'd come out to Vins Fantaisistes in the hopes of finally getting Sasha to see her. To talk to her. It was one thing for her to ignore texts and calls, but surely Sasha wouldn't be able to ignore her goddaughter? It was perhaps an unfair tactic, using her tiny daughter, but Abby was desperate. Smiling down at her, she hooked her index finger into Sophia's palm. Even in sleep, she clasped her mother's finger with an intuitive trust. Who could resist this perfect little angel?

Abby had respected Sasha's need for space following the accident. But she needed her friend. She needed to talk to Sasha. Was she really going to keep punishing her? Sasha had to know she'd never deliberately do anything to hurt her. Knowing that she *had* hurt her, though, tore at Abby.

Each time Abby thought about that day, her stomach twisted and lurched, nausea pulsing upwards and burning her throat. The crash had been her fault and hers alone. Abby would have to live with that knowledge for the rest of her life. It wasn't something she wanted to excuse or justify. It was something she had done. Not owning it would have been a weak choice. A cowardly one.

It was time to face Sasha. To look at her directly. To own what she'd done.

She ran her knuckles along Sophia's cheek. It would be so easy to scoop her baby girl up and head back to the car. Strap her in and head home. Hide away from everyone and everything. She pressed her lips against her daughter's forehead.

She was done hiding.

Taking a deep breath and gathering her courage, Abby stood and stretched. She had rehearsed yet another apology, determined to deliver this one in person. Leaving it as an unanswered message on Sasha's phone was no longer an option. She had left countless messages, imploring Sasha to talk to her, to listen to her. She would apologise every day for the rest of her life, if that's what it would take to have Sasha start talking to her again. Swerving to miss that damn possum was a scene she replayed over and over again. And she knew it had been her

271

reaction time that had been off. All because she'd looked down and tapped her phone. Her *stupid* bloody phone. Every time she thought about looking at the phone, her skin prickled, guilt washing over her. More than anything, she wanted to go back and change her actions. But glancing at a pinging phone was such a conditioned response; it was Pavlovian. It was like your mouth watering when you smelt onion sizzling in butter, when you saw syrup drizzling over a hot pancake. It was almost impossible to ignore.

But no matter how many times she replayed it, the outcome was always the same. The possum *always* darted out in front of the car. And she *always* swerved to miss it as she looked up from her phone.

Would she make the same decision if she could go back and do things over? Obviously, she wouldn't have looked at the phone in the first place. But if that had remained constant, would she have had the nerve to hold the steering wheel tight and drive directly at the possum? Would she have been able to deliberately, *intentionally*, kill another creature?

Her mind shut down. She was simply incapable of even contemplating the act of taking a life.

Which Sasha knew. Abby bit her lip and frowned. Why couldn't Sasha even try to see it from her point of view? Her shoulders sagged. She knew why. Sasha had lost her entire career, her passion, her life's purpose.

Thinking like this was a waste of time. No matter how much she wanted to, she couldn't change the outcome. She couldn't change the fact that she'd lost control of the car and slammed into the tree. She couldn't change the fact that Sasha's hand had been injured so badly that she'd never be able to play the piano again. And she couldn't change the fact that her relationship with her best friend had been irrevocably altered.

She just had to hope it hadn't been ruined irreparably.

CHAPTER FIFTY-FOUR

SASHA ~ NOW

Sasha looked across at Joe. Crumpled on the ground, thinking he was about to die from a snake bite, he had a slug-like crusting of snot and sweat hovered above his lip. He was whimpering to Sam about the way she was talking to him.

Arsehole. This display of emotion wasn't because he felt guilt. Or remorse. Or sorrow. It was because he'd been caught. Pure and simple. He didn't care about Abby. Or about what he'd done to Abby. Fury scorched through her at that thought.

'Mate, you've gotta help me.' Joe clutched his leg, pleading to Sam.

Sasha felt like she was watching it all through a tunnel. As if she was on one end and Abby was on the other. A kaleidoscope of connectivity. Images and memories swirling.

When Abby turned 30, Joe forgot her birthday. Scratch that. He *ignored* her birthday. There was a big difference. He had pretended to forget, knowing the display of dismissiveness would dig into Abby and hurt her. In the scheme of things, it wasn't the worst he'd done. Sasha had been furious, but Abby had swept it aside, saying that he showed his love in a thousand other ways. Which was absolute crap. He loved showing what he could *do*. He loved *controlling* Abby. That was about the extent of how deep his emotions ran.

Could Abby see Joe now? See *him* hurting? Sasha hoped so.

Joe squatted in the dirt, hands wrapped around his calf and hunched on the ground like a toad shrivelling in the midday sun.

There was no feeling of satisfaction. No vindication. Sasha thought she'd at least feel... better.

I just feel empty, Abs.

There was no sense of victory or elation.

I'm so, so sorry, Abs. I should have been a better friend.

She felt empty.

The emptiness made room for clarity. Joe was going to pay. One way or another, she would make damn sure he did.

The writhing on the ground continued, words dribbling from Joe's mouth. Words Sam was listening to and would use to put him away. Which was just as well, because all of her efforts were going into not picking up a branch and brandishing it like a cricket bat against the side of Joe's head. Would it be so bad to see him topple forward and splat face down in the dirt?

Sasha looked up again. Light filled the tunnel and Sasha swore she could see Abby smiling. Which was completely ridiculous.

But then, Abby always did know her thoughts.

She always saw the best in a situation and in people.

Sasha was going to be that person. The one Abby believed she could be.

CHAPTER FIFTY-FIVE

ABBY ~ RECENTLY

A rustle startled Abby. The wind blew and clouds scudded across the sky. Still crouched by Sophia amidst the vines, she shivered as a chill rippled along her spine and down her arms. The thick foliage and early-morning shadows concealed anything she might have been able to see. She jerked to her feet and looked around, scanning the path between the rows. Was it Joe? Had he followed her to the vineyard? She wouldn't put it past him. But what reason would he have to follow her to Sasha's home? A light breeze wafted through the rows of vines, the leaves at the top responding with a lazy wave. Apart from the distant voices of staff from the restaurant's veranda, Abby could see, could hear, no other movement or sign of life.

She was acutely aware how deserted the area was. There was no one around. Visitors to the vineyard wouldn't start arriving for at least another hour. It was just Sophia and her. And whoever was out there. Anything could happen and there'd be no one to see.

She raked her eyes along the vines, searching for some indication he was there. She shivered again, even though the breeze was warm. She spun towards the cars parked behind the restaurant. The staff carpark.

And there it was. A blue Kia Cerato. Neatly and unobtrusively parked between two similar-sized cars. She couldn't see the number plate, but she knew it was his.

Terror slammed into her gut.

He'd been to her house, *in* her house. And now he was here. It wasn't a coincidence. She was convinced of that.

She looked at Sophia, still asleep. She needed to place as much distance as possible between him and her baby. She couldn't allow him anywhere near her daughter.

Abby scanned the area. Could she make it to the house? Even the vineyard restaurant? It might be too early for diners, but it would be open while the staff prepped for the day. She inhaled and slowed her breathing. She needed to think clearly. More than anything, she had to keep Joe away from Sophia. The thought of him even looking at her precious baby girl revolted her. Just his presence was pure contamination.

She crouched low, her legs wobbly.

A voice broke through the silence. 'I can see you. I know where you are.'

Abby spun around.

'Joe?'

She scanned the area frantically, one hand on the ground, the other on Sophia's baby carrier, ready to propel herself forward. Nothing. *Was* it Joe? The voice was muffled. Almost tinny.

'You need to get moving. Now!'

Abby's stomach turned to liquid. He sounded so close. But she couldn't see him.

'Move. Now!'

Acting and reacting with a mother's need to protect her child, Abby could see only one option. She had to draw Joe away from her daughter. She looked at Sophia, impossibly long eyelashes feathered over her cheeks. Her baby girl. Her whole life. Her chest burned. There was no way she could cover the distance from the rows of vines to the shelter of the house if she was carrying the baby car seat. Joe would stop her without even trying. And then what? Waiting around wasn't an option.

She'd have to leave Sophia. She jammed her fist against her mouth, nausea swirling in her stomach. It was the only way.

Feeling as if her heart was being ripped out, Abby looked at her daughter and pressed her fingers against her tiny chest, covering her heart and trying to pass as much love and strength through her touch as she could. Be strong, sweet girl. I'll be right back.

Biting her top lip and casting a last look at Sophia, Abby darted from the shelter of the vines.

'That's it! Keep moving!'

Abby didn't wait. The voice rang in her ears, an electric shock urging her forward and away from her daughter.

She stumbled across the empty carpark, the open space around her leaving her exposed. Vulnerable.

And then she saw him. Joe. Strands of sun highlighted his thinning hair. He was so close to her daughter. *Don't you dare go near her!* She wanted to scream the words. But she needed to keep his attention focused on her. She paused, drawing his gaze to her. That's right. Keep looking at me. Chase me.

Her heart thudded in her chest. Her feet started moving in time with the rapid rhythm. Bile rose in her throat, a bitter, burning liquid mixed with fear and adrenaline that threatened to choke her.

Joe said nothing. But Abby could sense that he'd moved. In front of her, she could see people by the riverbank, moving at a consistent pace. She dimly registered it was a race of some sort.

But they were too far away to hear or see her. She was on her own.

The vineyard's jetty wasn't far away. Could she make it there? People were always milling around the area. People who could probably help her. She looked over her shoulder and saw Joe lengthening his stride.

Relief mixed with fear. He was moving away from her baby girl. But what would he do to her? She ran towards a line of trees. Diving behind a cluster of low-lying shrubs, she huddled against the trunk of a eucalyptus, desperate for protection, but deliberate in her efforts to keep Joe's attention focused on her.

Breathing heavily against the tree, Abby could hear Joe moving steadily towards her. He was closing the distance between the two of them. And lengthening the distance between him and her daughter, just as she'd hoped. She exhaled slowly, trying to steady her heart rate.

The ground was slick with damp leaves, despite the heat from the mid-morning sun. Bracing herself against the tree, Abby made herself peer around the trunk and into the open space. She'd left Sophia less than two minutes ago, but it felt like hours. Slow, torturous hours. Every fibre of her being cried out with the separation and risk she was taking. Sweat trickled from her hairline to the corner of her eyes, stinging them. Joe was still making his way towards her.

She turned back to the river. Just as she'd hoped, people were gathering at the vineyard's jetty. A couple of kayakers were also paddling towards the same point. But they were still too far away to hear her if she called out to them. If she could reach the jetty, she'd be safe. Or safer than she was alone.

She needed to move at just the right pace, ensuring Joe followed her and would be swept up in the people around him. Only then would she be able to get back to Sophia.

A sob burst out of her. Her baby girl was *alone*. How had it come to this?

She looked over her shoulder. Joe was closing the gap between the two of them. He was close enough that Abby could see the look on his face. Her breath caught in her chest. She knew that look well. It was mean. Cruel. He continued to advance steadily.

To anyone observing from a distance, he was merely strolling down towards the riverbank, casually observing the scenic view of the Swan River. There was no urgency, no rush.

Abby knew better. A low moan escaped as she steadied herself. There was still about 100 metres to the jetty. The ground sloped steeply by the tree line, shaded and slippery, the sun not yet able to dry the ground. Abby waited another few seconds.

She wanted him to be close enough that he'd think she had no escape. She needed him to be forced to react rather than acting with premeditated calculation. She wanted him to be flustered and confused when he neared the group of people.

She wanted him out of her life.

She wanted her daughter.

Looking around the eucalyptus tree, Abby stared straight into Joe's eyes.

Gotcha, he mouthed at her, his thumb and forefinger cocked like a gun and pointed at her.

With a slight shake of her head negating that one word, Abby darted out from the tree line and along the grass. She lunged forward, urging her legs to move. Her feet slipped as she lengthened her stride, her smooth-soled leather sandals not intended to grip to the dew-slicked undergrowth.

A cry slipped out and she wished that Sasha or even her parents might suddenly appear. It was a futile wish. She was alone.

Her pace slowed as she tried to navigate the uneven ground beneath her feet. Loose stones, branches, leaves and clay-like mud forced her to keep her eyes on the ground. The squawk of a cockatoo above her was the only indication her distress had been noted.

In the distance, Abby could hear the rippling sounds of a piano, the unmistakable touch of Sasha. No. Not Sasha. It would never be Sasha sitting at a piano again. She had seen to that. It would be a recording. But the sound gave her courage.

She turned at a sudden noise behind her. Joe's pace had increased. She spun her head back to the front, the whip-like action making her head spin, her balance falter. Her ankle twisted under her as she landed on an over-turned divot of grass. Early morning birdlife loved the soft, moist ground.

Abby gasped at the jolt of pain in her ankle that shot through her leg. She had to ignore it. She had to keep moving. Her uninjured foot landed on a slippery patch of grass. The ground swept up to meet her, a smooth arc of rushing air. The pain was intense. A branch pierced the soft skin beneath her collarbone. The cry that escaped sounded distant and foreign. Her speed propelled her forward, following an invisible trajectory down the grassy bank and towards the water.

Time was suspended. Yet she was powerless to prevent the impending rapid collision with a single rock jutting out next to some exposed tree roots. She could do nothing to prevent the back of her head from connecting with that rock.

Sunlight shimmered off the surface of the river, a mesmerising mix of brilliant blues and greens with stars of light adding a magical dimension.

Sophia would love these patterns, Abby thought.

It was her final thought.

Less than fifty metres from where Abby fell, guests from the vineyard continued to gather on the jetty. Two kayakers secured their crafts and climbed out. Competitors in a local fun run skirted the edge of the road that led to the jetty, their efforts focused on the hill in front of them that would demand their attention and energy. A race marshal pressed the side of a two-way radio and called out words of encouragement: *"You need to get moving. Now! Come on – don't let them catch you."*

No one noticed the woman slipping into the water. No one heard the splash as she tumbled, lifeless, into the murky depths. No one paid any attention to the figure standing on the bank, staring into the water before retreating, disappearing from view.

No one noticed the body caught in the branches of a tree grazing the surface of the river, her fanning hair acting as a filter for river debris.

CHAPTER FIFTY-SIX

SASHA ~ NOW

Four hours had passed since the police pulled Joe from the reserve. And by pulled, Sasha meant *hauled*. They had hauled his sorry arse to a waiting ambulance where he was checked and it was declared that he had, in fact, received a dry bite from the dugite. *Shame.* She would have liked to have seen him writhe and whimper a little longer. Maybe suffer a bit. Or, a lot. Any power he thought he'd had, any control, was long gone.

She wasn't about to apologise for feeling happy about the possibility of Joe suffering, though. He wasn't worth the emotion. He deserved everything he had coming to him.

Sasha turned and sat on a park bench overlooking the beach, the setting sun warm on her face. She and Sam were taking the long way back to his place after sharing a burger. They had walked along the coastal footpath, like they used to do before the accident. Leaves drifted past their feet, at the mercy of the salty wind being flung off the Indian Ocean.

Sam had shown the paramedics where the hut was and they'd rushed the guy off to hospital. Sasha still felt bad about leaving him there. Not that it'd been for long. Turned out he was an ex-colleague of Joe's who had dipped his toe into the illegal side of Joe's business, but then had a change of heart. He hadn't gone to the police because he knew his own involvement would have been exposed. Or something like that. Sasha's attention had mainly been on Sam. Once she knew there was no way Joe could get away, she could only look at Sam.

She gazed at him now. He was beside her on the seat, his shoulder pressed against her arm, his hands resting on his thighs. No. Not resting. Gripping. She reached across and laid her injured hand on top of his, not yet able to curl her fingers around and clasp his. But that didn't matter. Not now. Sam's fingers relaxed and she felt his shoulder drop against her arm. He'd been holding his breath. Nervous. Unsure. She'd done that to him.

'Sam–' Sasha began.

He turned her hand over and wrapped it in his, his fingers long and expressive. It felt intimate, but comfortable. This was where she was meant to be.

Sasha took a breath. 'God, Sam. I made such a mess of everything. Why are you still here?'

'I was never going anywhere, Sash.' He gave a small hitch of his shoulder. 'You needed time to process it all.'

'But I was so mean to you.' Her breath stuttered and she blew out slowly between closed lips. 'And Abby. I was so foul to her. And now there's nothing I can do about it.'

Sam squeezed her hand. 'She knew you needed time. She wanted to respect that.'

Her nose clogged with snot and emotion, making her snort. 'She wasn't meant to *die*.' She hiccupped on the last word. 'We would have worked it out.'

Sam stroked her back and pressed a kiss against the side of her head. 'I know. And she knew that, too.'

Sasha gulped when she heard the past tense. *Knew.*

Sam continued. 'She was meant to be here. With Sophia.'

Sasha loved that he didn't try and say anything trite or clichéd. Like, *We can't change that*, or *It's not your fault*. He just let her *feel* everything. Besides, she knew all too well that she couldn't change anything. Technically, she knew it wasn't her fault. But there were prickles of guilt that she knew would never completely go away.

'I'm such a mess, Sam.' The sun spilled over the horizon, shades of red, orange and purple bleeding into the ocean like leaking cans of paint. 'I thought seeing Joe being caught would help. But it doesn't. There's nothing that can make him pay enough for what he did to Abby.' She swung her gaze to Sam. 'He *will* pay, won't he?'

'I don't think everything he did can be prosecuted, Sash. What Joe did was reprehensible. Will he serve time for what he did to Abby? No. Not directly. But we have to be okay with the time he'll serve for his other crimes. There's a lot to unravel and uncover with what he was doing. It'll take time. But it *will* happen.' His fingers played a soothing pattern between her shoulder blades. 'You can't hold onto the anger. It'll just eat away at you. And that wasn't Abby. Abby was about moving forward. Living life. Seeing the good in people and situations. Do you know what I mean?'

Sam was right. That's exactly what Abby did. It was why she'd ended up with Joe in the first place, convinced that people weren't born bad, that circumstances shaped people. Sasha plucked at the fabric of her leggings, the sound slapping her thighs and puncturing the warm air.

At some point though, people had to be held accountable for their actions. She stared out at the point where the sun had now dipped and disappeared, leaving a shimmering mirage of the day's memories. You couldn't always blame the past. Or things that people did to you. The only thing you could control was the way you responded. Joe never got that. He wanted to control people, things, everything around him. *How's that working out for you now, Joe?*

'Yeah,' she said, a lengthy sigh ballooning her cheeks. 'I know what you mean.'

EPILOGUE

FOUR MONTHS LATER

It seemed as if everyone had been drawn to the Swan Valley region this weekend. Traffic was moving at a crawl as drivers and passengers alike gazed out of car windows at the lush fields and bucolic hills. The leaves on the vines had turned various shades of buttery yellow and burnt orange. But rather than merely signalling the end of a season, the vibrant colours created a stunning contrast with the still-green grass, encouraging a continual stream of visitors to return time and time again.

Sam swung the car through the entrance gates of Vins Fantaisistes, following the curve of the road as it wound its way towards the main building. The grass verges were filled with cars lined up like automotive soldiers, which meant that the restaurant would be running at capacity. The wisteria flowers had long dropped, their boughs naked. But there was still enough warmth in the air for guests to be sitting on the deck, savouring the sunshine afforded by the now-sparse branches overhead.

Sasha spun in the front seat of the car to face Sophia. 'Are you ready to see Nana June and Poppa Dave, gorgeous girl?'

Sophia gurgled happily, intent only on trying to separate her toes from her feet, twisting them and then pushing them into her mouth when detaching them with her hands didn't work. Her eyes widened in wonder as she realised the delight that came with sucking her big toe.

'Yes, sweetheart, you really are such a clever girl.' Sasha couldn't help the indulgent smile.

How was it that in the space of a few short months, this tiny human had managed to completely consume her every waking – and sleeping – thought? Sasha adjusted the overalls she had put Sophia in for the day, ones adorned with gumnuts and bottlebrush. She was impossibly cute. Not that Sasha was biased. Everything Sophia did was adorable. Even waking her at 2am. Although she might change her mind about that one. She was human, after all. A human with flaws and failings, but – hopefully – the wisdom and awareness to learn from them.

'Are you ready to go and see the room Nana June has set up for you?' Sasha asked the toe-sucking infant. Her mum had thrown herself into the role of grandparent as if she'd been counting down the days for it to happen. June claimed she had set the room up so Sophia could stay and give her and Sam some time together. Sasha smiled, knowing full well it was as much for her mum as it was about giving them time as a couple. She didn't blame her. 'Are you going to show Nana your new trick?'

Sophia blew a series of slobbery bubbles in reply while also sending herself cross-eyed as she extracted her big toe from her mouth and lifted it higher to inspect it. She was completely mesmerised by it. Sasha had no idea why they had been buying toys when clearly, toes proved so much more fascinating. It really was one of life's greater mysteries. Each time Sophia saw her toes, it was like she had discovered the meaning of life.

Which was kind of what Sasha did each time she watched Sophia. Discover the meaning of life, that is. Not be mesmerised by her toes. Although they were a rather delightful shade of rosy pink. She glanced down at them and wriggled them in her sandals.

Sasha shuddered suddenly. Sam reached over and wrapped his fingers around her hand, his eyes still on the road. Grief still hit her unexpectedly. And each time it did, the intensity was still the same. It slammed into her, loosening her stomach and tightening her chest.

All Sasha could do was accept it. Some days, she welcomed it. Sasha wanted to embrace it: to slam her hand against a wall; feel the slap of pain; the sting of her selfishness. She deserved every bit of pain that came her way.

Other days, she could accept the grief and smile at a memory. Abby daring her to put ten marshmallows in her mouth at one time right before a performance. No one knew how to settle her nerves like Abby. Abby dancing while she played Rachmaninov. Who danced to Rachmaninov? Abby grinning from the front row of one of Sasha's performances, wearing a pair of those joke glasses with a huge nose and moustache. Sasha hiccupped a small laugh at the memory.

It was a balancing act. A bit like one of those bloody balance balls at the gym that were meant to strengthen your core and do all sorts of wonderful things for your body. Except she was hopeless at it, tilting wildly from one side to the other and never quite finding that calm, central, stabilising point.

But she was getting better at it. One wobbly day at a time.

Sophia helped a lot. Sasha reached back and tickled the baby's foot, earning an uninhibited belly laugh for her effort. Abby was in every laugh and precious breath that Sophia took.

If someone had asked her a year ago if she would be excited about teaching, Sasha would have laughed at them. A year ago, she thought that being centre stage and performing to a filled concert hall were the benchmarks of satisfaction and contentment.

Today, she knew better. She would never forget the thrill and excitement of performing in front of an appreciative audience, knowing she had played flawlessly and bared a piece of her soul.

Through teaching though, she could still do those things. She was thrilled when eight-year-old Jackson mastered the mechanics of an abridged Mozart piece and instinctively modulated the volume between bars, adding his own feeling and expression. She was excited when 76-year-old Mrs Blackwell managed to play *The Anniversary Waltz*, the song that was played at her wedding reception 50 years ago and that she now wanted to play as a surprise for her husband.

And she was satisfied when Sam asked her to show him how to play the opening bars of *Ode to Joy*. In fact, she may have ended up being satisfied in more ways than one, if she remembered that evening correctly. Sasha touched a hand to her cheek and then reached out to link her fingers through Sam's.

'Come on, baby girl,' Sasha said as she forced back the blush that threatened to erupt. Once the car had come to a halt, she reached for Sophia, depriving her of her toe-in-mouth wonderment. 'Let's go and find Nana and Poppa.'

Brushstrokes of golden sunlight streaked across the top of the vines, a glittering canopy atop russet foliage. Sasha hoisted Sophia onto her hip and breathed deeply. Life would never be the same. How could it? She dropped a kiss on Sophia's head.

Cormorants and cockatoos still lined the boughs of the banksia and eucalyptus trees. And the honey-like minted scent still mingled with the fallen leaves. Today though, their cries were a symphony of hope and joy; a song of new beginnings and lessons learned.

ACKNOWLEDGEMENTS

Thank you! Gorgeous readers like yourself are why I am now writing this. Thank you so much for choosing my novel and reading it. Unless you haven't read it yet and have skipped straight to the acknowledgements. Please tell me I am not the only oddball who does this? Either way, I hope that you've loved it (or will love it!) and that you always see your wondrous possibilities.

And if you're of the type to be triggered by exclamation points, please be warned: there are many! So many! That's just the way I roll, especially when I am overwhelmed by the immense gratitude I have for everyone who has made this book a reality.

My first and everlasting thanks unreservedly goes to my husband, Mark, and our three offspring, Caitlin, Sami and Philip. Not to mention our irrepressible grandson, Ollie-Boo. You are my absolute everything! Thank you for never thinking this writing thing was a crazy idea and for believing in me every single step of the way.

To Tyler Harrington, son-in-law extraordinaire. Plot knots cease to exist and escapades are aplenty with this young man. He throws concepts and solutions around with preposterous abandon that never fail to unlock ideas and unravel problems.

To the entire team at Bloodhound Books who saw the potential and believed in my story – thank you, thank you, thank you! You are dream-makers. To my lovely editor, Rachel Tyrer, whose insights and deft touches simultaneously challenged and reassured me. Thank you. And to Tara Lyons, who stepped in brilliantly when Rachel's timeline suddenly shrunk – you're amazing!

Handing over copies of a magazine to my Mum and Dad that I wrote, produced and sold (yes, I made them pay 50 cents for the privilege, even though they facilitated every single step; my 8-year-old assuredness – okay – arrogance – knew no bounds) was a highlight of my childhood. Their unfailing support and matter-of-fact acceptance that I was a *writer* has stayed with me always. Thank you so very much.

To my dear friend/mentor/teacher and best-selling author, Holly Craig. Thank you for your unwavering support and belief in my words; for your mentorship and tutoring that gave me the tools to find my voice. Hol, this book would not be here now without you and the incredible Write Club (#thewriteclubis-thebestclub). May the fun and adventures never stop!

To the inimitable Kate Thompson Beaufoy; best-selling author, giver of truly insightful feedback and the most delightful person and friend! Thank you for all you've done and continue to do. You are beyond remarkable!

The members of Holly Craig's Write Club as well as our Thursday WAGS (Writing About Great Stuff) writing group offer encouragement and support that everyone should be so fortunate to experience. Writing sessions, classes, retreats and chatty lunches (with pretty drinks!) are now a much-anticipated part of my calendar. Thank you so so much to everyone in this beautiful community!

The perception of writing being a solitary endeavour can often be true. The time spent immersed with fictional words and worlds simultaneously fuels and soothes my introverted little soul. But I've had to rethink my ideas concerning social interactions, thanks to the incredible writing community. Cultivating a sense of belonging and community in a pursuit that is so subjective, so doubt-driven, is truly a remarkable feat. Fostering creativity within the embrace of friendships, free from judgement, is something I will never take for granted. The writing community honestly rocks!

To my beautiful friend, Julie Robinson, my OG writing buddy. This gorgeous soul truly listens and then responds with the most insightful thoughts and ideas. I would be lost without her. And she – somehow, and I do make this very difficult for her – manages to take photos of me that I adore!

To the lovely Sallyanne Bond. Who knew that meeting at a café in Margaret River would see not just the start of our amazing Thursday WAGS writing group but a very special friendship? Thank you for your constant source of encouragement and sanity. (Sorry, not sorry, but I've kept the wisteria!)

To the talented and sparkling Georgia Cabelle. You are one of the most awe-inspiring people I have ever met. Ever, ever! From Perth to Sydney to LA, we have paved a path of sparkling adventures and possibilities. Your book is going to be epic!

To the sublime Mandy Walsh. Writing friends who become true friends is honestly one of the best perks of this writing gig. Keep those words flowing, my beautiful friend. And yes – these words in this book mean you're stuck with me!

To the wonderful Kristy Sumich. You're an absolute superstar with your selfless offers of time, friendship, retreat venues and support. Thank you! You are one of the most genuine and selfless souls I have ever met.

To Carolyn Newton, fellow Bloodhound author and constant source of calm reassurance and encouragement, thank you! We're yet to meet IRL, but it also feels like we have.

To Rachel Hansen, the first industry professional who read my incredibly raw first draft yet still saw the possibilities and took the time to meet with me and offer invaluable advice. Thank you! Your words gave me the courage and belief to forge ahead.

Happy reading and may the pages always keep turning!

ABOUT THE AUTHOR

As well as an author, Deb Jordan is a pianist, primary school teacher and pretend athlete. Perth, Western Australia is now home after twenty years abroad spent evading kidnap attempts in Peru, serenading African presidents, escaping a marriage trade in Ghana (her husband was tempted when the price was ten chickens and three goats...) and circling jungle volcanoes in Costa Rica.

You can follow Deb on her website: www.debjordantheauthor.com and Instagram: Deb Jordan (@deb_jordan_author)

A NOTE FROM THE PUBLISHER

Thank you for reading this book. If you enjoyed it please do consider leaving a review on Amazon to help others find it too.

We hate typos. All of our books have been rigorously edited and proofread, but sometimes mistakes do slip through. If you have spotted a typo, please do let us know and we can get it amended within hours.

info@bloodhoundbooks.com